LITTLE DARLINGS

www.**kidsatrandomhouse**.co.uk

Jacqueline Wilson

LITTLE DARLINGS

TWO VERY DIFFERENT GIRLS —
ONE EXTRAORDINARY
FRIENDSHIP!

ILLUSTRATED BY
NICK SHARRATT

DESTINY

SUNSET

DOUBLEDAY

LITTLE DARLINGS
A DOUBLEDAY BOOK 978 0 385 61443 6

Published in Great Britain by Doubleday,
an imprint of Random House Children's Books
A Random House Group company

This edition published 2010

1 3 5 7 9 10 8 6 4 2

The Random House Group Limited supports the Forest Stewardship
Council (FSC), the leading international forest certification organization.
All our titles that are printed on Greenpeace-appproved FSC-certified paper
carry the FSC logo. Our paper procurements policy can be found at
www.rbooks.co.uk/environment.

Mixed Sources
Product group from well-managed
forests and other controlled sources
www.fsc.org Cert no. TT-COC-2139
© 1996 Forest Stewardship Council
FSC

Set in 13/17pt Century Schoolbook by
Falcon Oast Graphic Art Ltd.

RANDOM HOUSE CHILDREN'S BOOKS
61–63 Uxbridge Road, London W5 5SA

www.**kids**at**randomhouse**.co.uk
www.**rbooks**.co.uk

Addresses for companies within The Random House Group Limited
can be found at www.randomhouse.co.uk/offices.htm

THE RANDOM HOUSE GROUP Limited Reg. No. 954009

A CIP catalogue for this book is available from the British Library.

Printed and bound by Clays Ltd, St Ives plc

For Lisa and Millie

1

DESTINY

'*Happy birthday to you, happy birthday to you . . .*'

I wriggle up from under my old teddy-bear duvet and prop myself on my elbows.

'Happy birthday, dear *Destiny*, happy birthday to you!'

Mum takes hold of the duvet, trying to work the two big bears' mouths like puppets, doing growly bear 'happy birthdays'. She's played this game with me ever since I can remember. I suppose I'm way too old for it now I'm eleven, but never mind, it's only Mum and me.

'Thank you, Pinky, thank you, Bluey,' I say, giving each duvet bear a kiss.

I know they're not very exciting names, but I christened them when I was only two or three. 'And thank you, Mum.'

I put my arms round her and hug her close. She feels so skinny I'm scared of snapping her in half. She doesn't diet, she just doesn't find time to eat very much. Now we've moved to Bilefield she's got *three* jobs: she has her cleaning job at the university early in the morning, then she does her home-helping all day, and then Friday and Saturday and Sunday nights she's started working the evening shift at the Dog and Fox, only that's our secret, because she has to leave me on my own when she's down the pub.

I don't mind one little bit. She leaves me pizzas and oven chips, and any fool can heat them up, I can watch whatever telly I want or play all my secret games, and when I go to bed Mum's always left me a little scribbled note. Sometimes it's a

Danny Kilman quiz – complete the last line of the chorus, silly stuff like that. Sometimes it's a message: *Night-night, my best girl. Sleep tight and hope the bugs don't bite.*

We really did have bed bugs once, when we lived on the Latchford Estate. Mum let this friend of hers and her two kids from the balcony above live at our flat for a couple of weeks after the friend left her husband, and they must have brought them with them. They moved on, but their bugs stayed – awful little black wriggly things. Mum used to catch them with a bar of carbolic soap and she'd scrub and scrub the mattress, but they kept on wriggling. So eventually we gave up on the mattress altogether and hauled it in and out of the lift and lumbered it to the waste ground behind the dustbins where everyone dumps their rubbish.

Mum went down to the Social and begged for a new mattress. It was, like, well, you live on the Latchford Estate so you're the pits. We can't help it if you're dirty, we can't go providing you with new mattresses every five minutes. So Mum said stuff them and we made do without a mattress for months, huddled up together on the sofa cushions with Mum's duvet underneath us and my teddy duvet on top. I quite liked cuddling up together but it hurt Mum's back.

I think that was the main reason she took up with Steve. We went and lived in his posh house and he bought us all sorts of stuff. He didn't just buy us both a mattress, he bought us brand-new beds. Their bed was a really fancy four-poster bed just like in a fairy story. My bed was just ordinary. Mum wanted to get me a pretty new pillowcase-and-duvet set. She had one all picked out with white lace and embroidered pink rosebuds. I'd have loved it, but I didn't want to have to fawn all over Steve, so I said I wanted to stick to my old teddy duvet. And I was glad I did. When Mum and Steve were in their fancy bed, I could curl up in mine with Pinky one side of me, Bluey the other, and we'd go into the woods and have picnics, just like that silly old song.

I often don't sleep very well, and while Steve was around I couldn't climb in beside Mum, so I had a *lot* of picnics with Pinky and Bluey. Sometimes on really bad nights we'd scoot off on holiday together, flying off to different foreign lands, sightseeing and swimming and sunbathing. I don't play all that silly kid stuff now, of course. Well, not often. And Steve's history, and his fancy house and his four-poster bed.

He started slapping Mum about and she put up with it for a bit, but then he started on me, and she

4

wasn't having that. So we did a runner, Mum and me, with two suitcases stuffed with our clothes and my duvet and Mum's make-up and our little CD player and all Mum's Danny Kilman albums and her big Danny scrapbook. We couldn't literally run with those cases – we could barely *drag* them along.

We ended up in a refuge where all the little kids kept crying and the big kids were fighting and one of the women tried to nick all our Danny stuff. Mum didn't half clobber her when she caught her – my little mum against this huge hippo of a woman, a good twenty stone – but *no one* messes with Mum's Danny Kilman collection. Then we got rehoused on another rubbish estate not much better than Latchford, but Mum said she'd learned her lesson, she wasn't getting mixed up with any other bloke now, not even if he lived in Buckingham Palace.

She tried to make our new flat into a proper home, painting all the walls different bright colours and making proper flowery-patterned curtains for our windows – though it was so damp the ceiling went black with mould no matter how many times she painted it and the curtains were wringing wet with condensation every morning.

But then we got our lucky break! One of Mum's

special regulars, Harry Benson, a dear old gent she cleaned for on Thursday mornings, got pneumonia and went into hospital and died. Mum was sad because she'd loved old Harry. She'd nip out to the shops for him several times a week, buying his *Sun* and his Players and a pint of milk and a packet of his favourite Jammy Dodgers, and sometimes she'd put a bet on for him down the bookies. He must have been grateful because he left her all his savings in his will.

He'd often told Mum he was going to do this as he didn't have any proper family to remember. She was very touched, but she didn't get too excited because Harry lived in a council flat like ours and all his ornaments looked like stuff left over from a jumble: an Alsatian dog with his ears broken off, little jugs with cracks saying *A present from Margate*, a faded picture of a lady with a green face, that kind of thing. But it turned out he had nearly twenty-five thousand pounds tucked away in the post office!

Maybe some of his bets paid off big-time, maybe he'd just scrimped and saved all his life, I don't know. Mum cried and cried when she found out. She took me to the crematorium with her. She knew they'd scattered his ashes in the rose garden so she went and crouched there, whispering to

Harry that she was ever so grateful, and she made me say it too, though it felt a bit weird talking out loud to a lot of red and yellow roses. I kept looking worriedly at the petals in case they had little flakes of dead people on them.

I hoped Mum would take us on a fantastic holiday, a real-life version of my night-time fantasies, but she made do with a day trip to Blackpool. (I did get to paddle in the sea, though it was freezing cold and my toes turned blue, and I had fish and chips and two ice creams and won a toy gorilla on the pier, so it was a great day out.) She used all the money as a big down payment on our very own house.

It's only a very little house, an ex-council maisonette on the Bilefield Estate. It's meant to be the best of all the council estates – hardly any druggies, a lot of the flats privately owned, and Bilefield Primary is supposed to be a good school. Mum's dead keen on me getting a good education. So we've made this brand-new start – but I can't help thinking it's a bit rubbish. I *hate* the school because I'm in Year Six and everyone's got their own little set of mates and I'm the new girl stuck without anyone. Not that I'd *want* to be friends with any of that lot.

Mum says we're much better off now, but she

can't mean financially because the mortgage uses up all her money. She hasn't ever got anything left over for treats. I can't have new clothes or a computer or an iPod, or even my own mobile like nearly all the other kids in my class. Mum says it's worth it to have our very own house. I'm not so sure, to be truthful. I particularly think this at times like Christmas. And birthdays. Like today.

'Now you sit up nicely in the bed, Birthday Girl, and I'll bring you your special birthday breakfast,' Mum says, eyes shining.

She's still in her tattered pink silky dressing gown. I look at my alarm clock.

'Mum, it's half past seven! You'll be ever so late for work!'

Mum grins and taps me on the nose. 'No, I won't. I've got Michelle and Lana to cover for me at the uni, and Louella's going to do my first old lady. Today's special – it's my best girl's birthday. Hang on!'

She dashes to the door and bends over a tray on the floor. I hear the flare of a match. Then she picks up the tray, chuckling to herself, and carries it carefully over to the bed.

'Oh, Mum!'

She's spread a slice of bread with butter and golden syrup, one of my favourite treats, and stuck eleven pink candles all over it.

'Blow them out then, Destiny, quick! Blow them out all in one go and then you'll get a wish!'

I blow hard and expertly, and get every candle. Then I close my eyes, wondering what to wish for. *I wish I had a best friend? I wish Mum didn't have to work so hard? I wish I had a proper dad?*

Then I pick out my candles, sucking the syrup off the holders, and eat my birthday bread. Mum goes to make coffee, and when she comes back with it she's also got a tray of parcels: one medium size, one a bit smaller, one tiny, plus two envelopes, one large, one small, with my name on the front in Mum's swirly back-sloping writing: *Destiny*.

'*Two* birthday cards, Mum?' I say.

'Save the smaller one till last,' says Mum.

So I open the bigger card and it's one Mum's made herself. She's cut all sorts of pictures out of magazines – dogs and cats and rabbits and ponies and sandy beaches and flowers and flash cars and great big boxes of chocolates and giant ice creams – and stuck them on a piece of paper to make a crazy picture.

'It's all your favourite things,' Mum says.

I turn over the picture. Mum has inked a message in fancy lettering, pink and purple: *To my dearest darling dorter Destiny on her elevventh birthday. With lots and lots of love from Mum.*

I am ace at spelling but Mum isn't. I wouldn't point out her mistakes in a million years. I give her a great big hug.

'I do love you, Mum,' I say.

'You don't mind it not being a proper card?'

'I like your cards much more,' I say quickly.

I'm not expecting proper presents either. Mum often tries to make me stuff, or she gets things from boot fairs and cleans them up – but I'm in for a surprise. The biggest parcel is a pair of black jeans, brand new from Primark, still with the ticket on, and there's a new black T-shirt in the second parcel, really deep black and pristine under the arms, plainly never been worn or put in the wash. The only slightly weird present is the last one: a pair of little black net gloves.

'Do you like them? I found them on a market stall. I got me a pair too. They're a bit like the ones Danny wears in his early photos.'

'Oh yeah. They're cool, Mum. I love them,' I say, trying them on and turning my hands into little spiders scuttling up and down the bed.

'So, we'll have to find somewhere for you to go when you're all dressed up in your black jeans and T-shirt and your fancy gloves,' says Mum. She's fidgeting like she wants to jump up and down like a little kid. 'Open the other envelope, Destiny, go on!'

10

I open it up and find two train tickets – to London!

'Oh, wow!' I say.

I've only ever been to London once. That was on a weekend with Steve. At first he was in a very good mood and he showed us Buckingham Palace, where the Queen lives, and Trafalgar Square with the great big lions, and then we went to this huge great posh shop called Harrods and he bought Mum a dress, and Steve and Mum went out clubbing that evening – but the next morning Steve was in a very *bad* mood and didn't want to do anything at all.

'Where will we go, Mum?' I say. 'Buckingham Palace and Trafalgar Square?'

'We've seen them already,' says Mum.

'Oh great, so we can go to that shop, Harrods? Not to buy stuff, just to have a look round. We could play we're two rich Wags out on a shopping spree.'

'Yeah, well, we could do that when we get there in the afternoon, but we're going somewhere else in the evening. We're going to a *film premiere*,' says Mum.

I stare at her. She sometimes makes stuff up, just like me.

'No, we're not!' I say.

11

'Yes, we are! Well, we're not going to see the film itself – that's for the stars, naturally – but we'll be there looking at everyone arriving, standing on the red carpet. I've seen stuff like that on the telly. You can get really close up to the stars, even speak to them, and Destiny, guess who's going to be there – oh, guess!'

I look at Mum, shaking my head. 'I don't know,' I say, and I truly haven't a clue.

I don't know much about film stars. Mum's the one who hangs about for ages in WHSmith reading all the celebrity mags, not me. I can't quite get why she's so worked up, biting her lips, her fists clenched.

'Danny's going to be there!' she says.

'*Our* Danny?'

'Yes, yes!'

'But he's not a film star.'

'I read about it in the fan club mag. It's a film about a new band – it's called *Milky Star*—'

'Danny's got a new band?' I ask.

'No, no – oh, I *wish*! How wonderful to be able to see him play! No, according to this piece I read, Danny plays a major rock star, kind of similar to himself – but anyway, the film premiere's on Saturday and Danny will be there, it *said*. And I've been saving up for something special for your birthday for ages, so I thought I'd get us tickets, and buy you a new outfit – because it's time you met him, Destiny. It's time you met . . . your father.'

She whispers the last two words reverently. It's such a very private secret we hardly ever talk about it. Mum's never told anyone but me, and I wouldn't ever tell anyone else, even if I had a best friend in all the world, because this is such a sacred secret.

My dad is Danny Kilman. I suppose there wouldn't be any point telling people even if it wasn't a secret, because who would believe me? Mum met Danny when she was eighteen. She'd loved him ever since she was my age. She bought all his albums and had posters of him all over her bedroom walls. She'd had a few boyfriends, but Danny was the only man she ever loved. She was thrilled when Danny and his boys were playing at the Apollo and she managed to get a ticket. She went with her friend Julie and they screamed themselves hoarse, and then they went to the Midland Hotel and hung around in the hope of seeing the band there – and they were invited in for drinks.

Mum said it was the most amazing night of her life – she simply couldn't believe it. She was

13

actually talking to Danny Kilman! She was sitting on his lap! She was kissing him!

She said he wasn't a bit the way she'd imagined. He was quiet, even a little bit shy, and very gentlemanly, taking such care of her.

Mum says they only had a brief relationship but it was a truly passionate love affair – my little mum and rock god Danny.

'I should have left home and given up my job and followed him to London there and then,' Mum's often said sadly. 'I should have realized you can't really have a valid long-distance relationship, not with someone like Danny. I don't really blame him for starting to go out with Suzy. I don't want to sound catty, but she practically threw herself at him, everyone knows that – it was in all the gossip columns. I decided I didn't mind him having a little fling with her. I mean, his first marriage was already over, so he was free to do what he wanted, and Suzy was already quite a famous glamour model herself then and very pretty – though I've always thought she looks a little hard. But then, just around the time I realized I was going to have a baby, my Dan's baby, there's this devastating headline – DANNY KILMAN MARRIES SUZY SWINGER IN WHIRLWIND VEGAS WEDDING – and I realized it was too late. What could I do? I couldn't tell him and risk wrecking his brand-new marriage. It would be so unfair.'

I suppose Mum thought she would bide her time and wait. She never thought his marriage would last. But they'd only been married a few months when Suzy stopped partying with Danny half the night and started wearing loose tops and it became obvious she was going to have a baby. Danny's baby.

'Your half-sister, Destiny,' Mum said.

She's kept a separate scrapbook of the baby from the very first photos three days after she was born – 'Because she's family.'

I grew up knowing everything about this sister of mine I'd never met, Sunset.

'I bet Suzy chose the name,' said Mum, sniffing.

We have way more photos of Sunset than we have of me. I always liked the one of baby Sunset in her little white hooded playsuit with bunny ears. Mum tried to make me one, stitching ears on my tiny hoodie, only she got the shape wrong so the ears were too small and round and I ended up looking like a little white rat. Once Sunset was toddling around, Mum gave up trying to make me matching outfits because Sunset had such amazing designer clothes. When I was old enough, Mum and I would pore over them for ages, repeating the French and Italian designer names reverently.

The photo I like best in the whole scrapbook is one of Sunset and Danny on a white beach in Barbados. Suzy is there too, in the shade in the background, her tummy swollen over her bikini bottom because she's six months pregnant with Sweetie, my next little half-sister. Danny is lying stretched out on the sand, looking really brown and fit, wearing funny long bathing trunks down to his knees, and Sunset is sitting beside him, busy burying his feet in the sand. She's got her hair in a topknot and she's wearing huge sunglasses – maybe she's borrowed them from Suzy – and a red-and-white striped swimming costume. She's grinning mischievously at her dad, so happy. I'd stare at that picture until I could feel the sun on my skin, hear the lap of the waves, feel the powdery grit of the sand as I smiled at my dad.

2

SUNSET

'Smile, please!'

'Everyone smile! This way!'

'Look at me! You on the end, darling, give us a smile.'

'Little munchkin in the red boots – *smile*!'

That's me. I'm the only one *not* smiling. Dad is giving the press his famous lopsided grin, flicking his long tousled hair, striking a cool pose in his black gothic clothes and his silver-sequin baseball boots. He's not Dad any more, he's Big Danny, every inch of him, right down to the huge skull ring studded with diamonds distorting his little finger.

Mum's smiling too, showing off her new pink hairdo, exactly the same colour as her flowery ruffled dress, cinched in with a wide black studded belt, her long legs in black fishnets and then crazily high red-soled Louboutins. She doesn't model any more, but she still knows how to show herself off.

My sister Sweetie's like a mini model already. Her fair hair has been specially straightened for today. It swishes past her shoulders in a shiny waterfall. Mum's let her have a dab of purple shadow on her eyelids to match her purple ballet frock. She's wearing a little black velvet jacket over the top, studded with all her badges and brooches, black and purple striped tights and little black pointy boots. She coordinated her outfit herself, even though she's only five. Sweetie has known how to be a celebrity child ever since she could toddle.

Ace is still at the toddling stage and doesn't give

a fig about celebrity. He was supposed to wear a miniature version of Dad's outfit, but he screamed and kicked and said he didn't want to wear those silly clothes. He would only wear his Tigerman outfit or he would bite. So he's in his Tigerman costume – black and gold stripes with a long tail, and Mum has painted tiger stripes and whiskers on his face.

Everyone goes '*Ahhh*', and coos at him. Ace roars and they pretend to be scared. It's the simplest of routines, but Ace is happy to play Tigerman all day long and well into the night.

He's not so sure about all the flashing lights of the photographers. He blinks and ducks his head and grabs Mum's hand. She lifts him up and gives him a cuddle as he nuzzles into her neck, and he manages a little grin.

But not me. I can't smile. I'm not allowed to.

'Remember, you mustn't show your teeth – you'll spoil the photo,' Mum hissed as the Mercedes drew up at the start of the red carpet.

I have a gap in the front and snaggle teeth at the sides. Mum says I have to have extractions and braces but I am *scared of the pain* – and anyway, the orthodontist says we should wait several years. I'd like to wait a century or two. And anyway, I know I'll spoil every family photo even when my teeth are fixed. I'm not little and blonde and cute like Sweetie and Ace. They take after Mum. I take after Dad. I am dark and I have a wild mane of hair and big nose. They look fine on him but they look awful on me.

My clothes don't look right either. Mum picked everything out for me as she doesn't trust me to choose my outfit myself. I can't tell which top goes with which bottom (and I don't *care* anyway), and the only kind of shoes I like are comfy ones. I wouldn't mind a pair of sparkly baseball boots just like Dad's, but Mum says I'd look too much of a tomboy. I've got these dinky scarlet boots with really high heels. Sweetie adores them and can't wait to be big enough to wear them herself – but even Mum says five is too young to wear high heels.

I am wearing weird itchy black leatherette leggings that stick to me all over, and a blue velvet smock top. I hate the *feel* of velvet, especially because I bite my nails. Every time the little raw edges of my fingers touch the velvet it makes me shiver.

So no, I can't smile, please. Mum won't let me – and to be honest I don't *feel* like smiling. I hate red carpet stuff. This is the film premiere of *Milky Star*, a funny film about a young boy band, and my dad has a cameo role as a wild rock star. Well, he is a wild rock star, though he hasn't had a hit for a long time, and he hasn't done a proper show for years. I mustn't ever ever ever mention this, though.

However, Dad's still mega-popular – the crowd on either side of the red carpet are yelling his name.

'Danny! Hey, Big Danny!'

'I love you, Danny.'

'Sign my autograph book, Danny, *please*!'

'I'm your number-one fan, always and for ever.'

Always and For Ever is the title of Dad's number-one hit. It's the song that everyone knows. It was in the charts for weeks, and it's a Golden Oldie request on all the radio shows, and last year it was the theme tune of a romantic comedy series on television. It's the song that people always scream for at concerts. Some of the crowd are singing it now, arms in the air and swaying. They're nearly all women, mostly older than Mum. Some of them could even be grannies, but they're singing and screaming like teenagers.

Dad starts singing too, clowning around, going up to the iron barriers, signing autographs, smiling because the cameras are still flashing. Mum carries Ace and holds hands with Sweetie, close by Dad's side. I stumble awkwardly after them, my bad teeth clenched.

I see a girl in the crowd about my age, tall and

thin and dark, her hair scraped back in a pony-tail. There's a woman with her, maybe her mother or a big sister, because she's thin and dark too, with the same ponytail, and they're both dressed in black with little black mesh gloves – Dad used to wear them long ago, they were his special trademark.

They are both staring intently at Dad.

'Hey, Danny, look! Here she is – your destiny!' the woman shouts, and she points to her daughter, poking her in the chest. She doesn't seem to mind her mum's shouting and prodding. She sticks out her flat chest proudly, and yells herself.

'Yeah, I'm Destiny!' she shouts, eyes shining, her whole face radiant.

Is that her *name*? How can she sound so proud of it?

Destiny is another one of Dad's songs, though it's tucked away on an early album and only true fans have heard of it.

Destiny, you are my Destiny,
All the world to me.
Even though we're apart
You're always in my heart,
That's where you'll stay
For ever and a day.

When the wind blows,
When the grass grows,
Till the moon glows blue
I'll love you true.

It's not very good, is it? And Destiny isn't a proper name. I think there should be a law preventing parents giving their kids awful names. My own name gets ten out of ten in the terrible stakes. I'm Sunset. Yeah. I'm sure you're sniggering. Everyone does.

'Sunset!' Mum hisses in my ear. 'Come on, we're going in now.'

The photographers are all pointing their cameras down the carpet, where a blonde actress is squealing and clutching the front of her dress because one of her boobs has popped out.

'She's doing it deliberately, any fool can see that,' says Mum. 'Come on, Sunset, move.'

'Danny, oh, Danny, *please* don't go! Over here! Come over here!' Destiny's mum cries, sounding desperate.

'Can't you get Dad to say hello to them?' I ask Mum.

She sighs, eyebrows raised. The photographers are all flashing further down, recording the actress's wardrobe malfunction.

'There's no point,' Mum says. 'They've finished taking Dad's photo. Now, move it.'

I move, but slowly, looking over my shoulder. Destiny's mum is still shouting. Her eyes are popping, her mouth is wide open, she looks scarily demented. I look at Destiny – and she looks back at me. She's got such a strange, weird, yearning look on her face. She can't seriously be in love with my dad too. Surely he's way too old. She stares and I stare. It's almost as if we know each other.

I shiver and turn towards Dad. He waves to the crowd one more time, kissing his hand and pretending to waft the kiss through the air – and then he's inside the cinema, Sweetie hanging onto his hand. Mum's at his side, Ace on her hip. They're swallowed up inside too.

I'm all by myself on the red carpet, dithering. A huge security guy strides over to me.

'Are you Danny Kilman's daughter?' he asks.

I nod.

'In you go then, missy,' he says, steering me towards the entrance.

I look back at Destiny and her mum one last time. I think the mum's *crying*. I feel so bad, but there's nothing I can do. I walk uncertainly into the cinema, turning my ankle in my high heels, lost in a crowd of chattering people. I turn round and round, not knowing where to go or who to ask – and then Mum's hand clamps on my shoulder.

'For God's *sake*, Sunset, what are you playing at?' she whispers. 'Oh *hell*, you've made me break a nail!'

One of her false nails is stuck in my smock top like a little pink pickaxe.

'Come on, come in the ladies' room,' Mum says, tugging me. 'You need to pull up your leggings – they're all saggy and wrinkly and look ridiculous.'

'They *are* ridiculous,' I mumble, following Mum and Sweetie.

I can see Dad now, still clowning around, with Ace crowing on his shoulders.

The ladies' room is crowded out with beautiful young women in short black dresses. They clasp each other and kiss powdery cheeks and totter backwards and forwards in immensely high heels. They mostly take no notice of us, though a couple start cooing over Sweetie, admiring her ballet dress, peering at all her badges. She smiles at them happily, flicking her long glossy locks and telling them the significance of each and every one of her badges. She lisps a little, knowing it makes her sound cuter than ever.

'Be with you in just a tick, Sweetie,' says Mum,

and then she shoves me into a lavatory cubicle and squashes in after me.

'Come *here*,' she hisses, pulling at my horrible leggings. 'Let's sort you out.'

I blush, terrified that the beautiful women outside will think she's having to help me go to the toilet. I go hot all over. My leggings stick to my damp skin and make embarrassing squeaking sounds as Mum yanks at them. Then, when she's got them hitched up and smoothed out, I find that standing beside the toilet has made me suddenly bursting to *use* it. I have to go through the whole performance once more, wriggling the leggings down to my knees and then back again.

'Honestly!' Mum hisses, red in the face too from bending and tugging. 'You're the *oldest*, Sunset, and yet you're more trouble than Sweetie and Ace put together.'

I feel myself burning. My eyes start watering.

'Don't start blubbing!' says Mum, giving my shoulders a little shake. 'What's the *matter* with you? This is meant to be a special treat.'

When we emerge from the toilet at last there's a crowd of women waiting – but no sign of Sweetie.

'Oh my God,' says Mum, hand over her mouth – but then we hear Sweetie laughing.

She's in a room round the corner with more

mirrors, and she's borrowed a pair of high heels from someone and is flouncing across the carpet, flicking her hair and fluffing out her net skirt, and everyone is laughing, Sweetie most of all.

'Hey, Mum, look at me!' she cries, twirling round, her tiny ankles wobbling. 'My heels are much higher than Sunset's! They're much higher than *yours*! Don't I look grown up?'

'Oh yes, very grown up, at least twenty-two,' Mum says dryly, but her whole face is softened with love. 'Come on, sweetheart, give the kind lady back her beautiful shoes and stuff your tootsies back into your boots. We don't want to keep Daddy waiting.' There's an ominous edge to this last sentence. Sweetie picks up on it and kicks off her high heels quickly.

'Who's your daddy then?' asks the girl who lent Sweetie her shoes.

'My daddy's Danny Kilman,' Sweetie says.

'Oh wow!' says the girl, and everyone in the room gathers round, looking impressed.

'Imagine having Danny Kilman for your dad!' someone says.

'I'd sooner have him as my partner!' someone else says, and now they're all looking at Mum.

'You're so lucky,' one girl says, giggling foolishly.

Mum looks at them all, smoothing her skirt. 'Yes

I am,' she says. She holds out her hands. 'Come on, girls.'

Sweetie takes one hand and I'm forced to take the other, though it seems idiotic, a great girl of ten hanging onto Mummy's hand. We walk out and hear them muttering behind us enviously.

There are even more people jam-packed in the foyer now and a great buzz down one end, where the boy band Milky Star have just arrived.

'I want to see them! I really like Milky Star!' Sweetie clamours.

She must have seen them in one of her little girly comics.

'No, no, they're just silly boys. We must go and find Dad,' Mum says quickly. 'And don't go on about Milky Star to Dad, Sweetie, OK?'

Mum might dismiss the silly boys but we find Dad surrounded by silly girls, younger than the ones in the ladies' room, with even shorter skirts and higher heels. One of them is holding Ace, joggling him in her arms while he wriggles and squirms to be put down.

'*I'll* take my little boy, thank you very much,' says Mum, and she practically snatches him from the girl's arms. Ace is startled and starts whimpering.

'There, you're making him cry,' says Mum.

'Oh dear,' says the girl. She's not especially

pretty, her hair a little straggly, her mouth too big for her face, but there's something about her that makes you look at her.

'There now, Ace. He doesn't like to be held by strangers,' says Mum.

'Really?' says the girl. She raises her eyebrows at Dad. 'Most guys do.'

There's a ripple of laughter amongst all the girls. Dad laughs too. Mum looks furious, clutching Ace so tightly that he cries harder.

'Shh now, you promised to be a big boy so you can see Daddy's film,' says Mum. 'Let's take our seats.'

She starts to push her way through the crowd, Sweetie and me on either side of her – but Dad stays where he is, beside the girl with the big mouth. Mum turns and looks at him. Sweetie prattles on about Milky Star. Ace grizzles and whines. They haven't got a clue. Mum mouths something at Dad, looking pleading. Dad pauses – then turns his back on her. He leans towards the girl with the big mouth and whispers something in her ear. She laughs.

I feel so sick I think I'm going to have to rush back to the ladies' and throw up. Mum's looking greeny-white too, clutching Ace, her eyes swivelling in case anyone is watching.

Dad's saying something else, his head very close

to the girl's, so that her big mouth is nearly smearing his cheek with her shiny lipstick. People are pushing past them, ready to take their places in the cinema auditorium, but they're chatting and laughing together, totally relaxed, as if they're in a room by themselves. It's as if Mum and Sweetie and Ace and me have suddenly stopped existing.

Mum bites her lip, swaying a little. Sweetie tugs at her impatiently. Mum clearly doesn't know what to do. Should we go into the auditorium without Dad? What if he never comes to join us? Everyone will see the empty seat. And what about after the film when we go out? The photographers will still be there. 'Where's Danny?' they'll shout. 'Hey, what have you done with Danny? Why aren't any of you smiling? Little munchkin with the red boots, *smile.*'

I can feel my eyes filling with tears. Dad still has his back to us. *Dad*, I yell inside my head. *Dad, Dad, Dad!*

He turns as if he's heard me. He says one more thing to Big Mouth, and touches her arm, his hand cupping her elbow, then he casually strolls over to us as if nothing has happened. He gives me a wink, he blows Sweetie a little kiss, and gently tweaks Ace's snub nose.

'Come on, then, kids, let's see the film,' he says,

as if we're the ones who've been keeping him waiting.

Mum gives him a dazzling smile and hustles us along beside him. 'Cheer *up*, Sunset,' she hisses in my ear. 'For heaven's sake, this is meant to be a treat.'

I'm so muddled I try to smile to please her – and see her wince in irritation.

'*Hide your teeth!*'

I feel like *biting* her with my ugly teeth. I hold it together until we're sitting all in a row and the lights go down, and then I let my tears spill. I wipe my cheeks quickly with the cuff of my smock. Ace is still grizzling too, thrashing about on Mum's lap.

'Can't you shut him up?' Dad hisses. 'I *told* you he was too little.'

'He wants to see his daddy in the movie, don't you, Ace, darling?' says Mum. 'He'll hush in a minute.'

She tries giving him his dummy in the dark, but he keeps fidgeting with it, making silly slurpy noises.

'Look, I'll get some girl to look after him,' says Dad.

'You try to quieten him, Sunset,' says Mum, quickly plonking him on my lap.

I take hold of him firmly by the arms, not his

31

tummy – he can't stand that. 'I'm Mummy Tigerman and we're all cosy in our lair and we have to stay still as still or the bad men will come and get us,' I whisper in his ear.

I put my chin on his silky head and rub it backwards and forwards, and after a minute or so I feel him go floppy. He wriggles his bony little bottom further up my lap and lolls his head, silently suck-suck-sucking his dummy.

Sweetie is secretly sucking her thumb too, cuddling up to Mum, stroking the soft satin material of her skirt. Mum nestles close to Dad, while he sits wide-legged, slightly slumped, his arms over the backs of the seats on either side.

I wonder if the girl with the big mouth is sitting nearby. It feels as if she's squeezed up right next to me, whispering in my ear. *Watch out*, she's saying. *You sit there playing Happy Families, but I can get you.*

But slowly slowly I start to get involved in the film. I like Milky Star too, especially little Davie the drummer, the goofy youngest one. The other three are all ultra-cool, but little Davie always oversleeps, he's always the last to get a joke – he *is* the joke half the time as we watch him falling down the stairs and slipping on a banana skin. The other boys are pursued by girls – in fact one of the girls is Big Mouth, blowing kisses all over the place – but no one ever blows a kiss to little Davie.

Another film starts spooling in my head simultaneously, a film where I'm six or seven years older and Davie bumps into me in the street and we both laugh and apologize and then we go for a cup of coffee, and by the end of the evening we're girlfriend and boyfriend and Davie lets me play on his drums and I'm so good at it I get to be part of the band too, and Davie and I drum away together for the rest of our lives . . .

Then the audience laughs and I blink at the real Davie on the screen – and then see Dad. There he is, strutting down a Soho street, his hair tousled under his bandanna, his long black leather coat flapping, and round the corner all four Milky Star boys see him, then gasp and gibber and clutch each other. They get right down on their knees, crying, 'Oh, Danny, we're not worthy,' while Dad puts his boot up on their backs and stands proudly, arms raised, as if he is a lion tamer and they are four unruly cubs.

There's a great whoop of laughter in the cinema, and Dad throws his head back and laughs too. He sits up straight now, suddenly bigger, and his laugh is the fattest, funniest laugh of all. Mum laughs along with him, and Sweetie giggles, jumping up and down in her seat. Even Ace wakes up a little and speaks through his dummy.

'Ook at Dad! Ook at Dad!' he mumbles.

Well, I'm looking. I watch the film-Dad carefully as he struts down the street, waving one careless hand to the four Milky Stars. I see little old ladies in the street shriek at him and totter along behind, dragging their shopping trolleys, stumbling in their Dr Scholl's. They're playing *Always and For Ever* in the background, but it's slightly distorted and off-key – and when they get to the line at the end of the chorus, *When the wind blows*, there's a sudden blast of wind that nearly blows Dad's bandanna away and tangles his hair, making him totter too, like an old man.

Everyone in the cinema is rocking with laughter, but maybe it's not so funny. Maybe they're laughing at Dad the wrong way. Maybe they're laughing because Dad isn't young and cool and fresh like the Milky Star boys any more.

Dad's still laughing but not so loudly now. He's leaning forward, staring at the screen intently. His own enormous face stares back at him, every line and pore magnified. Then he's gone and we're back looking at Milky Star and the audience settles down again. Ace falls asleep but Sweetie starts fidgeting.

'When will there be another Dad bit?' she whispers loudly to Mum.

'Soon,' says Mum, though she sounds uncertain. 'Watch Milky Star – you like them.'

'Not as much as Dad,' says Sweetie.

The people in the row in front and the row behind all hear and go *'Ahhh!'* Dad's heard her too, and his arm snakes out. He gets hold of her and pulls her onto his lap. There's another *'Ahhh'* at Danny Kilman and his exquisitely pretty little daughter Sweetie.

That's what they called her in *Hi! Magazine*: *Danny Kilman with his exquisitely pretty little daughter Sweetie, enjoying very special family fun.* Dad was riding on a carousel at some charity fête last summer, sitting on a white painted horse with Sweetie in front of him, clutching the gold twisty pole. Dad's hair was all tousled then too, but he didn't look lined at all, maybe because he was laughing. Sweetie was laughing as well, wearing a little frilly white top and tiny pink shorts, showing off her flat golden tummy. It's so unfair. Why can't *I* be little and shiny with long fair hair and a totally flat stomach?

I stare at the screen and watch Davie, but this time he takes no notice of me whatsoever. Dad isn't in the film again, but when the four Milky Star

35

boys get their very first gig, they all tie bandannas over wild dark wigs and wear weird black clothes and huge rings, just like Dad. The whole audience creases up with laughter because they don't look cool, they look ridiculous. Everyone in their film audience laughs too, and boos them off the stage. Then they get a new manager and he whips off their wigs and throws away their stage clothes and jewellery and has them sing wearing ordinary T-shirts and jeans – and they suddenly look great. Their career takes off and they all get rich and famous and pull gorgeous girls, even Davie.

When the credits go up there are little cartoon versions of all the main people – and there's one of Dad too, strutting across the screen and then being blown right up in the air, arms whirling, legs dangling. His bandanna unravels and falls off, together with half his hair.

I hear Dad muttering something to Mum. When the lights go up they're both frowning. But then people start talking to Dad, calling along the row: 'Hey, Danny, you were fantastic!' 'Danny, you're such a good sport!' 'I think you totally stole the show!'

Dad smiles stiffly and acknowledges this, but he mutters more to Mum.

Ace is still asleep, clinging to me like a little

monkey, so I lumber along the row with him towards the exit. Sweetie is tired out too. She's very pale and she's rubbed her eyes so her shadow has smudged, but when she hears the people in front talking about the after-premiere party at Falling Rain, a nearby nightclub, she claps her hands.

'Oh, a party! Let's go to the party, and Milky Star will be there!' she cries.

'You're not going to any party,' says Dad. 'You're going home. It's way past your bedtime, missy.'

Mum looks anxious. 'I could get John to take the kids home and Claudia will put them to bed so we can party, Dan,' she says quickly.

There's no way she's going to let Dad party on his own, not with girls like Big Mouth around.

'I'm not in the mood for partying,' says Dad. He says it mildly enough but Mum jumps at it.

'Right. Fine. OK, let's hit the road.' She phones John to tell him we need him outside the cinema right this minute. There's an awful mad milling of people in the foyer again, but Mum pushes her way through, steering Sweetie, while I hang onto Ace.

When we get outside on the now-scuffed red carpet, Mum looks one way for the car, Dad the other. The photographers are mostly gone. There's just a few faithful fans leaning on the barriers.

'Hey, Danny, it's us! We're still here. Look, here's Destiny!'

It's the woman with the ponytail and the daughter, the one who kept staring so. I shiver, clutching Ace. Have they been standing out here in the cold for the last two *hours* while we've been watching the film?

'Danny, *please*, come and talk to us,' the mother yells, but Dad ignores her.

'Where the hell's John with the car?' he mutters.

'He'll be coming any minute, babe,' Mum says. 'Isn't that the Merc over there? Maybe he can't park any nearer. You keep hold of Sweetie and I'll run and look.'

She dashes off, running all wiggly because of her tight skirt and high heels.

'Danny! Quick, darling, now Suzy's out the way. Come and meet Destiny!' the woman screams.

Dad picks Sweetie up and walks back to the cinema entrance, not even looking round. 'Bring Ace over here, Sunset,' he calls.

I turn round too quickly, wobbling in my silly new boots.

'Whoops! Watch out, darling!' The ponytail mother reaches out, trying to catch me. Destiny is by her side, staring.

'You are so lucky,' she whispers to me.

3

DESTINY

We watch them getting into their silver Mercedes. Suzy's in the back, with Ace on her lap, Sweetie in the middle, then Sunset. Danny sits in the front with the chauffeur. Mum steps forward as if we're part of the family too, ready to squash into the car

– but when she's still a few paces away it drives off.

'Danny!' Mum calls, and she's got tears running down her face. She goes on calling his name, *'Danny, Danny, Danny,'* like some demented bird.

'Mum, he can't hear you. He's in his car. He's *gone*,' I say, giving her a little shake.

People are staring at us. There's a whole crowd of stars pouring out of the cinema now, going on to some party.

'Mum, please,' I beg, but she won't listen to me. She just stands there, shaking and crying and calling for Danny.

There's a sudden surge forward as the Milky Star boys come out in a little bunch. They laugh and chat to the fans, but the little one, Davie, is staring at Mum. The others look too, and one of them laughs. I clench my fists. But Davie is still looking concerned. He comes right over. He touches Mum gently on the arm.

'Are you all right?'

Mum barely focuses on him. She's still staring into the dark, looking at the long-gone car.

Davie looks at me. 'Is she with you?'

'Yes, she's my mum,' I say fiercely.

'What's up with her?'

'She's – she's just upset,' I say. 'It's OK. I'll – I'll take her home.'

'You want me to call a cab or something?'

'No, no . . .' Oh, definitely no. We took a taxi from the station to Leicester Square and it cost a fortune. Mum's only got a couple of pounds left in her purse. 'No thank you, we'll be fine.'

'Take care then, kid,' Davie says, patting me on the arm too, and then he goes off to join his Milky Star mates, and they all jump into a black stretch limo.

'Oh wow! Oh my God! Davie talked to you!' this girl gasps, jumping up and down.

'He's so cute. He's definitely my favourite,' says her friend.

'He *touched* you – and your mum!'

Mum blinks at them. She's stopped screaming, but she's still mouthing *Danny*.

'Come on, Mum,' I say, putting my arm round her. 'Let's go.'

She starts walking obediently. I've no idea where we're going. We walk across this big square, the crowds still jostling, everyone shouting and laughing on their night out. Mum and I are drifting along like a pair of zombies.

'Mum, do you know which way the station is?'

Mum looks around blankly. 'I don't know,' she says, shivering. 'I didn't think – it wasn't meant to happen like this. I was sure we wouldn't be going

41

back tonight. I thought . . . I thought we'd go off with Danny. I wasn't going to be pushy. I know he's got his other family too, but we've waited eleven whole years. I was sure, once he saw us, he'd realize straight away. Oh, Destiny, he didn't even *look* at us. Didn't he hear me? I shouted and shouted!' She's starting to shout again now, her voice very high-pitched.

'That woman's drunk, and that's her little girl with her too! Disgraceful!' someone mutters.

I want to punch them. My mum's never been drunk in her life. The most she drinks is a couple of glasses of cava at Christmas. How *dare* they! But Mum *sounds* drunk, shouting and rambling, and she looks drunk too, her eye make-up smudged all over her cheeks and her hair falling down.

I tell myself she'll be all right when we get on the train, but I'm starting to be so scared. It's like Mum's shrunk down into being a little girl and I'm the grown-up now, left looking after her.

We're walking and walking and yet we're not getting anywhere. I wait till I see a crowd of jolly middle-aged ladies, all linking arms and singing songs from *We Will Rock You!* I stop the kindest-looking one.

'Excuse me, but could you tell me if we're near the station?'

'I'm sorry, lovey, I'm a stranger here myself. We just came up to see the show – we're on a coach trip. Can't you take a coach home?'

'We've got train tickets,' I say, wondering if I'm going to start crying too.

'There's the station just down the street, dear!' a man interrupts. 'Just follow your nose, you can't miss it.'

I don't really believe him, but I drag Mum down the street anyway, and there it is, the railway station. It's definitely a railway station, but it doesn't look right at all. It's old, with a fancy tower in the forecourt. Mum doesn't seem to notice. I take her hand and we go inside. I hope in a mad kind of way that it will all suddenly transform itself into the *right* station – but it all looks so different, and when I look up at the train departures board, all the names are wrong.

I stop a man in uniform. 'Please can you tell us which is the train to Manchester?'

He looks at me as if I'm crazy. 'You can't get to Manchester from here! You have to go from Euston.'

'Where's Euston?'

'It's another station. You'd better take the tube.'

He points to where the underground is. We go down stairs and along tunnels, but then there are

43

machines that won't let us through. I unzip Mum's shoulder bag and find our tickets, but the machine still won't open its gates. Another uniformed man comes and peers at our tickets.

'No, no, they're just returns from Manchester to London. You need tube tickets too.' He's speaking loudly, as if we're both stupid.

I find Mum's two pounds but it's not enough for both of us.

'Couldn't we send the money later, when we get home?' I beg, but they won't listen.

I pull Mum away from the ticket office, and in desperation stop the next group coming chattering down the stairs. They're all girls a few years older than me, laughing and larking around.

'Please, I'm sorry to bother you, I'm trying to get the fare to Euston Station. Could you spare some change?' I ask.

They take no notice and push past as if they haven't even heard me.

Mum's heard though. Her head jerks like she's been slapped. 'Destiny! Stop it! Don't *beg*!'

'We've got to. How else are we going to get there?' I say, and I turn to another couple nearby. 'Please, I'm sorry to bother you . . .' I go through the whole spiel again, but they look disgusted – not with me, with *Mum*.

44

'How dare you make your poor kid beg for you!'

'Look at the state of her! It's obvious she's on drugs. She doesn't deserve to have a child, using her like that. She should be taken away from her.'

I clutch Mum. 'No, it's not like that! We've just not got enough money for the *tube*. Our train goes from Euston. Show them the tickets, Mum!'

But the man in uniform is coming over to us, looking angry – they're all angry now, and so Mum and I run for it, up the steps into the big wide street. We stand there panting and sobbing.

'Oh, Mum!' I say, hugging her.

'It's OK, it's OK,' Mum says, holding me tight. 'I'm not going to let them take you away.'

She sounds like Mum again and I lean against her.

'So what are we going to *do*?'

'Well, looks like we'll have to walk it,' says Mum. She glances down at our shoes. I'm in my trainers but she's in her best white high heels. She's already got sore red patches on both ankles. She wobbles on her heels for another couple of roads, but then she reaches down and takes them off. She's got these nylon pop socks on, with her big toes already poking out. By the time we reach Euston Station at long, long last they are in tatters

45

and Mum's limping, but she doesn't give a word of complaint.

'Thank God,' she says as we walk into the station.

At least it's familiar – but strange too. It's nearly empty – just a few lads messing about down one end, an old drunk man mumbling to himself, and a boy and a girl sitting on the cold station forecourt, oblivious to everything.

'Funny,' says Mum. 'Where *is* everyone?'

I look up at the departure board. There's nothing there, nothing at all until five forty-five in the morning.

'Oh, Mum, there aren't any more trains tonight,' I say.

'Don't be daft, Destiny, there must be trains,' says Mum, but then she sees the station clock.

'Oh no. You're right. We've missed it.' She takes a deep breath. 'We've missed everything.'

I'm scared she's going to start shouting and crying again. I hold onto her tightly. I can feel her trembling.

'What sort of a mother am I?' she mutters.

'You're a lovely mother, the best,' I say fiercely.

I'm looking all around but there's nowhere comfy we can curl up. We end up sitting on two hard bench seats by the locked-up WHSmith stand.

'We can't stay here all night,' says Mum, but we have to, we've no other option. We can't find a little hotel because we've no cash and Mum doesn't have proper credit cards any more because she used to find it too tempting to buy stuff, especially for our house. We got into debt, but we're paying it off, and we've kept the house, so we're doing fine. Apart from tonight.

I wish we had proper coats with us – it's so cold now. I nestle up as close as I can to Mum.

'Put your head on my lap, babe,' she says, so I do. She strokes my hair, gently running her fingers through my ponytail. 'There now. Shut your eyes. We're not in a manky old station. We're tucked up in a lovely big bed with gorgeous fresh white sheets and it's all dark and quiet, and in a little while you're going to go fast asleep . . .' Her voice is still hoarse from all the shouting but she's my lovely mum again and I listen quietly, lulled. Then her voice falters and I realize she's crying again.

'Don't, Mum. Go on, tell me more about the bed. You were making it so real.'

She shakes her head, her lips pressed together. 'That's the trouble, Destiny. I make things up so real that I start believing in them too. That's why we're sitting here, babes. I made myself believe we wouldn't be coming back tonight. Oh, I knew we'd have to come back *some* time – we wouldn't want to leave our house – but I thought we'd stay with Danny for a bit.' She sobs as she says his name. 'I thought – oh, Destiny, I thought once he'd seen you and me, once he heard your name, he'd remember, he'd realize. It's time you got to know your own dad, sweetheart. If anything happens to me, he's all you've got and you're his, quite definitely. You've only to look at you: you've got his eyes, his nose, his mouth, his chin, his wild dark hair. You a total Kilman, plain as plain. It's not as if we want to take liberties. He's still with Suzy and I approve of that, it's good he's faithful to her – though I can't quite see the attraction.

'Anyway, he's got all *her* kids. He's a real family man, you can tell. And *we're* family too – well, *you* are, Destiny, and I thought he'd be desperate to get to know you better. I knew Suzy wouldn't be thrilled, but I didn't know why she would mind so much – after all, I knew Danny before she did, and she's got him all the time now. I didn't see how she could begrudge us a day or two for you to get to know your dad – and I thought how lovely it would be for you to make friends with Sunset, seeing as there's less than a year between you.'

'*Mum!* A girl like Sunset would never want to be friends with me!'

'Yes, she *would*. I thought they'd ask us to stay overnight, and you could share Sunset's bedroom. They must have any number of guest rooms where I could bunk down. And then in the morning we'd have one of those really relaxed late breakfasts – lovely fruit and yoghurt and real coffee – and we'd chat for hours and then maybe all have a walk in a London park somewhere and go to a pub, and Danny would ask you all about yourself, and he'd be so thrilled if he heard you sing.'

'Mum! As if!'

'Well, you've got a lovely singing voice. You clearly take after your dad – I can't sing to save my life – and you'd tell him about school and how you're always top of the class.'

'I'm not always top. Raymond Wallis is heaps better than me at maths and science.'

'I just wanted him to see he's got another daughter to be proud of,' Mum persists. 'I didn't think he'd ask us to stick around for ever, but I was sure he'd want our address, want to keep in touch, start sending you proper birthday presents – maybe even send you to a posh private school—'

'I don't want to go to some snobby private school.'

'Yes, but you need to be educated properly. You're so bright, not like me. I'm dead ignorant, I know that, but you're my star and I want the best for you.'

'I've *got* the best, Mum – I've got you,' I say.

'I'm a dreadful mum,' says Mum. 'Look at us now, stuck here all night. And look at the scene I made! I don't know what happened, babe. I just lost my head. I couldn't bear it when Danny didn't spot us.'

'He *did* see us, Mum. He just didn't want anything to do with us.'

'No, no, that's not true. Well, he might have *seen* us—'

'And heard us.'

'Yes, all right, I know I was shouting – but he just didn't recognize us, take in who we were. If only we'd been on our own with him, I could have introduced you all quiet and polite, and then I just know it would have worked.' Mum pauses, winding my hair round her fingers. 'I know! We'll go to his house!'

'Mum, stop it. We can't do that. We don't know where he lives anyway.'

'Yes we do. He lives in Robin Hill – you've seen the pictures in *Hi! Magazine*. Remember I showed you their living room? They were all sitting on this big leather sofa when little Ace was just a newborn baby – and there was that lovely tender picture of Danny holding him in his arms. Oh, I'd have given

50

anything for Danny to have held you like that! Well, that was their house in Robin Hill. It's only about ten miles from London, I looked it up. We could go there now.'

'Mum! Stop it! Look, this is crazy. We haven't got any money. *How* can we go there? We can't *walk*. Look at the state of your poor feet already.'

'We could . . . we could hitch a lift. I always used to do that when I was fifteen, sixteen, and needing to get to places.'

'Mum, please.' I cup my hands round her face, looking into her eyes. 'Mum, you're going a little bit nuts again. Please stop it.'

'No, I'm not nuts, Destiny, I'm just trying to make it all come right. I blew it at the cinema, shouting my head off, I can see that now. But we've still got a chance. We can't go back to Manchester right this minute, we've got to wait till the morning, OK – so instead of sitting on our bums here, let's go and find Danny's house and we'll just say hello to him, keeping it very polite and low-key. What have we got to lose?'

'We can't just knock on his door!'

'It's not against the law, especially when you just happen to be Danny's daughter.'

'Anyway, *which* door? Do you know his whole address?'

'Not exactly, but Robin Hill's just this weeny little posh estate. There aren't many houses there, that's the whole point. They're all great big houses with huge gardens, swimming pools, stables, anything you fancy. Oh, Destiny, imagine getting up and going for a swim in your own pool and then having a ride on your own pony! Wouldn't you just love that?'

'Yes, but—'

'We'll find Danny's house, easy-peasy. We'll show him we're not just silly fans shouting our heads off. Oh, I could *slap* myself for yelling at him. How he must hate it. But I won't let you down this time, Destiny, honest to God. I'll be dead quiet and dignified, and he'll just need to take a proper look at you and he'll be bowled over. Oh, Danny's such a lovely man. He'll make us welcome, you'll see.'

I don't see at all. She's making it all up again, she can't seem to help it. I can't figure out a way to stop her. At least she's not angry now, she's not shouting. Her whole face is lit up. She looks like those people on *Songs of Praise*, devout and inspired, singing Danny's praises instead of God's.

We leave the station and Mum moves straight to the side of the road and holds up her hand like a lollipop lady. None of the cars take a blind bit of notice of her. No one even slows down.

'Come on, Destiny, you put your hand up too.'

We stand with our arms up until we get pins and needles, but we don't get anywhere. Then a man in a white van stops and Mum gives a shout of triumph and runs up to his window – but by the time I've run up too he's driven off and Mum's left on the pavement, her face red.

'What's happened, Mum?'

'He was a nasty man, dead crude. We wouldn't want a ride with *him*. Don't worry, we'll get a proper lift in no time.'

No time, no time. We seem to have stepped right into no time. Endless hours go by, and yet it's only minutes on Mum's watch. I've never been up this late in my life. I'm so tired. My eyes smart and I ache everywhere and all I want to do is lie down. I'd curl up on the mucky pavement given half a chance. My head feels way too big for my body, like it's going to snap straight off my neck any minute and roll along the gutter like a bowling ball.

A car draws up but it's full of young drunk men, and this time Mum doesn't even bother to ask if they're going anywhere near Robin Hill. They start yelling at us, making horrible suggestions. Mum holds my hand tight, our palms sweating. Then a taxi draws up, and thank heavens the car of drunks drives off.

'Are you OK, girls? Giving you grief, were they?' the taxi driver asks. 'Good job I saw you waving.'

'Oh, sorry. I wasn't hailing you. I was just trying to hitch a lift,' Mum says, still clutching my hand. I can feel her trembling.

'Are you crazy? You don't want to do that, especially not with the little girl.'

'I know, I know, but we've run out of money and I have to get us to Robin Hill,' says Mum.

'Robin Hill?' He blows through his lips doubtfully. 'You live in Robin Hill?'

'We're visiting someone there.' Mum pauses. 'Family.'

'Can't they send a car for you if they live in Poshville?' says the cabbie.

'It's a surprise visit,' says Mum.

He's looking at her like she's making it all up. She is making it up and I can't stop her any more. I'd give the whole world for us to be curled up in bed in our own little house. I screw my face up to stop myself crying. The taxi driver's looking at me.

'You all right, kid?' he asks.

'Yes, fine,' I mumble, because I don't want to let Mum down.

'Look, tell you what, I'm about ready to pack it in for the night. I live in Putney. That's more than halfway to Robin Hill. Hop in the cab and I'll take you as far as Putney High Street, OK?'

'Oh, you're an *angel*. Thank you so, so much,' says Mum, and she bundles me into the back of the cab and jumps in after me before he can change his mind.

'Yeah, that's right – see that shining plate above my bald bonce? That's my halo,' says the cabbie. 'So where are you girls from, then?'

'Wythenlathen. It's near Manchester,' says Mum. 'We've got our own house.' She always says it so proudly.

'You got a husband at home?'

'No, it's just Destiny and me,' says Mum, putting her arm round me.

'Destiny! That's an unusual name.'

'She's called after a Danny Kilman song.'

'I know it well. I've always liked Danny. You a big fan, then?' he asks.

'Oh yes, we're his number-one fans,' says Mum. She winks at me. 'I know him.'

I give her a nudge, not wanting her to say any more.

'Nice bloke, is he? A bit wild, I suppose, but that goes with the territory.'

'He was really lovely to me,' Mum says.

I look at her anxiously. He wasn't lovely at all,

he totally ignored her. I get that panicky feeling like when you have a bad dream and wake up in the middle of the night with your heart pounding and you don't know what's real and what's not.

The cabbie chatters on, talking about seeing Danny on telly, the famous interview when he got fed up with the silly questions halfway through and went lurching off, saying stuff that had to be beeped out. We've got a tape of it and we've played it so often we're both word-perfect for the full twenty-three minutes, and when we get to the end we always chant along with Danny: *Oh beep off, you silly beeping beeper*, and then roar with laughter.

Mum and the taxi driver are laughing now but I don't want to join in. I don't want to think about what's going to happen if we ever get to Robin Hill. It's all much too scary, so I lean against Mum and shut my eyes and sing a Danny song in my head to blot out their voices.

'Ah, has she nodded off?' says the taxi driver.

'She's had a very exciting day, bless her,' says Mum, patting my shoulder.

'You seem very close, you two.'

'Oh yes, we're all in all to each other, Destiny and me,' says Mum.

'Watch out when she gets to be a teenager. I used

56

to be real close to my daughter, and she thought the world of her old dad, she did – though, mind you, she could always twist me round her little finger. But *now* – oh, Lord help me, you ask her to do the simplest thing and she stamps around and sighs, and she's like, *Oh, Dad, you're so stupid.* If I'd talked to my old man like that I'd have got a slap round the earhole, but kids today, they're as lippy as anything, and there's nothing you can do.'

'Oh, I expect my time will come, but just now my girl's a total darling. I don't know what I'd do without her – or what she'd do without me.' Mum's voice goes shaky, and I yawn and snuggle down with my head on her lap, trying to distract her, worried she's going to start crying all over again.

I'm glad we haven't had much to eat because I'm starting to feel sick all hunched up like this, and it would be awful if I threw up in the guy's cab when he's been so kind to us.

It takes such a long time to get to Putney. I really do doze off and dream of a great high fairground roller-coaster. Mum and I are crouched in a car, swooping up and down, screaming our heads off. Way ahead of us we see Danny and his family. They're almost at the end of their ride. If they get off before us, we'll lose them for ever. Mum decides we'll have to jump for it, jump all the way down.

57

She keeps telling me it'll be fine, taking hold of me, shaking me, but I can't jump, it's too high and scary, so I'm stuck going round and round on the ride for ever—

'Destiny! Come on, sweetheart, wake up!' says Mum.

I'm back in the taxi and it's stopped moving. We're suddenly still.

'Did we crash?' I mumble.

'No, silly, we've just got to Putney. We have to get out now,' says Mum. 'Thank you *so* much for the lift. Here, I've only got a couple of quid – I know it's peanuts, but take them anyway as a kind of tip.'

'No, you hang onto what you've got, love. I hope you get to Robin Hill OK. I'd take you there myself but I'm bushed. I need to go and kip down, snuggle up with the missus. You going to be all right now, you and the kid?'

'We're going to be just fine – and thank you so much,' says Mum. 'Say thank you, Destiny.'

I thank him obediently. Mum leans over and gives him a kiss, but I don't go that far. She waves goodbye to him until the taxi is a little black dot and disappears.

'What a lovely guy,' says Mum. 'See, Destiny, there are still some genuinely gold-star people in this world. Imagine, a cabbie giving us that great long ride for nothing. Now all we have to do is hitch another lift . . .'

We walk along Putney High Street until Mum selects a suitable spot where the shop lights make us clearly visible. There are any number of cars still swooping past even though it's so late – no, so *early* now – but they whizz past in an instant. Then another taxi stops and Mum gives a little excited whoop, but this time the cab driver shakes his head at her when she says we have no money.

'Do me a favour, I've got a living to earn,' he says, and drives off.

So we're back to hitching again, and now I'm so tired I can hardly stand upright. Mum sits me down in a shop doorway and stands by herself on the edge of the kerb, waving her arms about. Cars stop every now and then, but either they think Mum's on her own and drive off when she calls to me, or they've never heard of Robin Hill.

'Maybe we'd be better off walking?' Mum suggests, sighing – but then a lorry stops.

'Where are you going to, darling?'

'Robin Hill.'

'Oh yeah? OK, hop in.'

'I've got my daughter.'

'She can hop in too.'

'You're actually going to Robin Hill?'

'I'm going to Kingtown. That's just past it, so I'll shove you out on my way, if that's OK.'

'Oh, it's more than OK, it's absolutely wonderful!' says Mum.

She takes hold of my hand and we clamber up into the cab. The lorry driver shakes us both by the hand.

'Hi, girls,' he says. 'I'm Ginger, for obvious reasons.'

He's got bright red curly hair and a cheery freckled face. He doesn't look like a madman who will axe us both to death, but I'm still wary, though Mum's grinning at him like he's her best friend.

'Well, nice to meet you, girls,' says Ginger. 'So how come you're out and about at this mad hour? Partying all night, eh?' He pauses. 'Oh dear, not doing a runner from the old man?'

'I haven't *got* an old man – and I don't want one either,' says Mum. 'It's kind of complicated, Ginger. We're going to be like surprise guests.'

'I see,' says Ginger, though he clearly doesn't. 'Oh well, it's great to have a little company in the cab. Someone to chat to. When I'm working nights I tend to get a bit dozy round about this time – don't worry, don't worry, I'm not about to nod

60

off . . .' He lowers his head for a split second and gives a snorty snore and then bellows with laughter. 'Your faces! No, don't worry, girls, you're safe with me.'

We are safe too, all the way down the dual carriageway. Then he slows down and stops in a hotel car park.

'Here we are. Told you I'd get you here safe and sound,' says Ginger.

Mum and I sit up straight, rubbing our eyes. I think we both dozed off. Mum's ponytail has collapsed altogether and the make-up's smeared round her eyes, but she still smiles radiantly.

'We're here, at Robin Hill?' she says.

'Yeah, just down that lane.'

'Then you're a gold-star darling, Ginger,' says Mum, and she kisses him on the cheek.

I mumble thank you and hope I won't have to kiss him too. We jump down from the lorry cab and Ginger blows kisses to us as he drives off, his snub nose wrinkling.

'Doesn't he look like a pig when he does that!'

'That's a horrid thing to say, Destiny,' says Mum, but she giggles. 'He didn't *act* like a pig though, did he? He was a total sweetheart – *and* the taxi driver too. We've been so lucky.'

Mum's still smiling, though she's wrapping her

arms tight round herself and stamping her legs, shivering.

'What are we going to do now then, Mum?' I say in a tiny voice.

She looks at me reproachfully. 'For a bright girl you can be very slow on the uptake, Destiny! We're going to find Danny's house.'

I look longingly at the hotel. I think of a hot bath, a clean bed with white sheets ... Mum's looking too. She fiddles with her tangled hair.

'It would be lovely to have a bit of a wash and brush-up first,' she says. She takes my hand. 'OK, let's give it a go.'

She walks towards the entrance of the hotel. I try to pull her back.

'Mum! We can't! We haven't got any *money*!'

'We can always do a runner in the morning,' says Mum.

My heart starts thumping. Is she *serious*? She marches through the glass door into the hotel lobby. She's serious all right.

There's no one in the hotel lobby. No one at the reception desk. No one. Mum peers around. She looks at the soft purple sofa right in front of us.

'Well, we can always have a kip on that,' she says. 'Go on, lie down, darling. You look all in.'

I stand there, swaying on my feet, and then

move unsteadily towards the sofa. I touch it cautiously, like it might be alive – and then I sit on the edge. It feels so good I can't help leaning back – and then I lie down properly and put my feet up.

'That's my girl,' says Mum. 'Here, budge up, make room for me.'

But as she comes to join me, a man walks out of a room at the back and stares at us.

'Good Lord, where did you spring from?' he says. He glares at me. 'You can't sleep there!'

I jump up off the sofa. He peers at the cushions, as if I might have left muddy marks all over them.

'My daughter's tired. We'd like a room, please,' says Mum, her chin up.

The man looks at his watch ostentatiously. 'Our guests don't usually arrive at this time,' he says.

'Well, we've been to a party,' says Mum. 'And now we'd like a room.'

He sighs, but turns on his computer. 'Is it just for one night?'

'Yes please.'

'May I have your credit card?'

Mum bites her lip. 'Surely we pay when we check out?'

'Yes, of course, but I need to take your credit card details now.'

'Oh, right.' Mum make a pantomime of checking

her bag and her jeans pocket. The man waits impassively. 'Oh no!' she says. 'I can't find it.'

'Now there's a surprise,' says the man.

'I don't know what to do,' says Mum.

'Well, I'm afraid you can't stay here. Goodbye,' says the man.

I grab Mum's hand. I don't want her to bluff any more, it's so awful. But she takes no notice.

'Where on earth can I have lost it?' says Mum. 'I'll have to ring the credit card people in the morning. Can't we simply have a room for the rest of the night and I'll sort out all the financial details later, after breakfast?'

'I'm sorry, it's a strict company rule. Guests have to provide their credit card details when they check in.'

Mum sighs. 'Well, can my daughter and I at least use your ladies' room – or is there a strict company rule that says little girls can't use your toilet?' says Mum.

The man taps his fingers on the desk impatiently. 'Very well. But be quick about it.'

We aren't quick at all. We don't just use the toilet. We wash our faces in the sink. Mum takes her top off and washes under her arms and soaks her filthy feet. She reapplies her make-up and combs her hair and fixes a fresh new ponytail, and then brushes mine into place too. We don't have toothpaste or brushes. Mum tries rubbing a tiny bit of soap around her teeth instead but it makes her gag.

'There, we look a bit better now,' she says. 'Do you want to wash your feet too, Destiny? Mine feel so much better now.'

'No, Mum. We've been ages. That man will come banging any moment. Please let's go.'

'You're such a little worrypot,' says Mum, giving me a kiss on the end of my nose. Then she has to scrub it with toilet paper because she's left fresh lipstick marks all over it.

'Dear, oh dear, we can't have you looking like Rudolph the Red-nosed Reindeer when you meet your father,' she says.

The man is waiting just outside the door of the ladies' toilet, looking grim. He pokes his head inside, obviously checking to see we've not smeared the sinks or peed on the pristine floor.

'I told you to be quick about it. What were you doing, having a bath?'

I snigger anxiously, but he's not being funny.

'Now hop it, both of you.' He glares at Mum. 'You're lucky I haven't called the police.'

'Oh, is it a crime now to ask for a room in your

poxy hotel?' asks Mum. 'Don't you fret, I wouldn't stay here if you paid me now.'

She takes my hand and marches out in her high heels, ponytail swinging, while I scamper along beside her.

'Oh, Mum, you don't think he *will* call the police, do you?' I ask.

'Don't be daft, Destiny. Of course he won't. Cheer up, darling. We're here, in Robin Hill.' She strokes the street sign lovingly, as if it's a cat. 'There! Come on.'

There's a white wooden barrier across the road and a hut beside it, but thank goodness there's no one in it. We walk along the pavement into the Robin Hill Estate, feeling like Dorothy stepping out of her front door into Oz. We're only a few steps away from the busy main road and yet we seem to be right in the countryside: there's a canopy of trees overhead and thick hedges like the grassy path. Birds are already starting to sing in the trees, though there's still no sign of dawn. It's so dark here. I grab Mum's hand and hold it tightly.

'Isn't it lovely here?' she whispers. 'I knew Danny would live in a wonderful place.'

'Do you really think you'll know which is his house?'

'Of course!' says Mum, but now she doesn't sound so sure.

As we walk on we discover there are many houses, but most of them are hidden away down long gravel driveways. All you can see are big security gates. Mum climbs up a rung or two on one gate to see if she can spot the house and a light comes on out of nowhere, making us both gasp. Mum jumps down and we make a run for it, right up the lane and round the corner. We flatten ourselves behind a tree, hearts thudding, waiting for shouts and running footsteps and police sirens, but the light has gone off now and there is utter silence.

'Whoops!' Mum says, giggling shakily.

'Mum, they'll think we're burglars and lock us up!'

'Oh, Destiny, stop it, you're doing my head in. I'm trying to stay positive here. I'm pretty sure that wasn't Danny's house. He's got a lovely garden. I've seen photos of him playing with the children in it. He's obviously such a lovely caring dad. Can't you see, you've been missing out all these years, darling. I want him to start caring for you too, just a little bit. It's high time.'

'But, Mum—'

'Shut *up*, Destiny. Why do you always have to

argue with me? I'm your mother and I know best. Now come along.'

So I walk along beside her, not saying anything. She's starting to limp again, but she keeps her shoes on, wanting to keep her feet clean. She's humming, but so softly I can barely hear her. I don't have to listen to know what tune it is. It's *Destiny*, my song.

We stumble up and down grassy lanes, getting glimpses of huge houses, one with a big lake, one with tennis courts. I imagine Danny rowing, Danny running round with a racket. Another house has a huge Alsatian that leaps towards us as we peer through the gate. It can't get at us but we run anyway, frightened its loud barking will alert someone.

'That can't be Danny's house. He'd never have a mad dog like that with children around. It would swallow little Ace for breakfast,' Mum pants.

I'm starting to think we'll spend the rest of the night stumbling around Robin Hill, probably going backwards and forwards past Danny's house several times without ever realizing. But right at the end of the lane there's a big gate with limp bouquets of flowers and little teddies tied to it, and all along the wall there are smudges and blobs of writing, though we can't read them in the gloom.

We don't need to. It's obvious they are passionate messages from fans. This *must* be Danny's house.

Mum squeezes my hand tight. 'We've found it, Destiny!' She gives a little chuckle. 'They'll be so surprised when we knock on the door!'

'Mum! We can't knock *now*. It's much too early.'

'Oh, darling, we can't wait now,' says Mum, pacing up and down in her punishing high heels. 'I can't wait, I can't wait!'

'Mum, what would we think if there was a knock on *our* door at three o'clock in the morning? It'll worry them so – and they'll get angry too.'

'Not when we explain,' says Mum, but she's started to waver. 'Maybe you're right. We'll wait till it's daylight, OK? It'll give us a chance to get a bit of beauty sleep.'

So we sit down on the path and lean against the wall. In spite of the cold and the worry and the excitement we both fall fast asleep.

4

SUNSET

I wake up early, even though I was awake half the
night. Mum and Dad rowed for hours and hours.
They were yelling so loudly that Ace woke up and
started crying too. I got to him before Claudia
and lifted him out of his bed and took him back

into my room. Sweetie came too, burrowing into me with her little sharp elbows and knees, her long hair tangled all over my face.

We lay there uncomfortably while the shouting went on. I tried pulling the duvet up over our heads. I made Sweetie and Ace pretend we were bears in a cave, but it only distracted them for a minute or two and then they got hot and poked their heads out of the duvet again. Mum was screaming now and Dad was shouting very, very rude words. Ace started muttering them too, but I put my hand over his mouth.

'Stop it, Ace. You mustn't say that.'

'Dad is.'

'Dad's being very bad.'

'Why is he so cross with Mum?' Ace mumbled. 'I hate it when Dad's cross.'

'Mum's *crying*,' said Sweetie. 'Shall we go and stop them, Sunset?'

'No, then they'll be cross with us. Shh now.'

'I want Mum!' Ace said.

'Well, you've got me just now. Come here, little Aceman Spaceman. Time to dream your way over the moon and in and out the stars.'

I stroked his hot head and his silky straight hair while he nestled close, and in a few minutes he was breathing deeply, fast asleep.

'He didn't do a wee in his pot,' Sweetie whispered. 'Watch out, Sunset, he'll wet the bed.'

'No he won't,' I said firmly, though I worried she might well be right.

The bed's still dry now, and I should lift him out quick and put him on his pot, but if he wakes up he'll wake everyone and it's so quiet and peaceful. Sweetie's stayed in my bed too. She's stretched out like a starfish, taking up most of the space. She's still got purple shadow on her eyelids. I stare at my sister, sighing. It's so unfair. Why can't *I* be little and pretty. I'd give anything to be tiny and blonde and beautiful like Sweetie. She doesn't have to bother to be nice to people all the time. Everyone likes her just because she *looks* lovely. I comb her long locks gently with my fingers and put my head very close to hers so that *I* have long fair hair falling past my shoulders.

Sweetie murmurs in her sleep and pushes me away.

'Excuse me, but this is *my* bed,' I mutter, but she doesn't budge.

So I slide right out of the bed and stand and stretch. Then I tiptoe across the carpet and carefully open the doors to Wardrobe City. I have a white fitted wardrobe the whole length of one wall, but I've managed to squash all my boring dresses

72

and jackets and tops and trousers up at one end. That means I can use more than half of it for Wardrobe City.

It started off with my doll's house. *Hi! Magazine* gave it to me when Sweetie was born. They did a twelve-page photo feature on Mum and Dad and their new baby girl. They showed Mum in bed with Sweetie (in her bunny sleeping suit) and Dad bringing Mum breakfast on a tray; Mum and Dad lying back on the bed with Sweetie in their arms; Mum working out while Dad cradles Sweetie; Mum and Dad in party clothes sitting on the big velvet sofa with Sweetie in a long white christening robe on Mum's knee; Sweetie in her own fairy-tale rocking cot with Mum and Dad kissing her goodnight. I'm in that one too, with my finger up to my lips, saying shush (teeth hidden). Then they wanted a photo in my bedroom with me sitting on the floor with Sweetie on my lap and all my teddies sitting in a ring around us, but they felt the wall looked a bit white and bare so they *sent out for a large doll's house* to fill in the blank space!

I don't think I'd ever even seen a doll's house before. I forgot all about my new baby sister and just wanted to kneel in front of this wonderful pink and white house with its glossy white-tiled roof and white pillars and three little white steps up to the rose-coloured front door. It had a tiny brass lion-head knocker that you could really tap, and a little letterbox slit for fingernail-sized envelopes. The door was hinged so a small doll could knock and then slip indoors. I longed to squeeze through the front door myself. I crouched down to peer through the lattice windows to see if I could spot any dolls inside, waving tiny pink plastic fingers at me.

'Do you want to see inside?' said Mark, the photographer's assistant. He touched a hook on the side of the house. It swung right open, exposing all three storeys of the doll's house, rudimentarily furnished – a bed here, a rug there, a stove in the kitchen and a tiny toilet with a little seat in the bathroom.

I fetched my smallest thumb-sized bear and walked her round the doll's house, laying her down on the bed, sitting her on the rug, standing her by the stove to cook porridge and then squatting her on top of the toilet. I forgot all about my teeth. I was smiling from ear to ear.

Sweetie had got bored by this time and the nanny (not Claudia – was it Rhiann or Agnieszka or Hilke then?) fed her so I could play undisturbed for twenty minutes. That teddy was called Furry and had always been the baby of the bear family, but she grew up rapidly in the doll's house and became Mrs Furry, proud owner of a miniature mansion. I fashioned her a little apron out of a tissue and she bustled about the house, diligently dusting with her paw.

When Sweetie was fed and changed and ready for the cameras again, I reluctantly laid Mrs Furry down for a rest on her bed and sat on the floor with my sister, trying my hardest to look winsome. I was hopeless at it. I couldn't keep my lips over my teeth and my head kept lolling self-consciously to one side, and I was so worried about blinking each time the camera flashed that I stared, cross-eyed and rigid, into the lens. Sweetie was newborn but she already had the knack. She couldn't quite smile yet but she opened her blue eyes wide and pursed her little rose-bud lips and clasped one of my fingers in the cutest way, already playing to the camera.

When we were done at last, and the photographer and his assistant were packing up all the weird white dishes and silver paper and endless cameras and stands and batteries and cables, I went and knelt by the doll's house. I woke Mrs Furry and she trailed wretchedly round each room, kissing each bedknob on the bed, the woolly edges of the rug, the rings of the cooker. She even bent down and kissed the toilet.

'What's she doing? Is she being sick?' asked Mark, kneeling down beside me.

I blushed in case he thought I was being rude. 'She's saying goodbye to the house,' I whispered.

'Doesn't she want to live there any more?'

'Yes, it's her absolute dream home!' I said, which made him laugh.

'Then tell her she can stay there. It looks like the doll's house is yours to keep.'

'Really!'

'We tried to hire it, but it was going to cost so much we bought it outright. I don't see the point of lumbering it back to the studio. You keep it, sweetie.'

I thought for one stomach-churning moment that he meant it was my baby sister's doll's house. 'I'm not Sweetie, I'm Sunset,' I said, crestfallen.

'I know, darling. I call everyone sweetie.' He very gently pinched the end of my nose. 'And you're a total sweetie.'

Oh, I loved Mark so much. For a long time I pretended that he and I lived in the pink and white house together, with Mrs Furry as our housekeeper.

Mum bought me two doll's house dolls but I never liked them very much. They had china heads and stiff white cloth bodies so they couldn't sit down properly. I had to prop them up or let them lie flat on the floor as if they'd suddenly fainted. They were dressed in Victorian clothes, the lady in a purple crinoline and the man in a grey frock coat and pinstripe trousers. Mum said I should call them Victoria and Albert. I didn't really want to. It made them seem stiffer and stranger than ever. I started having bad dreams about six-foot monster dolls with painted heads and staring eyes, ready to fell me with one flick of their stiffly stuffed arms. I banished Victoria and Albert to the very bottom of my sock-and-knicker drawer.

I invited the next-size-up teddy into the doll's house to keep Mrs Furry company. This was Mr Fat Bruin, a tubby bear with a big smile who told jolly stories, especially after I'd given him a drink out of a miniature liqueur bottle.

I decided Mrs Furry and Mr Fat Bruin might like some children, so I gave them Chop Suey, a tiny Chinese cat permanently waving his paw, and Trotty, a pink glass horse, and a baby, Peanut, specially made out of pink Plasticine.

Mum got cross with me when she found me playing with my new family.

'Why are you cluttering up your lovely doll's house with all this *junk*? I bought you proper dollies to play with. These silly things aren't *dolls*. They look all wrong. They're too big or too little.

And you know I hate you playing with Plasticine – it gets everywhere.' She squeezed Peanut, mangling her terribly.

I said I was sorry and agreed I was silly and took my family out of the doll's house – but as soon as Mum had gone out of the room I brought them all back. I asked Mrs Furry to stand by the stove to cook them my favourite meal of sausage and mash and baked beans. Mr Fat Bruin flopped on the sofa with a tiny folded-up scrap of newspaper. Chop Suey played marbles with tiny beads. Trotty did her ballet exercises wearing a wisp of pink feather. I tenderly moulded Peanut back into shape and tucked her up in her matchbox cot. I'd keep my family safe and splendidly housed no matter what.

They still live in the doll's house now, years and years later. I've got new dolls, little sturdy smiling ones, and five tiny felt mice, all in different outfits, but they're just friends and cousins to my proper family. I've got lots more furniture now too: a four-poster bed with a set of rose-silk covers, a television, a tiny bird in a white cage, rugs in every room, pictures hanging on the walls, curtains at each window, but the original key pieces are still my favourites. Mrs Furry has a whole set of saucepans and can serve her meals on special miniature willow-pattern plates. Mr Fat Bruin's sofa has velvet cushions with little braid tassels. Chop Suey and Trotty and Peanut have roomfuls of tiny toys, including a perfect miniature doll's house. It has a little hook at the side so it can swing open. I've made minute Plasticine replicas of my family inside, playing with another even smaller doll's house. I like to imagine that inside *that* one there's another weeny family playing with a crumb-size doll's house, on and on until it makes me feel giddy.

The doll's house is still my favourite possession, even though I suppose I'm much too old to play with dolls now. Sweetie wanted to play with the doll's house too as soon as she could crawl, but she just chewed on the furniture. She very nearly swallowed Peanut.

I tried gently distracting her, but it only made her more determined. She started using the doll's house to pull herself up, hanging onto the little window ledges and buckling them. I couldn't bear it and tapped her little scrabbling fingers – and Mum saw and shouted that I was a bad, jealous, selfish sister and I must learn to share my toys with Sweetie. I was willing to share *most* things with her, but not the doll's house. So I dragged it laboriously inside my wardrobe and shut the door on it, so that Sweetie couldn't get at it.

I kept the doll's house in the wardrobe, very sensibly, because Ace proved to be a total menace when it came to wrecking my things. In this week alone he's spoiled the points of every single one of my felt pens and pulled the head right off Suma, my biggest teddy bear.

But Wardrobe City is safe behind locked doors. I only open up my world when Sweetie and Ace are out or asleep. I've made three more houses out of shoe boxes stuck together, furnishing them all myself, and built a towering apartment building out of wooden bricks. After various terrible castrophes I had to use up several tubes of Evostik cementing the bricks together.

There's also two shops. One sells little packets of cereal and small pots of jam and miniature alcohol bottles and a variety of Plasticine ready-meals. The other is a clothes shop specializing in a denim range – lots of little jackets and jeans that I made out of an old pair of dungarees. There's also a small farm so everyone has fresh milk and eggs every day, and a garage with a fleet of Dinky cars. I'm secretly saving up for a castle, though it's going to be a bit of a squash fitting it in.

I don't ever tell anyone about Wardrobe City. They'd think me weirder than ever at school. I hate school. I've been to four different schools already and they're all horrible. I didn't mind lesson time at my last school, but Ridgemount House is awful because there aren't any rules. We don't even have to do proper lessons if we don't feel like it. The other kids mess around all the time. I don't fit in at all. They don't like me. They call me Wonky Gob. I haven't got a single friend.

I can't tell Mum or Dad. They'll just go on about the tough schools they attended when they were little kids and say I have to learn to lighten up and join in with the fun and then I'll soon make friends. Like Sweetie. She is in Year One at my school and every single child in her class wants to be her best friend.

I hear a howl and a scratch-scratch-scratching outside my door.

'Go back to sleep, it's too early,' I hiss.

I want to rearrange the bedrooms in my doll's house in peace – but Bessie grumbles and moans and complains so bitterly that I have to shut Wardrobe City up and go to her.

I open my bedroom door and pick her up. She's an old lady cat now, but she's still beautiful, a big fat black cat with white paws. Someone gave her to Mum after she's done a modelling job with kittens, but Mum doesn't really look after her, and Dad doesn't like cats. Sweetie's supposed to be allergic to them, and Bessie avoids Ace because he chases her, so basically I'm the one who looks after her now.

'It's not breakfast time yet, Bessie,' I whisper, rubbing my cheek against her soft furry head.

Bessie disagrees. It's *always* breakfast time as far as she's concerned. I carry her downstairs to the kitchen and empty a tin of her wet goo into a bowl. She gollops it down eagerly while I keep her company with a bowl of cornflakes. No one else is stirring. Claudia lies in as long as Ace will let her. Margaret, our housekeeper, doesn't come to do breakfast until late on a Sunday. Her husband, John, doesn't start mowing the lawn or fixing stuff till midday so that Dad isn't disturbed. It's very peaceful in the early morning.

Bessie finishes her bowl before I finish mine. She goes to the back door and starts yowling again to be let out. It's hard working getting all the locks and bolts sorted but I'm a dab hand at it now. I open the door and Bessie shoots out, across the long lawn, round the pool, under the trampoline, up the path to the wild woody part where the grass is high and she can hide.

I follow her out in my pyjamas, snatching John's old gardening fleece from the peg on the back door. I feel less inclined to stick my feet into his gardening boots so I wander out barefoot. The grass is wet and tickly. It feels a bit like paddling. I skip about, waving my arms in the air, kicking my legs out, being a ballet dancer.

Mum once sent me to dancing classes when I was about five. Maybe it was to get me out of the way when Sweetie was born. Mum said it would help me to look graceful. I stuck it out for a whole year. I liked Miss Lucy, who taught us. She was very kind and never ever got cross even when I kept starting on the wrong foot and twirling the wrong way. I was the only child in the class who couldn't skip. I'd feel myself getting hot and red, and I could see all the other little girls sniggering as I staggered about. But Miss Lucy always said, 'Well done, Sunset. I can see you're trying hard, dear.'

Then one day Mum couldn't take me because she was having extensions at the hairdresser's and the nanny had to take Sweetie to the doctor's, and Margaret and John were having a weekend off, and the temp girl from the agency didn't turn up – so Dad took me dancing.

He sat with all the other mums while they twittered and fussed because they were actually sitting next to Danny Kilman, and most of them had had crushes on him since they were little kids. Dad just sat basking in the attention, leaning back, hands behind his head, his long skinny legs stretched out, his cowboy boots pointing upwards – and I was so proud that he was *my* dad. But when I started dancing he sat up straight. After a while he hunched over, head bent, as if he couldn't bear to look at me any more.

As soon as the dancing lesson finished, while I was still doing a wobbly curtsy with all the other little girls, Dad took me by the hand and hauled me out of the room.

'Do you like dancing, Sunset?' he asked.

'I don't know,' I mumbled.

'Well, I don't see the point of you going, darling, because you're absolute rubbish at it,' Dad said – and I never went back.

I know I'm still rubbish, I'm not daft, but I love whirling around and leaping about, and so long as I can't see myself I can pretend I'm in a sticky-out white dress with pink ballet shoes on my feet. I do a figure-of-eight around the pool, a wafting float through the long grass, and then start a serious wood-nymph ballet in and out of the trees. I'm getting seriously out of breath now, so I slow down and sweep a deep curtsy to my imaginary audience while they clap and cheer and throw flowers at me.

I can hear clapping! *Real* clapping, muted but

unmistakable. I look up and there's a face at the top of the wall, elbows, two clapping hands. I feel myself blushing all over. I must look such a *fool*. Who is it? A girl, not very old, only about my age. A thin dark girl with her hair pulled back in a ponytail.

Do I know her? She looks sort of familiar. She's not one of the girls at school, she's not any of the girls who used to come round to play, she's ... She's the girl from last night at the premiere, the girl who said I was lucky!

What is she doing *here*? And how did she get up the wall? It's a good six feet high. I stand dithering, still brick-red, not knowing what to do. Maybe I should run right back into the house. Perhaps I should find John – he's meant to be our security guy. I should tell him there's a girl climbing the wall.

'Hello,' she says tentatively.

'Hello,' I say, as if it's the most normal thing in the world for us to meet like this.

'I liked your dancing,' she says.

My heart thumps but she doesn't seem to be teasing me.

'I must have looked a right idiot,' I mumble.

I realize I *still* look incredibly stupid in my pink teddy-bear pyjamas and John's old fleece. She looks so effortlessly cool in her black T-shirt. She's still got her little black mittens on. Her mum was dressed identically.

'Where's your mum?' I ask.

'Oh, she's here, but she's asleep just now.'

'What do you mean, here?'

She nods to her side of the wall. 'Here!'

'What, your mum's sleeping on the *pavement*?'

'Yep.'

'Is she all right?'

'I think so.' She peers down and nearly slips. 'Whoops! Hang on a minute.' She pulls hard, wriggles a lot, and then somehow gets one foot up on the wall too.

'Oh, careful, you'll fall!'

'No, no, wait a minute.' She levers her foot further across, wriggles a bit more, gets her leg right up – and then suddenly there she is, sitting triumphantly side-saddle on top of the wall.

'How did you *do* that? How did you get right *up* it?'

'I'm good at climbing. And there's the creeper-thingy so I hung onto that. I could jump right down into your garden, if that's OK with you?'

'Well . . .'

'I'd come through the gate, but it's all locked up and it's one of them ones with a security code, isn't it?'

'Yes, I think so.'

'So how do your friends nip round to see if you want to play out?'

'They don't. I suppose their mum and my mum might fix it up first, on the phone,' I say uncomfortably, not wanting to let on that I don't *have* any friends just at the moment.

'Well, *I've* come round on the off-chance, haven't I? Can I come in?'

I know I shouldn't let her. Mum would go bananas. She's always going on to Dad that we should have more security. She tried to get the wall built even higher, with jagged glass at the top, but the other Robin Hill residents objected, saying it wouldn't be in keeping with the rest of the estate. Mum was furious, saying they were all a load of nosy interfering snobs, and they simply didn't understand our security problems because they just had boring old managing directors for their husbands, not world-famous rock stars. We didn't just have to worry about burglars – the kids could well be stolen and held to ransom.

But this girl with the ponytail is clearly not a burglar or a kidnapper. It's so strange: I don't *know* her, I don't even know her name, and yet I don't feel shy with her. I feel I can say anything and she won't laugh or screw her finger into her forehead or call me weird.

'Yes, of course you can come in – but do be careful. Look, wait . . .' I take John's fleece off, roll it up and put it on the ground by the wall. 'This should break your fall – or I could try and catch you if you like.'

'I'd knock you flying!' she says. 'It's OK. Watch!'

She suddenly leaps, landing neatly and gracefully on the fleece, bending her knees and then straightening up and flinging her arms wide, just like a gymnast.

'Now I'll clap *you*,' I say, doing so.

'I hope I haven't got your dressing gown muddy,' she says, picking it up and shaking it out.

'That's not my dressing gown!' I say. 'It's John's fleece.'

'Who's John?'

'Well, he's mostly our gardener,' I say, embarrassed.

'Oh, yes. I can't imagine Danny Kilman doing the gardening,' she says.

'Do you – do you have a big crush on Danny then? You were at the premiere last night.'

She hesitates. 'It's . . . complicated,' she says, in a very grown-up way, though she looks uncomfortable.

'It's OK. I think I'm getting a crush on Davie in Milky Star. I think he's cute.'

'Oh, yes. I like him too. He *spoke* to Mum and me last night.'

'Did he?'

'Yes, he did, honest.' She's peering through the trees towards the house. 'You've got the biggest garden in the whole world, Sunset!'

'How do you know my name?' I say, blushing.

She laughs at me. 'You're in all the celebrity magazines, silly.'

'I hate those things. I mean, I know my dad and my mum are in them and that's OK, because they're famous, but I just mess it up.

'You're famous too! And what are you on about? You always look great in the photos. You've got such lovely clothes. I love those red boots you've got – and that little leather jacket! You're so lucky.'

She's still acting like she really means it. The leather jacket doesn't fit me properly any more: it's so small it cuts in under the arms. This girl's as tall as me but much thinner. It would probably fit her. Shall I offer her my jacket? But would she think me rude and patronizing? Would she be offended?

'Would you like a leather jacket like that?' I ask cautiously.

'That's a daft question!' she says, but she's laughing.

'Well . . .' I start, but she says something that distracts me.

89

'My absolute favourite photo of you is one where you're quite little and you're playing with Danny on the beach? Do you remember that one?'

I shake my head.

'Well, what about when baby Sweetie was just born, and you're playing with your doll's house. Do you remember *that*?'

'Oh, *yes.*'

'It was such a lovely doll's house, all pink and white. Is it Sweetie's now?'

I hesitate. 'Well, she's got all her own stuff.'

'So it's still in your bedroom?'

'It's in my wardrobe actually.'

'Hey, you must have a ginormous wardrobe! Do you sneak inside and have a little play with the doll's-house people when no one's around? *I* would!'

I nod, because I know she won't laugh. I wonder about inviting her right into the house, taking her up to my bedroom and showing her Wardrobe City. I know she'd love it. I'd introduce her to Mrs Furry and all her friends, and we could do the housework together and go to the shopping centre and hang out at the farm, me and my friend . . .

'What's your name?' I ask.

She hesitates, catching her teeth on her lower lip. 'Don't laugh,' she says.

'As if I would! You don't laugh at me, and Sunset's a very silly name.'

'It's Destiny. Destiny Williams.'

'That's – that's a pretty name,' I say. I don't get it for a moment. Then, 'You mean, Destiny like my dad's song?'

'*You are my Dest-in-eee*,' she sings, raising her eyebrows. She's got a strange, lovely voice, very deep and grown up.

Then we both giggle.

'Imagine what it's like for me at school. I don't half get teased.'

'Oh, I do too,' I say, which is true, though there are lots of kids with odd names at Ridgemount House – Kester, Bambi, Starling, Plum, Primavera . . . 'I hate school.'

'Me too. But you don't need to go to school, do you? Couldn't you have, like, a private tutor, seeing as you're so rich?'

'I wish! Yes, a tutor that just teaches stuff like art and English.'

'They're *my* favourites too!'

'It's weird, we've got so much in common,' I say.

'We have, haven't we!' She sounds thrilled too. 'We even look a bit alike, don't we? Do you think?'

I'm not so sure. We're both dark, I suppose, but

she's thinner than me and looks older and *much* prettier. I wish I did look like her.

'Maybe we look a *bit* alike,' I say.

'Yes, we really do,' she says, and she's smiling all over her face now.

Then we hear someone calling, in a high, frightened voice.

'Destiny! Destiny, where *are* you?'

'Oh God, that's my mum,' says Destiny. She runs back through the trees towards the wall. 'It's OK, Mum, I'm here. I'm in the garden,' she calls.

'What? Whereabouts?' She sounds frantic.

Destiny runs right up to the wall and tries to climb up it, but she can't get a grip. She tries harder, but falls down, scraping her hands.

'Don't! You're hurting yourself. Come to the gate,' I say quickly. 'Oh, your poor *hands*!'

'It's OK, only a graze. I'm tough as old boots, me,' says Destiny. 'Mum, can you hear? Sunset says to go to the gate.'

'Sunset! You've met up with her at last!' she calls from the other side.

'You wanted to meet *me*?' I say to Destiny.

She shrugs. 'Perhaps my mum had better explain. She'll tell it all to Danny.'

I swallow. How will she talk to my dad? He doesn't talk to anyone he doesn't know. You have to set up a special meeting with him via Rose-May, his manager – and then he mostly doesn't turn up, not unless it's for the media. And he doesn't even talk to us in the morning. We're not allowed to go near his bedroom before twelve, not even Sweetie.

I follow Destiny anxiously as she walks along beside the wall. She spots the swimming pool and raises her eyebrows. 'You've got your own huge swimming pool!' she says. 'Oh my God, it's *guitar* shaped. How cool is that!'

'It's a bit odd swimming in it with all those curvy edges,' I say. 'You can't do proper laps.'

'So you can swim OK then? I'm rubbish at it. I only went to our swimming baths once and someone pushed me under and the water went right up my nose, and I bawled my head off and wouldn't ever go back. So, you can lie out in your loungers after a swim and get suntanned and drink piña coladas?'

'Well, I don't have proper cocktails. I have this thing called Over the Rainbow – it's all different juices and lots of fruity bits.'

'You really *do* have cocktails? You're not joking me?' Destiny shakes her head. Then she squints towards the house. 'Sunset, your house is massive! It's bigger than our entire block of flats. So which is your bedroom?'

'That window up in the turret bit.'

'Oh, that's *exactly* the room I'd choose. It's just like a fairy tale. Do you have to share it with Sweetie?'

'No, but she comes into my bed sometimes. And Ace does too – *not* a good idea, because he sometimes wets it,' I say.

She laughs. 'I love all these things they leave *out* of *Hi! Magazine*,' she says.

Then we get to the gate – and there's Destiny's mother, pressing against the iron railings. She's smaller than I remembered, not much bigger than us. Her ponytail makes her look like a little girl, yet her face is lined and eerily pale, and her eyes are staring so. It's hard not to feel a little frightened of her – but Destiny rushes up to her and squeezes her hands through the narrow bars and pats her mum's thin shoulders.

'I'm so sorry I worried you, Mum. It's just you were so sound asleep and I thought I'd have a go at hitching myself up the wall to have a quick look and I spotted Sunset here, dancing in the garden—'

'Making a fool of myself,' I say. 'How do you do, Mrs Williams.'

'Hello, dear,' she says softly. She looks from me to Destiny and back again, shaking her head. Tears start spilling down her cheeks.

'Don't cry, Mum!' says Destiny.

'It's just I'm scared I'm still dreaming,' she says, wiping her eyes quickly with her black-mittened fingers.

'You come in and be part of the dream,' says Destiny. She looks at me. 'She can come in, can't she?'

'Yes, yes, of course,' I say uncertainly.

Destiny tugs at the gate but it just rattles, not budging an inch. 'Tell us the security code then, Sunset.'

'I – I don't really know it,' I say.

'You *must* know it, else how can you get into your own house?' says Destiny, staring at me.

'Well, the only time I'm out is when John or Claudia or Mum takes me in the car, and they just press this little zappy thing. But you can press another one indoors. I can go and press it now and the gate will open then,' I gabble. 'Stay there. I won't be a minute, I promise.'

'You will come back, won't you?' says Destiny sharply.

'Destiny!' says Mrs Williams, sounding shocked. 'Don't talk to Sunset like that!'

'No, it's all right. I promise I'll come back,' I say. I'll be *less* than a minute, you'll see.'

I turn and rush through the garden, round the

swimming pool, past the flowerbeds and the play lawn with Sweetie's Wendy House and the jungle gym and the trampoline, across the patio, then round the back to the kitchen door. I'm scared Margaret might be there, or Claudia having an early cup of coffee, but the kitchen's completely empty, thank goodness. Maybe I can make Destiny and her mum a coffee, fix them some toast.

I won't actually take them into the house. I could bring their breakfast out into the garden – we could all sit by the pool. Then I can try to explain that Dad won't actually come and talk to them, but I could find them a Danny Kilman signed photo instead. I know where there's a whole stack, and I could maybe find them a special-edition boxed set of CDs – they'd love that.

But first I've got to get the gate open. The control panel is in the hall and I'm not allowed to go near it, so my hand goes a bit trembly as I reach out and press the switch twice. I hope that's it, that there isn't another code. Then I rush back to the kitchen, fill the kettle, put it on to boil, go back out of the door, and charge into the garden.

It's worked! The gate is wide open, and Destiny and her mum are standing just inside, holding hands.

'There!' I say. 'Come right in. If you'd like

to sit down by the swimming pool, I'll fix you—'

'Cocktails?' Destiny interrupts, laughing.

'I'll fix you breakfast!' I say.

'It's so kind of you. You're such a nice girl, though we knew you would be, didn't we, Destiny?' says Mrs Williams.

'Come this way then,' I say, and lead them towards the pool.

But before they can sit down there's shouting coming from the house, and then Mum comes speeding across the garden in her grey Pineapple tracksuit.

'Sunset? I was just going out for a run. What the hell are you doing?' Then she sees Destiny and her mum and she gasps. 'What are you two doing in my garden? Get out!'

'No, Mum—' I try to interrupt her but she won't listen.

'I'm giving you five seconds to get out of here!' she says. 'How dare you break in like this!'

'They *didn't*, Mum. It was me. I let them in. They were outside, sleeping on the pavement.'

'Be quiet, Sunset. Go back into the house. Dear God, how could you be so stupid?'

'Please, Suzy, don't be cross with her, it's not her fault,' says Mrs Williams.

Mum flinches at being called Suzy by a stranger.

'Will you just go, please. You're trespassing on private property,' she says. 'Do you want me to call the police? I've had it up to here with you crazy fans.'

'No, Suzy, you're getting it all wrong. We're fans, of course we are, but we're much more than that. Now, if we could just have a word with Danny . . .'

'Look, you saw him last night. I remember you two hanging around by the red carpet.'

'But we didn't get a chance to have a proper chat.'

'Don't be ridiculous! You can't just come barging in here demanding to talk to my husband, acting like you know us.'

'But we *do* know you,' says Destiny's mother. Her pale face shines and her strange staring eyes glitter. 'You're family.' She turns to Destiny and puts her arm proudly round her shoulder. 'This is Destiny – Danny's daughter.'

I gasp. Destiny looks at me, biting her lips and blushing.

'You're dad's daughter too?' I whisper.

'Yes, dear, she is. Don't you see how alike you are? Oh, it's wonderful to see you two sisters together!' says Destiny's mother, clapping her hands.

'You're talking total ludicrous rubbish!' Mum

shrieks. 'Stop it!' She raises her hand as if she's actually going to slap Mrs Williams.

'Don't you dare hit my mum!' Destiny says fiercely.

'It's all right, Suzy, I can see it's a big shock having it sprung on you like this. But I promise you don't have to worry. It was just before you and Danny got together. I'm sure he'd never be unfaithful to you. Any fool can see how happy he is with you, a devoted family man – and I'm so pleased for you, truly. I've got no illusions. I might still love my Danny to pieces but I know I don't stand a chance with him now.'

'Get *out*, you demented muckraker! What are you trying to do, blackmail us?' Mum shrieks.

Destiny's mum takes a step backwards, looking totally bewildered. 'Of course not! I don't mean any harm. I just thought it was time for the girls to get to know each other, seeing as there's only six months between them – and Destiny needs to get to know her dad now, for all sorts of reasons.'

'You're completely crazy. She isn't Danny's child! You've never even met him!'

'I met him when he did the *Midnight* gig. He came to Manchester nearly twelve years ago. I met him afterwards, in the private bar of the hotel. It was a whirlwind romance – just like his song, *Destiny*. He wrote it for me, I know he did.'

'John! John, come here!' Mum shouts. Then she marches forward, almost spitting with rage. She takes Destiny's mother by the shoulders and pushes her hard. 'Get off my property, you stupid sleazy groupie! Go away!'

'Stop shoving my mum! Stop it!' Destiny yells, trying to grab my mum's hands.

Oh God, they're all *fighting*. I can't bear it. I don't know what to do. Should I help my mum – or Destiny and *her* mum? Is it really true? *Is* Destiny my half-sister?'

Then John comes running, and he seizes Destiny with one big burly arm and her mother with the other, and he's *dragging* them towards the gate.

'That's it, get rid of them! I'm going straight back into the house to phone the police, so I wouldn't hang around if I were you,' says Mum.

'No! Please! Let me see Danny just for a few minutes. He's got to meet his daughter.' Destiny's mum is begging.

'She's *not* his daughter! Stop talking such rubbish. Stop it! As if Danny would ever have any-thing to do with a slag like you!' Mum shouts.

Destiny starts screaming stuff back at Mum, hitting and kicking John, but he's got his arm right round her and she can't get away. He's dragged them almost to the gate – he's hurting them, it's so dreadful, and there's nothing I can *do*.

'Sunset! Sunset!' Destiny's mum is calling to me now. 'You tell your dad. Please, please, ask him if he remembers me, Kate. Tell him about Destiny. Tell him to get in touch. She'll need him—'

But then they're through the gate, and John shoves them hard, so they both fall down.

'Stop it! Please don't hurt them!' I whimper helplessly.

Mum takes hold of me and slaps me hard on the face. 'How dare you let those creatures into the garden!' she says. 'Get to your room this minute.'

'But they just wanted to see Dad, that's all. Mum, is it true? Is she really my sister?'

'Of course not! It's just a stupid con trick to get money out of us. Don't you *dare* ever mention it to your father. Now get to your room and stop that ugly blubbering. What do you *look* like!'

She pulls John's fleece off me and drags me back into the house so fiercely she rips the sleeve off my teddy-bear pyjamas.

5

DESTINY

It takes us all day to get back home. The whole morning is taken up with hitching back to Euston Station. No one will stop for us, and then when this great fat guy in a white van gives us a lift he drives us the wrong way. We end up in a derelict factory site, and then he gets really leery and Mum and I are scared stiff. He gets hold of me, but Mum punches him right where it hurts most and then we jump out of the van and run like crazy. Thank goodness he's built like a tub of lard on legs. He tries to chase after us but he can't keep up.

Still, we're properly lost now until some nice woman stops because Mum's crying. We tell her about the creepy fat guy and she wants to take us to the police to report him, but we talk her out of it. She drives us to the main London road and we're just starting to get out when she suddenly says, 'No, get back in. I'm going to worry about you. I'll take you up to town myself.'

We can't believe she's so kind, especially as it takes ages because we're stuck in awful traffic jams.

'I'm so sorry,' Mum keeps saying.

The woman reaches over and pats Mum's knee. 'Come on, us girls have to stick together.'

She shares a Kit-Kat with us too, which is great, because we're both *starving* by this time. She puts on a CD, and you'll never guess who the singer is – Danny Kilman! Mum starts crying again when she hears the music. I hope she isn't going to tell the woman everything because it was all so weird and horrible. I couldn't stick that Suzy treating us like we were dirt. She didn't even believe Mum.

That's the worst bit. I'm not totally sure I believe her either. When we get to the station at long last there's another battle to fight, because our tickets aren't valid any more, but Mum's still crying and the ticket collector relents and lets us through the gate. When we're on our way I go to the toilet and have a good long stare at myself in the dingy mirror. I turn my head slowly from side to side, tilting it up and down. Do I look like Danny? We're both dark, but that's about it. Maybe I look a little like Sunset, but she's all posh and glossy and talks like someone on the telly.

At least she was nice. Really friendly, and not a bit snobby. Thank God she's not like her mum. I hate that Suzy. Danny should have stuck with Mum. *If* they were ever an item.

When we get back home at long long last there are two bills waiting on the doormat. Mum looks at them listlessly and then drops them on the carpet. She goes to the bathroom and is in there a long time.

I go to the door and knock. 'Mum? Are you OK?'

'Mm? Yes, yes, I'm fine. Just a bit of a tummy upset – you know what I'm like. Can you put the kettle on for a cuppa, love?'

I go and start boiling, and then peer into the fridge to see if we've got anything to eat. There's just a hard knob of old cheese and some soft tomatoes. I find the end of a loaf in the bread bin and cut it carefully in half. We can have cheese on toast with grilled tomatoes. I wish I could run out to the chippy. My mouth waters as I think of fish and chips, but I know Mum's purse is empty.

I feel down the sides of the sofa and chairs and go through all our pockets and find a single penny, not even enough for one chip. It'll have to be cheese on toast then. I make it carefully and lay it out on a tray.

Mum's looking very pale.

'Are you OK, Mum?'

'Yes, I'm fine,' she says quickly. She starts scurrying around, tidying.

'Sit *down*, Mum. You look ever so tired. In fact, why don't you go to bed? I could squeeze in beside you and we could both have tea in bed.'

'Don't be cross, darling, but I'm really not very hungry. I just don't fancy anything right this minute.'

'You've got to eat, Mum. Look how thin you're getting.'

But she just sips at her tea and then wearily walks to her wardrobe, shuffling like an old lady. She pulls out a jumper, her tight skirt, those white heels . . .

'Mum? What are you doing? What are you getting dressed for?'

'I'm going to work, sweetheart.'

'But you're absolutely knackered! You *can't* go to the pub!'

'I'm fine,' she repeats, painting a grisly red smile on her lips.

'You're *not* fine. Mum, I won't let you!' I take hold of her by the shoulders and try to steer her towards her bed, but she wriggles away from my grip.

'I have to turn up tonight or they'll give me the sack. We need to pay all these bills – and the mortgage – and everything else.' She says it as if she's reciting multiplication tables, with no emotion at all, but suddenly there are tears streaming down her face.

'Mum?'

'I'm fine, I'm fine,' she says, wiping her eyes with the back of her hand. 'It's just I so hoped we might stay with Danny for a day or so, and that he'd be so thrilled to see what a lovely girl you are he'd maybe want to buy you stuff, be like a proper father to you.'

'I've got a proper mother. I don't want him for a father, not now.'

'No, no, you mustn't take that attitude, babes.

Don't blame him. If he'd realized you were there then he'd have been so thrilled. It was just that Suzy – and it's clear that she's really, really insecure.'

'Really, really a prize cow,' I say. 'You know what, Mum? I feel truly sorry for Sunset. Imagine having Suzy for your mother!'

Mum gives me a wan smile. 'Yeah, it beats me what Danny sees in her,' she says. 'OK, sweetheart, I'm off now. Try to get to bed early. You need to catch up on your sleep.'

She gives me a kiss. When I look in the mirror again I see a ghost red mouth on my cheek. I finish my toasted cheese and Mum's portion too, and then I prowl around the house, too wired up to sit and watch television. I think about Sunset in her great big mansion. She'll have one of those televisions as big as a cinema screen. Perhaps there's one in every room in the house. There must be so many rooms. Would they really use them all? I imagine sitting for ten minutes on a huge leather sofa in one room, then walking to the next room and curling up in a big velvet chair, then two minutes later going to loll on a Victorian chaise longue, changing seats dozens of times throughout the evening, with kitchen intervals to fix myself snacks.

Perhaps she has a whole suite of bedrooms too –

one for each day of the week, with individual themes and colour schemes. I think up an ultra-girly pink room with rosebuds in pink glass vases and pink teddies and a candy-striped duvet and Sunset's very own pink candyfloss machine. Then I invent a blue room with blue fairy lights and a blue moon painted on the ceiling and an *en suite* blue bath with dark-blue dolphin taps. I decide on a sunshine room with a huge cage of singing canaries and big bowls of bananas and smiley suns all over the walls, and by contrast an entirely black room with a black velvet duvet and black satin sheets and an enormous black toy panther curled up on top. Then she might have a Victorian room with a four-poster bed and a scrap screen and a rocking horse, or an ultra-modern room with elegantly stark furniture and odd glowing lamps and a trapeze hanging from the ceiling. Best of all, she could have a round bedroom with a soft curved bed and shelves of round Russian dolls and a little trap-door in the middle of the room, so that when she gets hot she can put on her swimming costume, open the trapdoor, and slide all the way down to a turquoise swimming pool in the basement.

I get my homework jotter out of my school bag, tear out a page, and do tiny drawings of each bedroom, so that I'll remember each one.

Then I go into my own bedroom. I look up at the big damp patch on the ceiling (the roof leaks every time it rains). I look down at the fraying carpet squares on the floor. I look at my old bed with my faded duvet bears waving wanly at me.

I go to bed but I can't get to sleep. I toss and turn for hours until I hear Mum's key in the lock at last. I hear her tiptoeing about in the dark.

'It's OK, Mum, I'm still awake,' I call.

'You're a bad girl then. Go to sleep at once!' says Mum, but she's not really cross.

She takes off her clothes and crawls into my bed, and we spend the night huddled together under Pinky and Bluey. Neither of us sleeps much, even though we're exhausted. Mum gets up first and brings me a cup of tea on a tray – but I don't want to wake up now.

'I've set your alarm for eight. Promise you'll get up then,' Mum frets, sipping her tea as she gets dressed. 'Destiny? Promise!'

'Maybe,' I mumble, sliding back down under the duvet.

'You do as you're told,' says Mum, prodding me. 'Come on, babe, promise me you'll go to school. No bunking off. You're going to get a good education if it kills me.'

She has to leave or she'll be late for her cleaning

job at the uni. It's a good forty-minute walk to the campus but at least she's not in her high heels now, she's in her old trainers – though she's still blistered from yesterday.

'I wish you didn't have to walk so far, Mum,' I say, propping myself up on one elbow.

'You'll be walking there yourself in a few years' time,' Mum says. 'Doing some fancy degree course. *If* you get a good education.'

I sigh. 'OK, OK. Don't nag.'

'That's what mothers are for,' she says. She gives me a kiss goodbye. She sings the usual verse from a Danny song: '*Goodbye, my babe, it's time to go, don't wanna leave, I love you soooo.*'

I generally sing along with her but I shut up this time. When my alarm goes off at eight I shuffle around the house eating cornflakes straight out of the packet. I stop and stare at each Danny poster on the living-room wall. There are so many we don't need wallpaper. I look at the biggest poster, a young Danny striking a pose, head back, singing into his mike. *My Destiny* is printed at the top.

I suddenly tug hard on the poster and it falls down with a crash, the edges tearing, lumpy with dried Blu-Tack.

'I don't want to be your Destiny, you silly old fart,' I say, kicking the poster.

Then I pick up my school bag and slam out of the door, turning the key and then slipping its string down my neck, under my school blouse. I'd give anything not to go, but I promised Mum.

I go the long way round, of course. If I took the short cut through the estate, someone would be sure to spot me and they'd start chasing me. There are two major gangs on the estate, the Flatboys and the Speedos. They're silly baby names but they're not all little boys playing at being baddies. Some of the bigger guys carry knives, real serious flick knives, not kids' penknives. Jack Myers is in my class and his eldest brother is the leader of the Flatboys. The Speedos captured him recently, and when he swore at them they cut him down his arm and tattooed him on either side of his eyes with a lead pencil to show he was a marked man. So then the Flatboys caught one of the Speedo kids and hung him by the ankles from the top-floor balcony and very nearly dropped him.

The Flatboys and the Speedos mostly pick on each other. They don't often hurt girls, but you never know. Both gangs would go after me because I'm a Maisie. They call me that because our house is one of the maisonettes around the edge of the estate. Everyone hates the Maisies and thinks we're snobs. You're *especially* hated if you own your house instead of renting.

So I trudge all the way round the outside of the Bilefield Estate. My school shoes are too small for me and cramp my toes but I don't want to tell Mum because she'll only worry.

I hope she's feeling better now. My own stomach cramps thinking about her. I try to remember Sunset's seven different bedrooms to distract myself. I count them on my fingers. Then I make up different outfits for her. It's almost as if she's walking along beside me, keeping me company. She isn't wearing any of her cool designer clothes, she's in her pyjamas and huge fleece, and she's a bit embarrassed about it too, but I promise I'll flatten anyone who dares tease her. I can do that, easy-peasy, with most of the kids in my class. Well, I'm a bit wary of Jack Myers and Rocky Samson and some of the other boys already in Flatboys/ Speedo gangs, but I'm just as tough as any of the girls, even Angel Thomas, and she's twice my size and should have been christened *Devil* Thomas. I can fight and be really mouthy if I want, but most of the time I'm dead quiet at school. I don't even talk to the teachers much.

I liked my last school more, especially the teacher I had in Year Five, Miss Pendle. She lent me storybooks and gave me a gold star in literacy and said I had a Wonderful Imagination. I didn't even mind when the other kids teased me for being a teacher's pet. I *wanted* to be Miss Pendle's pet. But now I'm in Year Six at Bilefield and I'm still looked on as the new girl. I'm not really anyone's friend. The Year Six teacher is Mr Roberts. He's very strict and shouty and is always giving us tests. He smells of tobacco and has a silly beard and gets damp patches under his arms, and no one in the world would want to be *his* pet.

He doesn't shout quite so much now because we've finished all our tests and half the time we're mucking around instead of doing proper lessons. Mum's daft to think I'd be missing out on anything by bunking off school now, but she won't listen.

I don't listen much when Mr Roberts starts chuntering on about us being the top of the school – we'll soon be starting a whole new scholastic life at secondary school and isn't it exciting? Yes, very exciting to be going to Bilefield Secondary, where the big kids stick your head down the toilet and nick your mobile and your money as soon as you start in Year Seven.

Then he goes on about our Year Six end-of-year entertainment. I can't get interested. He wants to call it *Bilefield's Got Talent* – oh, very witty. Everyone groans and moans, especially when Mr

Roberts says we've *all* got to do an act whether we want to or not. Jack Myers says he's not poncing about on a stage making a fool of himself, but Mr Roberts suggests he might like to get together with some of the other lads and do some kind of street dancing – and that shuts him up. *All* the boys want to street dance. They divide up into Flatboys and Speedos, apart from silly Ritchie and Jeff, who want to dress up in frocks and do a daft ballet dance, and Raymond Wallis, who actually can do ballet properly and wants to do a special acrobatic solo. Most of the girls want to dance too, singing along at the same time. There are two groups of girls who want to do Girls Aloud numbers.

'Fine, fine, but we could do with a little *variety*,' says Mr Roberts. 'Can't any of you think of an act that's a little bit different?'

'Yeah, OK, I'll do a pole dance, Mr Roberts,' says Angel Thomas.

'Well, maybe that's a little *too* different,' says Mr Roberts. 'We'll put that idea on hold, Angel. Perhaps you can do some kind of exotic dance, but a pole dance would get us both into a lot of trouble.'

Natalie and Naveen and Saimah and Billie-Jo are whispering together.

'We want to do a play, Mr Roberts. Can we do our own play?' asks Natalie.

'That's an excellent idea,' says Mr Roberts. 'But you'll need to do it properly, write it out and rehearse it, and it can't be longer than ten minutes maximum. I'll help you rehearse, girls. And boys, you need to choreograph your street-dance routine. We'll see if Mrs Avery can help you get started, choose the right music. I want you all to take this very seriously. We're going to entertain the whole school *and* your parents, so I want you all to give a cracking performance. We'll sort out some kind of voting system and give a proper prize to the over-all winner, OK? Now, who hasn't chosen their act yet?'

'I can't do nothing, Mr Roberts,' says Hannah, sighing. 'I can't sing and I can't dance.'

'Maybe you could join up with Natalie and co. and be in the play.'

'I can't act either,' says Hannah.

'Can I do magic tricks, Mr Roberts?' says Fareed. 'My dad's shown me how to do heaps of card tricks, and I can even pull a rabbit out of a hat. Almost.'

'Excellent! Well, Hannah, perhaps you could be Fareed's assistant. Magicians always have a lovely lady assistant.'

'Yeah, you can saw her in half, Fareed,' says Angel, laughing. She catches my eye. 'And make Destiny disappear. For ever.'

115

I give her a little sneer, acting bored. It would never ever do to show Angel that I'm just like the others, dead scared of her.

Mr Roberts is looking at me too. 'Yes, Destiny, what about you?' he says in the same false bright tone he used for Hopeless Hannah. He obviously has me down as one of the sad thickos. Well, see if I care.

'Perhaps you don't want to sing or dance. Tell you what, how about doing a recitation?'

Oh, sure. Poetry. The other kids would have a field day, shouting, *Off, off, off!* And throwing tomatoes at me.

He doesn't understand.

'I could help you find a poem. It doesn't have to be too long. Maybe you could read it if you find it hard to learn it. You're a very good reader, Destiny,' he says earnestly. 'You just need to gain a bit of confidence.'

'I'll sing,' I say, just to shut him up.

He looks surprised. I never join in his stupid music lessons. I *hate Kumbaya* and *Lord of the Dance*. I don't even bother to open my lips to mouth the words.

'Do you know any songs?'

Stupid question. I know every track, genuine or bootleg, of every single Danny Kilman album, from his debut songs with the defunct rock band Opium Poppy to his last recorded tracks six years ago.

I just nod vaguely, but he clearly doesn't trust me.

'Which song?'

It might as well be the obvious.

'I'll sing Danny Kilman's song *Destiny*,' I say.

Some of the kids snigger uncertainly. I don't think they've even heard of Danny. Though Mr Roberts looks surprised but enthusiastic.

'Of course! Brilliant choice. Actually I'm a big Danny Kilman fan.'

Oh God.

'Tell you what. I could accompany you on my guitar if you like – do that little melancholy riff in the middle—'

No!

'I thought I'd leave that bit out,' I say quickly. 'Just sing the word part. If that's OK.'

'Yes. Yes of course,' he says, but he looks disappointed. I feel a bit bad but I'm not having him mucking up my special namesake song even if I've decided I don't want Danny for my dad any more.

I don't say anything to Mum when she comes home – but she sees I've torn the big poster down straight away. She gasps as if the real Danny is lying crumpled on the carpet. She kneels down and smoothes the poster out, wincing at the tear marks. She fetches the Sellotape and mends him very carefully on the back of the poster so that he doesn't have to have shiny Sellotape bandages across his face. Then she gets a whole new packet of Blu-Tack, stands on a chair and puts him up in his place again, taking the greatest care not to stick him on a slant or give him any creases. She doesn't say a single word to me while she's doing this, but her lips are moving. I think she might be whispering to Danny.

She looks terrible. She hasn't had time to wash her hair so she's still got it pulled back in a ponytail and it droops lankly down her back. Her face is grey-white, with shadows like bruises under her eyes. I don't know if it's because her hair is scraped back so tightly, but her eyes look truly scary, as if they might pop right out of her head. When she raises her arms I can see all her ribs through her T-shirt, and the knobs of her elbows look as sharp as knives.

I go into the kitchen, put the kettle on, and look for food in the Aldi carrier Mum's dragged home. I stick two big potatoes in the oven. Then I cut some bread and butter and bring it into the living room on a tray, with a cup of tea.

Mum is sitting down now, sifting through the

post. I think it might be more bills. Her hands are shaking.

'Here, Mum, have some tea,' I say, sticking the tray on her lap.

'Oh, that's lovely of you, sweetheart,' she says. She sips her tea but doesn't touch the bread and butter.

'*Eat*, Mum.'

'I'll have it a bit later, darling.'

'No, we've got baked potatoes with cheese later – and maybe baked beans? But you need to eat something now, Mum. You look awful, like you're starving to death.'

She flinches.

'I'm sorry, Mum, I didn't mean to upset you, it's just that you're scaring me. Look, you've not gone anorexic, have you?'

'What? No, no, of course not.'

'Because you're way too thin as it is. You'll be a skeleton if you carry on not eating.'

'OK, lovey, I'll eat. Look!' She takes a big bite out of the bread and butter. 'There now – and you've made a lovely cup of tea. You come and share the bread and butter with me.'

She pats the armchair and I squash in beside her. I have a little peer at the letters. Yep, more bills. I pull a face.

'It's OK. We'll manage,' says Mum. 'It's worth having to scrimp and scrape so we can live here. Imagine if we were still stuck in that dump of a flat on the Latchford Estate. We haven't done too badly, have we, Destiny? Our very own house!'

'Yeah, Mum,' I say, trying to sound enthusiastic, although there's so much needs doing to the house, and I can't help thinking the Bilefield Estate is almost as bad as Latchford, and it does your head in trying to avoid the Flatboys and the Speedos all the time.

'It's just – I wish we had someone here to look after us,' says Mum.

'We don't need someone else. We look after each other,' I say indignantly.

'Yeah, but it would take all the pressure off if you had some kind of father figure around. I mean, we both know who your real dad is . . .' We look at the poster and Mum sighs. 'He'd have so wanted to meet you, darling. I know he'd be so proud of such a lovely new daughter.'

'Mum. Stop it. He walked straight past me at that film thing.'

'He didn't understand.'

'Suzy understood – it made her shout and scream at us. Mum, just shut up about Danny Kilman and his family. It all went *wrong*.'

Mum squeezes her eyes tight shut. 'It was my fault. I made a mess of things and I so wanted it to be lovely. I always do that. I just seem to screw everything up. I mean, look at the time Steve came along. Remember his house, how lovely was that? Remember the four-poster?'

'Yeah, and I remember him using you like a punchbag too.'

'I just seemed to get on his nerves after a bit. Maybe I shouldn't have kept arguing with him.'

'*What?* Oh, Mum, stop that. Of *course* you argued. He was a total pig, you know that.'

'But he did look after us for a while – and he was very fond of you, really. He was just narked if you got a bit lippy.'

'You're *crazy*, Mum! He hit me. He was horrid. What *is* all this? Why aren't you happy just being us? It sounds like you're desperate to get a boyfriend again.'

'No, I'm not. I just worry so. You need a proper family.' Mum plays with a strand of her hair that's come loose, winding it round and round her finger. 'What do you think about visiting your grandma?'

'Now I know you've gone totally bonkers!' I say.

Mum's mum, my grandma, is a hateful old bag who kicked Mum out when she was expecting me. She doesn't act like a real grandma at all. Last time we went to see her, she just gave us our tea and then she was off down the pub with *her* boyfriend, not the slightest bit interested in talking to Mum or me.

'What was it Grandma said about me?' I say, pretending to think. 'Oh, *I* know – I was a cocky little madam and goodness knows why, because I was a gawky little kid with wonky teeth. Yeah, remember?'

'That was awful of her – but she'd think you're lovely now, Destiny. You're growing up gorgeous,' says Mum. 'And she *is* family.'

'I don't want to be her family. *We're* family, just you and me. Now shut up with all this daft stuff. I need you to help me with my homework.'

'I'd love to help you, sweetheart, but you know I'm useless at literacy and maths and all that stuff.'

'You're a total Danny expert. You could get a flipping *degree* on Danny Kilman – so I want you to help me with his song. I've said I'll sing *Destiny* at the stupid school concert. Can I practise with you?'

'Oh, darling!'

I've distracted her at last.

'You've been picked to sing at a concert!'

'We've *all* been picked, every single one of us in my class.'

'But your teacher must think you've got a lovely voice – and you *have*.'

'It's not like anyone else's voice though. Miss Belling at Latchford said I sounded overpowering, like I was trying to drown out all the others.'

'Well, that's just typical of that rubbish school. They can't recognize talent when it's right under their noses. Good for Bilefield! And how lovely to be singing your very own song! I'm so proud of you. Danny would be too. You're a chip off the old block, darling.'

6

SUNSET

I keep thinking about that girl Destiny. Could she *really* be my sister? Mum's so angry about it, it's almost as if she's got something to hide.

'Don't you *dare* mention it to your father!'

Well, I *do* dare. And I'll tell him Mum slapped

me round the face. I put my hand up to my cheek. The slap doesn't hurt any more, it hasn't left the slightest mark, but I can still feel it. Sometimes I think Mum hates me. And sometimes I hate *her*.

I wait till late in the afternoon. I'm not daft – no one goes near my dad in the mornings, especially on Sundays. We all have a very late lunch. Sweetie and Ace babble away but I keep my lip buttoned tight. Mum's not saying much either, but she keeps looking at me anxiously. She just picks at a tiny piece of chicken, nibble-nibble with her perfect teeth.

I wait till she goes off with Claudia and Ace and Sweetie. Dad slopes off down to the pool with the Sunday papers. He's not said much either. I'm not sure if he's in a good mood or not. But I have a cunning plan. Destiny's given me an idea.

I go to the drinks cabinet and pour a whisky and soda just the way Dad likes it – *lots* of whisky with just a splash of soda, in one of the fancy crystal glasses. I tie a tea towel round my waist, put the whisky on a tray, and then carry it very carefully to the pool.

Dad's rifling through the tabloids, looking for photos from last night. Mum's done that already, of course, but there's no Danny Kilman pics at all, just lots of snaps of Milky Star.

'What do you think of Milky Star, Sunset?' he asks me, scratching his head.

He hasn't combed his hair properly and his bandanna has been tied on so carelessly I can see his scalp, weirdly pink under his very black hair. It makes me feel sad for him.

'I didn't reckon them much,' I say, wrinkling my nose.

'Yeah, can't see what all the fuss is about myself,' says Dad. 'They're so bland and boring, you can't tell one from the other. Can you? Which one do you like best?'

'I *said*, Dad, I didn't really like any of them. I couldn't tell which one was which,' I fib. That's the way to keep him in a good mood. You just repeat back everything he's said, simply changing the words round a little.

'What's this then?' says Dad, nodding at my tray and tea towel.

'I'm Sunset, your cocktail waitress. Care for a drink, sir? My speciality is whisky and soda.'

'Yes please, you funny little kid,' says Dad.

I serve him his drink and then sit down beside him. I kick off my flip-flops and dangle my feet in the pool.

'It's so great having you for my dad, Dad,' I say, *really* sucking up to him.

126

He smiles and sips his drink.

'It's great for Sweetie and Ace too,' I continue, splashing my feet in the water. I pause. I wait till half the whisky has slipped down. 'And I bet Danny Junior and Topaz are dead chuffed to have you as their dad too,' I say.

I don't look at Dad. I keep on splashing. We don't ever mention Dad's *first* family. Dad had another wife, Ashleigh, long before Mum. I've never met her, but Danny Junior and Topaz used to come and stay with us sometimes, mostly before Sweetie was born. Danny Junior drank a lot and Topaz didn't eat anything at all. They didn't act like they wanted to be friends with me.

Dad makes a grunting noise, not commenting further. He finishes his drink.

'Let me get you another, sir. I am your ever-willing cocktail waitress,' I gabble, and then charge back to the living room.

Oh, shoot, Mum's there – but she starts as guiltily as me. She's checking something on her mobile. No, not hers – that's little and pink. She's checking *Dad's* mobile. He's left it with a pile of change and his car keys on the big coffee table. Mum's clicking through all the messages. She nearly drops it when she sees me.

'Hi, Mum.'

She glares at me, suddenly focusing. 'What have you got draped round your hips? It looks awful, showing off your tummy – take it *off*, Sunset. You've got no more sense of style than a monkey in the zoo.'

I gibber and pretend to scratch under my arms, to show her I'm not a bit hurt – though I *am*.

'It's a tea towel! What in God's name are you doing wearing one of my tea towels?'

'It's my apron, ma'am. I'm your friendly cocktail waitress. I've just been serving the gentleman by the poolside, but I'll be right back to mix you a vodka and tonic – slimline naturally – *or* I have a very delicious dry white wine.'

'For heaven's sake, you're ten years old. You're not supposed to be messing around with alcohol.'

'I'm not *drinking* it, I'm serving it. Ma'am.'

'Well, *stop* serving it. It's a stupid game.'

'I have to serve the gentleman. He's wanting his whisky.'

Mum sighs. 'Well, serve it then – and then go and amuse yourself sensibly. I don't know what the matter is with you, Sunset. You've got your own plasma television, an Apple Mac, a Nintendo DS – I'd have given anything to have all this stuff when I was a kid – and yet all you do is play silly baby games or lock yourself in your wardrobe and mutter to yourself. I think you're a bit simple in the head.'

I pull a simple face at her, pour another whisky and soda in double-quick time, and get out of there. Dad is lying back on the lounger, his eyes closed. His mouth is turned down in an I-don't-want-company manner, but I can't give up now. I rattle the whisky glass and he opens his eye.

'Your repeat order, sir,' I say, holding out the tray.

He sits up a little, shaking his head. 'You're a funny kid, Sunset,' he says, taking the glass.

'Yes, I know I am,' I say, squatting down by his feet. I take the tray and swivel it earnestly round and round so I don't have to look him in the eye. 'Dad?'

'Mmm?'

'Dad, you know we were talking about all your kids?'

'Were we?'

'How many have you got?'

'What?'

'How many—'

'I'm not in the mood for trick games, poppet.'

He sounds very curt even though he's called me poppet. But I have to persist now.

'It's not a trick question, Dad. How many kids have you got?'

'Three.'

'*All* your children.'

'OK, five then. You know I have.'

'Yes, but are you quite sure you haven't got one more?' I say, my voice going husky now because my throat's so dry.

'One more?'

'Because – because I met this girl, Destiny – you know, called after your song – and she says you're her dad.'

'Well, lots of kids have crushes on me, you know that,' Dad says. 'She'll be pretending I'm her dad, bless her.'

'No, she's not pretending, she says it's real. And her mum does too.'

'So who's this mum?' Dad asks, taking a long swig of his whisky.

'She's called Kate Williams, a very thin dark lady, and she says she was your girlfriend before Mum, and Destiny is your daughter. Destiny is a little older than me and she looks a bit like me, but she's dead cool – though guess what, Dad, she's got my weird teeth—'

'Give it a rest, Sunset, you're burbling. You and your silly stories,' says Dad, finishing his drink in one last gulp and thumping the glass on my tray.

'But it's not a story, Dad.'

'Enough! Run away and play. And stop spouting nonsense, do you hear me?'

I hear him all right. But I still don't *know*. He hasn't said yes, but he hasn't said *no*. Though he's clearly not going to talk about it any more. And Mum won't either.

It's an awful afternoon. We have to go to tea with this famous tennis player who's just moved to Robin Hill. He's got a little girl of seven and she wants to play tennis with me. I don't want to play in the slightest – I'm rubbish at most games – but Mum glares at me and tells me not to be a spoilsport. It's a nightmare. She is as small as Sweetie but she's brilliant at tennis, whereas I can hardly hit the ball over the net. I fall over and skin my knees and very nearly cry in front of everyone.

Later on the tennis player and his wife have a match with Mum and Dad. Dad's always gone on and on about his prowess at tennis but he's pretty useless too, and he drops out after a few games, saying he's hurt his ankle. Mum's not played tennis much but she's quite good at it, nipping briskly around the court. The tennis player starts giving her a few tips, holding her arm and her back, teaching her how to improve her serve. Dad watches with a sour expression – and when we go

131

home at long last he starts sounding off about Mum flirting.

Mum just laughs at first and tells him he's being silly – but Dad gets really mad at her. Then Mum suddenly loses it and says something about his secret texting – and then they really start. Claudia hustles Sweetie and Ace away quickly and gets them ready for bed. I slope off to Wardrobe City and try not to listen to the big argument. It doesn't sound as if anyone's going to come and say goodnight. Claudia pokes her head round the door about ten.

'Aren't you in bed yet, Sunset?'

She doesn't tell me what to do because she's not my nanny, I'm too old to need one. Claudia's only been with us a few months. She's not foreign like most of the others, and she's very posh. She talks like people in an old-fashioned film. She *looks* old-fashioned too: she wears a black velvet Alice band to stop her straight mousy hair falling in her eyes and she has very crisp white shirts and irons her jeans. I heard Mum and Dad giggling about her once, taking off her accent. They're not giggling now. They're shouting at the tops of their voices so you can hear them clearly in my bedroom. They're calling each other all kinds of things. Claudia is pink in the face and her eyes don't quite meet mine.

132

'Night-night then, Sunset,' she says.

'Night, Claudia.'

She pauses. Dad bellows something and then the front door slams. Mum yells something after him and then starts sobbing. I hear the car rev up and drive away.

'I'm sure everything will be hunky-dory in the morning,' Claudia says softly.

'Mmm.'

She hesitates, then comes right up to me in the wardrobe and gives my shoulder a quick pat. I freeze because I don't like anyone coming near me when I'm in Wardrobe City. All my people freeze too. They can never show they're real when strangers stare. And now I'm getting older and a little bit ashamed of playing pretend games, they won't become real even when the strangers go. I am abandoned outside the city wall with a handful of shabby little ornaments and worn-out toys.

Claudia doesn't understand. 'Night-night,' she repeats dolefully, and backs out of my room.

Oh dear, now she'll think I don't like her. No one really likes poor Claudia, not even Sweetie and Ace. We should be friends, because no one really likes me either.

I sit back on my heels and shut my eyes tight so that I don't start crying. I can still hear Mum.

Maybe it's all my fault this time. I heard her shrieking something about a girl. Perhaps she feels dreadful that Dad has another daughter. Maybe I should have shut up about her.

But I can't help thinking about Destiny. I wish I knew her email address. I need to tell her mum that I kept my promise. I did tell Dad. I want to email Destiny. It's not just because she might be my sister. I want her to be my friend.

I go out in the garden early next morning in the mad hope that they might have come back, but there's no one there. It suddenly feels so lonely standing all by myself in our huge garden.

I go to check the garage. Dad's car is still missing. I wrap my arms around myself. I can feel my heart thumping. Dad's gone, and maybe it's all my fault.

Mum doesn't come down to breakfast either, but I know she's here. I try going into her bedroom but she shouts at me to go away. She's got her head under the duvet so I can't see her, but it sounds as if she's still crying.

I don't think Sweetie and Ace know that Dad's still out, but they can guess something's wrong. Sweetie is extra whiney and won't eat her yoghurt and banana, and cries when Claudia tries to brush her hair.

'It hurts, it hurts! I want *Mummy* to do it, and I hate horrid plaits anyway,' she moans, sticking her lower lip out.

'Mummy's not feeling too good, Sweetie. Do keep still. You know you have to have plaits at school,' Claudia says, trying her best. 'Ace, you need your hair brushed too. It's sticking up all over the place.'

'I'm Tigerman and I never never never get my hair brushed,' he says. He reaches for his juice, not quite watching what he's doing, and spills orange all down his white T-shirt.

'Oh, Ace, now I'll have to get you changed all over again,' says Claudia.

'I'm Tigerman and I never never never get changed. I don't wear clothes at all, I just have my stripy skin,' Ace declares. He pulls off his T-shirt, his shorts, even his underpants, and runs around naked, growling.

Claudia looks as if she's about to burst into tears.

'Come here, Tigerman. You're just my little cub and I'm the great big Daddy Tiger, and you have to do as I say or I'll smack you with my giant paw,' I say. I catch him and lift him up and blow a raspberry on his tummy so that he squeals with helpless laughter.

I carry him off and sponge all the sticky juice off

him and stuff him into clean clothes, keeping him happy by starting up a tiger-roaring contest, seeing which of us can roar the loudest.

'For God's sake, stop that ridiculous noise, you're giving me a headache,' says Margaret, the housekeeper, going downstairs with a breakfast tray. 'You kids are the giddy limit. No wonder your mum's taken to her bed with a migraine. You should be ashamed of yourself, Sunset, a great girl like you playing silly games and egging your brother on when you should be getting ready for school.'

It's so unfair that my eyes prick with tears.

'Now now, don't turn on the waterworks,' says Margaret, pushing past us.

Margaret can be really mean sometimes. She likes Sweetie best – she's always making her special fairy cakes and chocolate cookies, and letting her lick out the bowl. Sweetie plays up to this and cuddles up to Margaret and says sickening stuff like, 'Oh, Margaret, I do love you. You're the best lady in the world next to my mummy.'

I get lumbered taking Sweetie into the Infants while Claudia drags Ace into the Nursery. All the kids smile and wave and call to Sweetie the moment they spot her, but she hangs back, clutching my arm.

136

'What?' I say irritably.

'Mum and Dad were quarrelling *again*,' she mumbles.

'Yes, I know.'

'Sunset . . . do you think they're going to split up?'

My tummy lurches. I wish she hadn't put it into words.

'Of course not, Sweetie. All mums and dads quarrel,' I say, trying to sound very grown up and certain. 'You mustn't worry about it.'

'But Daddy hasn't come back. I went into Mum and Dad's room when I woke up and he wasn't there,' Sweetie wails.

'He just had to go to this club to see some of his friends,' I suggest. 'You know what Dad's like with his music mates – they stay out till all hours.'

I'm trying to convince myself as much as Sweetie. She's still frowning at me, biting her lip. Her hair's lopsided and straggly because Claudia hasn't got the knack of plaits, and she's got a rim of orange juice round her mouth. She still manages to look breathtakingly pretty.

'Come here,' I say, spitting on a tissue and scrubbing at her.

'Leave off!' she says, struggling, but when I've

wiped off most of the orange she leans against me. 'Sunset, if Mum and Dad split up—'

'I said, they're not going to.'

'Yes, but *if* – what will happen to us? Will we live with Mum or will we live with Dad?'

'They'll both want you, Sweetie,' I say. 'Maybe they'll have to chop you in half.'

It's just a silly joke but her face crumples.

'Don't cry! I didn't mean it, I was just being silly. Oh, Sweetie, don't worry, they're not splitting up, I promise, but if they do, then maybe they'll take turns looking after us, or we'll stay with Mum during the week and Dad at weekends – whatever.'

'But will we still live at *home*, with Margaret and John and Claudia and Ace?' asks Sweetie.

'Yes, of course,' I say, and she relaxes and runs off to join her little friends.

I trail round to the Juniors. The bell's already gone so I'm late, but I don't care. I'm thinking about Mum and Dad and home. I'm especially thinking about Wardrobe City.

John comes to collect Sweetie and me in the car at the end of school (Ace goes home with Claudia at lunch time). John's his usual silly self, telling us very bad jokes and making funny snorty pig noises, and Sweetie laughs and laughs, but as we draw up on the drive she quietens and starts sucking her thumb. But Dad's Jag is there. I blink hard – yes, it really is there. He's back, so maybe everything's all right.

We go into the house and there are flowers in the hall, flowers all over the big living room, the lily smell so heady it makes me feel dizzy. Mum and Dad are sitting together on the big cream sofa, holding hands. Mum's wearing tight white trousers and a white lace top with a wide apricot belt and strappy gold high heels. Dad is all in black but he's wearing an apricot-coloured bandanna and three big gold rings. They are a matching pair, smiling smiling smiling, speaking softly in turn – because they are being interviewed.

The journalist is sitting opposite them, taping every murmur with her little recorder, but she's scribbling in her notebook too, her long false nails getting in the way.

I hang back, especially when I see the photographer setting up his gear in the corner, but this is Sweetie's cue to be cute.

'Daddy! Mummy! I'm home from school,' she trills, and goes rushing up to them, giving them both a big hug, though she knows to be very care-ful. Woe betide her if she gets grubby fingers on Mum's white lace or knocks Dad's bandanna askew, showing his bald bits. Mum and Dad smile at her fondly and she wriggles between them, quaint in her red and white checked school dress, one sock up and one sock down, her red hair-ribbons trailing. Dad laughs and pulls her plaits; Mum shakes her head and ties her ribbons and pulls up her socks, but oh, so fondly.

'Oh, what a sweetheart!' says the journalist. 'She just obviously has to be Sweetie. So where's your other daughter?' She looks around the room and her cold blue eyes spot me skulking in the corner.

'Yes, come here, Sunset, darling,' says Mum, holding out her arms.

I have to do the hugging bit too, lumbering above them both, too big and awkward to cuddle in between them.

'Oh, let's have a family shot!' says the journalist. 'Haven't you got a little boy too?'

'Run and find Ace, Sunset, there's a little darling.'

So little darling goes off on an Ace-hunt. He's not in the playroom with Claudia or in the kitchen with Margaret. I look in the office and find Rose-May and Barkie. Rose-May is Dad's manager. She's got a soft flowery name and speaks in a soft whisper. She even looks soft and flowery: she's got fluffy blonde hair and she wears floaty tops and lots of perfume. However, she is so not soft and flowery herself. She's the only person I know who tells Dad what to do. She never shouts. When she's cross her voice gets even softer, but it's like she's a rose who's grown very sharp thorns. Dad doesn't argue with her, he does exactly what she says.

Barkie's not really called Barkie – her name's plain Jane Smith – but Dad always used to call her Barking Mad and now Barkie's her affectionate nickname. She doesn't mind. When she comes round she says on the intercom, 'Woof woof, it's only me.'

Barkie's known Dad since way back, when he first started his career. She was one of his number-one fans, following him from gig to gig. It was her idea to start up a fan club and she's been running it ever since. She's not exactly a *fan* now, because she's a middle-aged lady and she knows Dad too well, but she still melts whenever he looks at her. She's very nice but very, very plain, with goofy teeth even worse than mine, so Mum doesn't mind her staying close to Dad all these years. He treats her like his pet dog, patting her bony shoulders and ruffling her hair. He calls her his Number-One Girlfriend.

'Hello, Sunset,' says Rose-May. 'What's the matter?'

I'm not looking at her, I'm looking at Barkie.

Maybe she used to know Destiny's mother.

'I'm looking for Ace,' I say. 'That journalist wants to see him.'

'No, no, it was meant to be a Danny solo interview. I didn't even want Suzy in on the act,' Rose-May whispers, her little pink mouth puckering. 'It was meant to be about a new album, a new tour—'

'Is Danny *doing* a new album and tour then?' Barkie asks eagerly.

Rose-May sighs. 'We're testing the water, Barkie. Calm down. Oh well, it looks as if it's going to be a family interview now. With photos.' She looks me up and down. 'Perhaps you'd better change, Sunset – and maybe get Claudia to fix your hair,' she murmurs. 'I think she's upstairs with Ace. I'll go and chivy them along.'

She moves off purposefully, leaving a cloud of her flowery perfume in her wake. I wrinkle my nose and sneeze.

'Bless you,' Barkie says kindly, tapping away on her computer. 'Wouldn't it be exciting if Danny *did* do a new album, Sunset? Oh my, wouldn't the fans be overjoyed?'

'Barkie, you know you've been a fan for ages yourself, before Dad got together with Mum? Well, do you remember who Dad was going out with then?'

Barkie smiles at me, showing all her bad teeth. 'Your daddy's had lots of girlfriends, dear,' she says, with a little giggle. 'He used to be quite a lad in the old days.'

'Do you remember him seeing this very thin dark lady, Kate Williams?'

'Your dad didn't introduce his girlfriends to me, sweetheart.'

'No, but I think this lady might have been special to him,' I say. I don't think I should tell Barkie about her maybe having Dad's baby. It might upset her terribly, the way it did Mum. 'She certainly still thinks the world of Dad,' I add.

Barkie smiles and taps her screen, where she's updating the fan club membership details. 'So many ladies think the world of Danny,' she says.

Something clicks inside my head. 'Barkie, can you see if there's a Kate Williams on the fanbase?'

'Well, it's supposed to be confidential.'

'Oh, Barkie, please, I *know* her. Well, I know her daughter, and I need to get in touch. I don't know their email address. Please just have a peep for me. Quick, before Rose-May gets back.'

'All right then,' says Barkie, typing *Kate Williams* onto the screen.

143

'Oh no, there are *heaps* of them!' I groan, peering at the result.

'We've still got nearly a hundred thousand fans all over the world,' Barkie says proudly. 'Look, one of these Kate Williamses lives in Malta. And here's another in the States.'

'It won't be them. And it probably won't be *this* Kate – she only just joined.' I sigh in frustration. 'But I suppose she could be any of the others.'

I think hard about Destiny's mum. I hear her desperate voice. She has a familiar broad accent. 'She talks sort of northern, like they do in *Coronation Street*,' I say.

'Then *this* will be her, most likely. This one lives in Wythenlathen,' says Barkie. 'That's part of Manchester, dear. There's no email address though.'

I seize Barkie's biro and scribble down the postal address on the inside of my wrist before she can stop me. Then I rush off to change. I put on the terrible leggings, but they wrinkle and twist so that it feels as if I've got my legs on backwards, and when I pull on the velvet smock I discover I've spilled strawberry ice cream all down the front. I pick jeans instead, with a stripy top and a little bolero thingy, trying hard to be creative. I hope I might look funky – but judging by Mum's expression when I go back into the living room, I've failed miserably. None of us children match. Sweetie is still in her school dress, and Ace is in his Tigerman costume and his wellies.

The journalist claps her manicured hands and says we look such *real* children. What else could we be, puppets? Rose-May is frowning and she only allows a couple of quick photos before saying softly, 'I'm so sorry but the children must go and have their tea now, mustn't they, Suzy? You'll need to supervise them, won't you, darling – but don't worry, I'll sit in with Danny for the rest of the interview and see that everyone's comfortable.'

So we are all cleverly dismissed. We sit at the kitchen table munching Margaret's pizza while Mum prowls restlessly up and down in her gold high heels. She's beautifully made up, but if you look very carefully you can make out dark circles under her eyes and they still look very red.

'I'm so glad you and Dad are friends again, Mum,' Sweetie says happily, swinging her legs.

'What do you mean, darling? Daddy and I are always friends,' Mum says sharply.

I flash a warning look at Sweetie. Can't she see they were only cosying up together for the journalist's benefit? Sweetie doesn't even see me looking, but Mum does.

'Don't wrinkle your nose like that, Sunset, it makes you look hideous. And what on *earth* are you wearing? That skimpy little bolero's much too small for you now. And you've got your school shoes with your jeans! What do they *look* like! Where are your boots? Honestly, I spend a fortune on your clothes and you dress like you've just been to a jumble sale.'

She goes on and on, wanting me to answer back so she can tell me off for cheek, but I don't say a word. I just sit there with one of my hands up my sleeve, stroking the inky words on my arm.

I've stroked a little too much. When I'm on my own in my bedroom at long last, when the stupid journalist and photographer are long gone, I examine my arm and see the writing's all smudged – but I can *just* about make it out. I write it out in the back of my school jotter so I have it safely for ever.

Then I go to my wardrobe. Wardrobe City calls to me – but this time I look at all my clothes crammed tightly on the left, and click through all my hangers until I find the little black leather jacket. It is very little. I try it on. It's much too tight under the arms and it won't meet properly across my chest. It's no use to me now – and Sweetie never has my hand-me-down clothes, she

146

always has brand new. It's no use to anyone stuck in my wardrobe, is it?

Even so, I feel guilty as I take it out and wrap tissue paper round it. It's so soft it folds up neatly into a manageable parcel. Then I search for writing paper. I've just got an old stationery set with goofy teddy bears dancing round the edges. I think it was a going-home present at a party. It's horribly babyish now. She'll probably laugh at it, but it'll have to do.

I sit on the edge of my bed, rest the notepaper on a big book, and start writing.

Dear Destiny,
I hope you don't mind me writing to you. I got
your address from the fan club list. It was
lovely to meet you (and your mum) on Sunday.
It was such a surprise to discover that you
might be my sister!!!

I cross out 'might be' and substitute 'are' because it sounds as if I don't believe her.

I'm so sorry Mum got so cross.

I start to write, *She is a mean pig*, because she *is*, but I scratch that out because it sounds so disloyal. I think about *Hi! Magazine* and the words they use when some celebrity shouts and screams.

She is going through emotional turmoil.

I'm pleased with that phrase. I hope I've spelled it properly.

I did tell my dad, just as I promised, but he got a bit cross too, and wouldn't talk about it properly. But don't worry, when he's in a good mood I'll try again.
    Meanwhile, as a tiny saying-sorry present I'm sending you my leather jacket because you said you liked it. I do hope it fits you OK. I think it will suit you much more than it ever suited me.
Love from Sunset
My email address is sunsetsmiles@mac.com. What's yours?

I tuck the letter inside the jacket, then I stick the tissue in place with Sellotape. I want to parcel it up properly right this minute so I risk creeping downstairs again.

I listen hard. There's no shouting, no sobbing. I can hear music coming from the television room, Danny Kilman music. Maybe they're cosied up

148

together on the sofa, reminiscing. I breathe out happily and tiptoe into the office. Barkie is long gone, of course, but all her office supplies are here. I help myself to her biggest Jiffy bag, the sort she uses for mailing the souvenir Danny Kilman boxed set to other number-one fans.

My little leather jacket just about fits inside, and I stick the top down and write the address. Barkie's got her own franking machine so it's easy-peasy getting it all ready to post. She has a big sack of stuff for John to take to the post office tomorrow. I delve into the sack and position my Jiffy bag right in the middle.

There! I'm so pleased with myself I decide to creep into the kitchen to celebrate. Margaret goes back to her own flat after she's served supper. I can hear the dishwasher chugging away. It'll mask the sound of me opening the Smeg. I know exactly where we keep the ice cream.

My mouth is watering already but it dries as I slip inside the kitchen door. Dad's there, his back to me, and *he's* searching inside the freezer. Is he after ice cream too? I start grinning. Dad is actually meant to be on a diet. Rose-May keeps nagging him about it, saying rock stars have to stay skinny, especially when they're more mature. Dad's meant to eat stuff like fish and chicken with steamed veg, though he often asks Margaret for one of his favourite fry-ups. He's not supposed to have any puddings at all – though he's fishing out a Magnum now and nibbling at it as he chats on his mobile.

I shake my head at him even though he can't see me. Maybe if he's in a good mood I'll be able to tease him about it. I'll wait till he's off the phone and then I'll sneak up on him and go 'Gotcha!' It might make him laugh.

He's laughing now, but very, very quietly. 'You are such a bad, bad girl,' he whispers.

Who's he talking to? He doesn't talk to any of us like this, all warm and husky, not even Sweetie.

'But you *mustn't* ring. You especially mustn't text – Suzy practically hit the roof when she saw that last message.'

I swallow, standing absolutely still.

'I know, I know, I'd give anything to be with you too, baby,' Dad murmurs. 'Last night was so wonderful – but I can't risk it. Rose-May's trying to get this album deal set up now that the film's on general release next week. Yeah, yeah, I know it will be good publicity, but I'm seen as a family man now, it's part of the package. Yeah, I know it sucks. We'll be together soon, baby, I promise. I can't wait.'

I back out of the kitchen, shivering. I stand in the hall, hearing *Always and For Ever* playing in the living room. Always and For Ever! Dad's planning to dump us, walk out on all of us.

I run into the living room. Mum's lying on the sofa, her white top all rucked up, her hair a mess – but she smiles sleepily at me. She's got a glass of wine in her hand. It looks like she's already drunk a lot more.

'I thought you were in bed, Sunset,' she says indistinctly. She holds out her arms to me, forgetting she's got the wine glass.

'Oops!' she says as it spills over her top. 'Clumsy! Come here, darling. Come and watch your clever old dad. See the way the crowd's singing along with him, all those arms waving, all those girls mouthing the words.'

'Mum—'

'They all want him but he's *ours*, Sunset. He's our Danny, and we love him, darling, don't we? He might stay out half the night and break our hearts – but he always comes back.'

'Mum, what if one time he didn't come back?' I say. 'What if he went off with some other girl?'

'What? Stop it, don't talk like that! Why do you always have to spoil things? Do you think it's clever? Just go to bed, go on. And see what's happened to your dad. He was meant to be fetching another bottle of wine.'

She says I always spoil things. I could really spoil things now. I look at her lying there in her crumpled clothes, glaring at me. She looks like Sweetie in a temper. She looks too *young* to be a mum.

So I don't tell her. I stand out in the hall, not sure if Dad's finished talking on the phone or not.

'Dad?' I call. 'Dad, Mum wants you.'

7

DESTINY

So, OK, Mr Roberts has got us all in the hall and we have to take turns going up on the stage to do our party pieces. And it's weird – this is just a first practice and it's only *us*, plus Mr Roberts and Mrs Avery, our PE teacher, but we're all nervous. The girls have gone squeaky and giggly, the boys push and shove, and even Angel is acting anxious, prowling up and down, clicking her fingers.

'This is a mad idea. We're going to look stupid,' she says.

'Yeah, we don't *have* to do this stuff,' says Jack Myers.

'Yes, you do – or I'll beat you with my very big stick,' says Mr Roberts.

'You can't hit any of us, you'll end up in prison, Mr Roberts,' says Jack.

'Wonderful! No more kids, no more lesson plans, no more marking. It'll be a doddle,' says Mr Roberts. 'Now, who's going first? How about you go first with your little gang, Jack, then you can relax for the rest of the session. Come on, boys, give me your music.'

'We haven't practised properly or nothing. We're going to be rubbish,' says Jack.

He's right, they *are* rubbish: they just jump about the stage, Jack leading, all his mates copying, not even looking where they're going so they all bump into each other. They end up red-faced and sheepish. If I were Mr Roberts I'd say, *Yes, you* are *all rubbish* – but he does his best to be positive.

'I'd say you have a lot of raw talent, lads – with

the emphasis on *raw*,' he says. 'What do you think, Mrs Avery?'

'Yeah, you've got a lot of potential, guys. Jack, can you do a somersault?'

'Sure,' says Jack, spitting on his hands and flipping over.

'Cool. We'll make a feature of that. I can help you sort out a routine, all you guys dancing in unison. Maybe we can work in one or two surprise elements.'

'That's not fair, miss, if you're giving them all this help and coaching,' says Rocky Samson, who's in the Speedo dance group.

'Mrs Avery is here to help everyone, Rocky,' says Mr Roberts. 'She's a positive saint, prepared to give up her dinner hour every day to help you lot, so I hope you're properly grateful to her. And to yours truly.' He gives an ironic little bow.

Some of us are going to need more help than others. The girl dancers are not too bad. They've been practising in the playground already and they've mostly copied routines off the telly. Raymond's dance is brilliant, not the slightest bit sissy, though the boys were all set to laugh at him. They *don't* laugh at Ritchie and Jeff, though they're supposed to be funny. The girls' play is hopeless – they just waffle, and then there's a sudden argument and they all start shouting so loudly and so fast you can't even hear what they're saying.

Mr Roberts sighs. 'Girls, girls, girls! Lower your voices – and speak *slowly*.'

'But we *have* to speak quick to get it all in, you said we've only got ten minutes, Mr Roberts,' says Natalie.

'Then we must cut the words, not gabble them,' says Mr Roberts, taking notes. 'I can see my dinner hours are going to be chock-a-block too.'

Fareed isn't very inspiring with his magic tricks, dropping his cards twice, and Hannah just hangs her head and stands beside him, not doing anything.

Mr Roberts sighs. 'I think we need to build a little razzmatazz into the act, kids,' he says, making notes. 'But don't worry, it's going to be fine.'

Angel is in a sulk and hasn't got an act prepared at all. 'There's no point if you won't let me do a pole dance,' she says.

'Maybe you and I could work out an acrobatic dance together, Angel,' says Mrs Avery. 'Like a solo street dance? Do you have a favourite song – something with a real beat to it? I'll help you work out a routine.'

'Whatever,' says Angel, still sounding sulky, but you can tell she's really pleased.

Now it's me. Mr Roberts smiles at me encouragingly.

'OK, Destiny, your go. Do you still want to try this Danny Kilman number?'

'Yes, I do.'

'Well, do you have the backing music?'

'No.'

He looks delighted. 'Then maybe you'll need me to accompany you on my guitar after all?'

No, no, no!

'If – if you don't mind, Mr Roberts, I'd sooner sing by myself, like I said. The guitar might – might put me off,' I stammer.

'Very well. But you're probably going to need a little back-up for the actual performance. That's a truly difficult song to pitch *a cappella*.'

I don't know what he's on about. I don't want his *Kumbaya* dithery guitar noises mucking up my song. I don't need to hear any backing. I've heard *Destiny* almost every day of my life. I know every little note and nuance the way I know the sound of my own breath.

Mr Roberts is looking doubtful. The boys are looking bored, the girls spiteful, ready to snigger. Angel is yawning, rocking back on her chair. I

157

suddenly feel sick. Maybe I'm going to make a total idiot of myself and ruin Danny's song into the bargain.

Your dad's song, says Mum, inside my head.

I close my eyes. I'll sing it just for her. I open my mouth and get started. As soon as I've sung, '*You are my Destiny*,' I'm there in the song, on a different planet, and I'm feeling the words, the soar and sweep of them making the hairs stand up on my arms, and I carry on to the last beautiful long note, letting it all out.

Then there's silence.

I open my eyes. Everyone's staring at me. I feel myself getting hot. I'm sure I'm blushing. I *have* made a fool of myself. They clapped everyone else. They even clapped Fareed and Hannah, and they were hopeless.

Why are they all just sitting there looking so stunned?

Then Mrs Avery starts clapping. She actually *stands up* and claps, and the others join in. Mr Roberts claps too, in a weird uncoordinated way, as if he isn't quite sure his hands are still on the ends of his arms.

'For goodness' sake, Destiny,' he says eventually, sounding sort of cross. 'Why didn't you tell me?'

I peer at him. Tell him *what*?

158

'You've got the most amazing voice.' He's still peering at me as if he can't quite believe it. 'You've never sung like that before. Why didn't you sing like that in my music lessons?'

I shrug.

'Well, I'm still astonished, Destiny. I'm not sure I've got any advice for you. Just sing your heart out.'

I can't wait to get home to tell Mum. I can sing, I can sing, I can sing! Well, I've always *known* I can sing. Mum says I've inherited my dad's voice, but actually I don't sound a bit like Danny Kilman. Maybe I take after my mum. We always lark around singing together when we're dusting or decorating or scrubbing the floor.

Actually Mum hasn't been singing much recently. But this will cheer her up. Mr Roberts is going to put me on last in *Bilefield's Got Talent*. We're meant to be all in with an equal chance but it's obvious I'm in the top spot. There will be an afternoon performance for the rest of the school, and then another one at seven for all our families, both with panels of judges. It's a Friday and Mum starts her evening shift at the Dog and Fox spot on seven. I'll just have to hope she can swap shifts with someone.

I hurry home, knowing she won't be back till half six at the earliest. She's got this new client,

Maggie Johnson, who likes Mum to put her to bed with a cup of tea and a Tunnock's teacake, and then they watch *The Weakest Link* together. Mum has to join in too, even though she's not an Anne Robinson fan and never knows any of the answers. Maggie doesn't know many of them either, but it cheers her up to have a go. Mum's tried to make me go round to this Maggie's house because she worries about me being on my own and she thought it would cheer Maggie up. It didn't work. I can't stand Maggie's home because it's dark and it smells and there are wet knickers and nighties drying all over the radiators and the backs of chairs – and Maggie herself isn't a sweet rosy-cheeked old lady, she's a mean old bag who glowered at me, and kept asking in a loud whisper, 'What's she doing here?'

I wish Mum didn't have all these awful mouldering clients monopolizing her. She's my mum and I want her looking after *me*. But wait till I tell her about Mr Roberts's reaction to my singing! I let myself in and find a note telling me that someone's tried to deliver a parcel. They've left it with Mrs Briggs next door.

A parcel? We never get parcels. I clutch the key and run round to Mrs Briggs's. She takes ages getting to her door, creaking along behind her

160

zimmer frame. I call through the letterbox, 'It's just me, Mrs Briggs, Destiny, don't worry!' but she still puts her door on the chain and peers through the crack suspiciously.

'Are you kids plaguing the life out of me again?' she demands.

'It's *me*, Mrs Briggs!'

'Ah yes, young Desiree,' she says. She's never quite got the hang of my name. 'Yes, you'll never guess what, dear, someone's sent you a parcel. Is it your birthday?'

'Well, it *was*, last week.'

'You never said! I would have got you a card. So how old are you, darling?'

We go all round the moon discussing me being eleven and Mrs Briggs being eighty-seven when all I want is *to get my parcel*! But eventually she lets me in and I pick up the huge Jiffy bag in her hall. I peer at the writing on the bag. I don't recognize it. It's not really heavy. You can still squash the bag, but there's definitely something inside. Thank goodness the postman didn't just leave it on the doorstep. It would have been nicked before his back was turned.

I thank Mrs Briggs and whizz back home to open it in private. It's so carefully taped up I lose patience and rip. Suddenly I'm holding a jacket, a beautiful leather jacket, soft as a kitten, beautifully styled, the most gorgeous jacket in the entire world. I stare at it, shaking, unable to believe it. I realize I've seen the jacket before. Oh my God, it's *Sunset's* jacket!

I pick it up properly to try it on and a letter flutters out. I slot my arms into the silkily lined sleeves and pull the jacket on. It fits perfectly, as if it were made for me. Then I pick up the letter and read. It *is* from Sunset. It's a lovely letter too. She did her best to ask Danny about me – and she hopes the jacket will suit me.

I go to the bedroom and look at myself in Mum's mirror. Oh, it *does* suit me, it truly does! I look just like a celebrity! I pick up Mum's hairbrush and start singing, pretending it's a microphone. I can't wait for Mum to get home. Now there are *two* special things to tell.

The moment I hear the key in the door I go, 'Mum, Mum, wait till you hear!'

'Hey, darling! I've brought Louella back for a cup of tea.'

Oh *rubbish*, why did she have to do that? I whip the jacket off quick and stuff it under my pillow and then walk reluctantly into the living room. Louella has already sat herself down in my chair. She nods at me.

'How are you doing, Destiny?'

'Fine, thanks, Louella,' I say.

She nods sceptically. 'I hope you're not giving your mother cause for grief. She's always worry-worry-worry over you. One little scrappy girl gives her more worries than my four give me.'

'My Destiny's a total love. It's my silly fault if I worry about her,' says Mum. 'I'll go and put the kettle on.'

Louella glares at me. '*You* should be making the tea for your mum, Destiny, a big girl like you. There she is, on her feet all day, caring for all those dear old souls. She needs a little care herself when she gets home.'

'I *do* make the tea sometimes. I'll do it now,' I say crossly.

'No, no, I'm *fine*. You two sit and chat,' Mum calls from the kitchen.

I don't *want* to chat to Louella and she doesn't look like she wants to chat either.

'Your poor mum's working herself to the bone,' she says. 'Skin and bone, that's all she is now. I keep telling her, you're working too hard, girl, always on the go. You need to take it easy, put a little flesh on those bones.'

Louella herself has more than enough flesh on hers. She's so fat she totally overflows my chair, her vast brightly patterned dress spread out around her. Her feet are wide apart, planted firmly. Pop socks and sandals are *so* not a good look.

'How's school then, Destiny?' she asks. 'You working hard?'

I shrug.

'Staying out of trouble?'

She's got such a cheek. Her twin boys, Adam and Denton, are only in Year Three and yet they're already famous throughout the whole Juniors for getting into trouble. They might hold hands and blink their big eyes at their mum and deny everything, pretending they've been picked on, but they're incredibly bad. Just last week they hid in a wheelie bin and jumped up at one of the dinner ladies and nearly gave her a heart attack, and the week before that they liberated the Year Three classroom gerbils in the girls' toilets. Her middle child, Jacob, is one of the most feared Speedos even though he's only nine. Her oldest, Cherie, who's twelve, goes round with this other girl in Year Seven and I've seen them wearing really tight tops and short skirts, both looking at least sixteen, going out as if they're *looking* for trouble.

Louella has *no* idea. She only sees her kids when they're all neat as ninepence and in

Louella-approved outfits, school uniform or Sunday best, with white socks and highly polished shoes.

'I'm not in any kind of trouble,' I say.

I so want to tell her that Mr Roberts and Mrs Avery treated me like a total wonder-child today, but I don't want to tell her before Mum.

Oh, Mum, come *back*. How long does it take to make a cup of tea? Louella is looking all round the living room, nosy as anything. She shakes her head at the Danny posters.

'Your mum and her Danny! I don't know what she sees in him myself. So scruffy and so old. If she must go for one of these golden oldies, why not plump for Cliff? He's always so smartly dressed,' Louella chunters. 'And does she really need all these posters? She could get some really good pictures at a car boot and they'd give the room a bit of style.'

'This is *our* style,' I say, even though I don't like the posters now. I don't like Louella either – but I can't resist asking her: 'These Danny pictures – look at them, Louella. Does he remind you of anyone?' I say, and I jut my chin and angle my own head in a Danny pose.

I want her to slap her huge thigh and exclaim, 'Oh my Lord, Destiny, it's you, you're the spitting image!' even though I'll deny it because we're not telling anyone, and definitely not Louella. But she doesn't seem to be struck by any revelation.

'He just looks like all those other hairy old rockers,' she says dismissively. 'I wouldn't even know what he sings like.'

'I'll put on one of his CDs if you want,' I tease her. 'Nice and loud.'

'*No*, thank you! I've got more respect for my ears,' she says. 'You want to listen to some *proper* singing, Destiny. You come along to our church on a Sunday and listen to our choir. They're so stirring they'll send shivers down your back.'

'We don't go to church.'

'It would do you the power of good – and you'd make lots of friends there, you and your mum. You two need to get out and mix more. It's so sad you've no friends, no family.'

'We've got each other. We're fine,' I say indignantly.

I long to push her right off my chair. What right does she have to barge in here and criticize? I leave the room in a temper and go and find Mum. She's just standing there in the kitchen. The kettle's boiled, but she's not making any attempt to pour it. She's leaning against the draining board, biting her lip.

'Mum?'

She jumps, flips the switch on the kettle, and starts throwing tea bags into mugs. When the kettle starts bubbling she whispers, 'Were you being rude to Louella?'

'She's being rude to me!'

'Shh or she'll hear! I wish you'd make an *effort* with her. She's a truly good woman. She'd do anything to help me.'

'That doesn't mean I have to like her.'

'Oh, Destiny, stop it,' Mum says. She looks so sad and I can't bear it.

'I've got something lovely to tell you, Mum. *Two* things,' I say quickly.

'What?'

'No, wait till *she's* gone, then I can tell you properly.'

Mum sighs. I hate the way her face goes when she breathes in sharply. It looks as if her cheek-bones are going to burst through her skin. She's so thin now you can work out exactly what she'd look like as a skull.

I get the biscuit tin and start buttering slices of malt loaf too.

'Are you peckish, babe?' asks Mum.

'No, this is for *you*. You need to eat more, Mum.'

I take the plates into the living room, one

holding Hobnobs, the other malt bread, but Mum just nibbles one crust. Louella hoovers up both platefuls, big fat fingers reaching out to the plate, *snatch*, *gollop*, again and again.

Mum desperately tries to make conversation. She tells me about the football birthday party Louella's planning for the twins, the bridesmaid's dress she's making for Cherie, her plans to take Jacob to judo classes, praising her as if she's a candidate for the Mother of the Year awards. I remain unimpressed.

Mum changes tack and tells Louella how well I'm doing at school. She says I'm going to sing my own Danny Kilman song at the end-of-term concert. I twitch to tell her that they think my voice is great, but I'm *not* saying it in front of Louella – she would only spoil it.

I sit glowering, willing her to go. At last she heaves herself to her feet, nearly tipping my chair over.

'Goodbye, Destiny. You be a good girl for your mother now. And if you get lonely you come round and play with my four, do you understand?'

I understand that if I went round to Louella's, the twins would plague me with tricks, Jacob would set all the Speedos against me and Cherie would squash me flat.

'Goodbye, Louella,' I say firmly, almost pushing her through the door. When she's gone at last I lean on the back of the door, doing a pantomime *Phew!*

'Destiny! Stop that! Why are you being so horrible? Louella's a lovely woman,' Mum says, frowning at me.

'Mum, she's *awful*. She's so mean and bossy and full of herself. I don't get what you see in her.'

'She's a good friend. If anything ever happened she'd be a good friend to you too. She'd look after you like one of her own, I'm sure of it,' Mum says.

I stare at her. 'Mum? What do you mean, if anything happened? I can look after myself! I'd sooner poke my eyes out than stay with Louella. Anyway, let's forget her. Wait till you hear! Sunset's written to me – and you'll never guess what she's given me as a present!'

Mum clutches me. 'You're not winding me up, are you, darling?'

'No, it's in my room. Come and see! I've been *dying* to show you, but you would go and lumber us with Louella.'

I tug her into the bedroom, pull the leather jacket out from under my pillow where I'd hidden it and slip it on.

Mum gapes at me. 'Oh, darling! It's really

Sunset's own jacket. We've seen her wearing it in all the mags!'

'I know. I told her I liked it when we saw her. She's sent it specially with this letter – look.'

'This is what I've always dreamed about!' says Mum, her eyes scanning the letter. 'Oh, Destiny, she's tried to tell Danny, she's going to try again. Oh, bless the child.'

'There! Isn't it a friendly letter? That stupid Louella was going on about us not having any friends. *She* doesn't have famous celebrities who are friends *and* relations. Only I want you to keep in with her for Friday the eighteenth of July just to cover you if you need to work late at all – and I hope you can get out of your shift at the Dog and Fox too – because you have a very important date, Kate Williams.'

'Do I? What?'

'You are coming to *Bilefield's Got Talent* – and guess who is going to be top of the bill? Mr Roberts's new singing sensation – *me*!'

I grab the hairbrush and start singing *Destiny*, putting my heart and soul into it. Mum watches, hands clenched, mouthing the words along with me. When I've finished she bursts into tears.

'Mum? I wasn't that bad, was I?'

'You were wonderful, but I shouldn't tell you that, you'll get big-headed.'

'No, no, tell me *heaps* of stuff. I want to feel great! Do you think I've got a chance of winning then?'

'If you *don't* win I'll want to know the reason why!' says Mum. 'Now, I'd better get the supper on. I'll whizz the vacuum round too – Louella pointed out the carpet was all over fluff.'

'Louella! Look, *I'll* do the vacuuming if we really have to.'

'No, you get your homework done – and you'll need to write a really nice thank-you letter to Sunset. I can't get over her sending you her jacket.' Mum holds it up admiringly. 'It's a real beauty, isn't it? Imagine what it would fetch on eBay. Sunset Kilman's very own jacket.'

'Mum, we're not putting it on eBay, it's *mine.*'

'Better not wear it on the estate, pet. One of them kids will nick it off you as soon as look at you.'

'I won't wear it outdoors, I'm not daft. I'll wear it *indoors*. Like right now!'

I slip it on and then write my letter to Sunset.

Dear Sunset,
Thank you very very very much for the leather
jacket. I absolutely LOVE it. I can't believe you
could just parcel it up and send it to me. It fits
me just perfectly too.

It was good of you to try so hard to ask your
dad – our dad! – about me. I expect it's an
awkward embarrassing subject for him. It
obviously is for your mum! I'm sorry she got so
cross. I hope she's OK now.

Hey, Sunset, you'll never guess what. I'm
going to be in this crazy end-of-term talent
contest, Bilefield's Got Talent – you know, like
the TV show – and I'm going to be singing my
very own namesake song, 'Destiny'. I don't want
to boast but my teacher Mr Roberts thinks I'm
very good at singing. I suppose that IS boasting
a bit – sorry. Do you like singing?

I know you said you like art and English best
at school (me too). What sort of school do you go
to? I expect it's a really posh private one with
lots of famous pupils. What's it LIKE, being
famous?
Love and lots more thank yous,
Destiny
P.S. I don't have an email address as I don't
have a computer. I love your notepaper with all

the teddies. I have two teddies on my duvet and, don't tell anyone, but I used to play silly games with them.

I get my felt tips and doodle all around my name, drawing a little sun on one side and a cloud with raindrops on the other. Then I carefully draw a rainbow arching through my name. I hope she thinks it looks pretty. I wonder if she will write back? I add another P.S.:

It would be great if you wrote back to me. Maybe we could be penfriends?

8

SUNSET

Dear Destiny,
I'm so pleased you like the jacket. I knew it
would look fantastic on you.

    I promise I will try talking to Dad again –
but he's been in a very bad mood recently for

several different reasons and I daren't say anything at all just yet.

It's great that you're going to be in a talent contest. I have never taken part in one, on account of the fact that I have no talent. I am useless at singing. I sound like an old frog croaking.

I suppose my school IS sort of posh. You have to pay lots of money to go there. I would pay lots of money NOT to go there. I hate my school. It is very progressive. That means there aren't any rules and you are encouraged to express yourself. I wish I went to a REGRESSIVE school, with heaps of rules, where no one's allowed to argue back. There are a few famous pupils. Well, they're famous because their mums or dads are famous, like footballers or film stars – or rock stars, like our dad. So I suppose that makes me a little bit famous, like you said. It's horrible. I can't ever be just an ordinary girl, I always have to be with the whole family, and people always notice us and come up and say stuff and take pictures with their mobile phones. The proper photographers are worse, always yelling at you to smile, and you have to make sure you're dressed up and look cool. Only I am the exact opposite of cool, worse luck.

Sometimes I would give anything not to have a famous dad.

Let's definitely be penfriends – that would be absolutely fantastic.
Love from Sunset

One of the reasons Dad is in such a very, very bad mood is he's worried he's not famous any more. Well, he *is* – there's this two-page article in one of the big newspapers. Rose-May fixed up the interview, a proper one. Dad's thrilled and thinks it's gone really well, and he even gets up early on Saturday to read it – and then he nearly hits the roof.

We don't know what's going on. Dad's ranting and Mum starts crying, and there are all these telephone calls, and then Rose-May comes rushing round and tries to calm them down.

'What's wrong *now*, Sunset?' Sweetie asks. She's in a bad mood too, because Mum's supposed to be taking her out this morning to buy a party dress for her sixth birthday and now it looks as if the shopping trip's postponed.

'I think someone's written something really bad about Dad,' I say.

'What, like they've called him bad names?' Sweetie asks.

'They've called him Bum and Poo and Knickers!' Ace says, naming all the bad words he can think of and giggling hysterically.

'Shut up, silly little peanut,' I say, picking him up.

He flings himself about wildly, spluttering the same stupid words over and over again.

Sweetie looks at him coldly. 'Isn't he a *baby*?' she says.

'Yes, a tiny baby, and if he doesn't calm down this instant we shall put him in a nappy and stuff him in a cradle,' I say.

'I'm *not* a baby. I'm Tigerman,' Ace says, struggling. 'I want my Tigerman outfit!'

I let him wriggle free and he runs off to plague Claudia to dress him in his stupid costume. Sweetie sighs and raises her eyebrows.

'I lots of times don't really *like* Ace,' she says.

I don't always like Sweetie, but I smile at her sympathetically. She's listening to the row downstairs.

'I can't hear what Mum's saying,' she says. 'Can't she take me shopping and let Dad and Rose-May do the shouting? I don't want Claudia to take me. She likes all those silly little baby dresses – *yuck!* I want something bee-yoo-tiful and cool.'

'You have a knack of making most things

beautiful and cool,' I say, sighing. 'Don't worry, Sweetie. I happen to know Rose-May's fixed up *Hi! Magazine* to come and take photos of your party, so they'll want to make sure your dress is absolutely perfect. I think Mum will take you shopping tomorrow, you wait and see.'

Sweetie sighs and starts picking the varnish off her nails.

'Don't do that, you're messing it up.'

'It's messed up already. Will you take it off properly, Sunset, and paint my nails a new colour? And then put little daisies on, like the lady who does Mum's nails?'

I give it a go, raiding Mum's bedroom for her varnish and remover. I try my best, trying to keep Sweetie happy. I think I make quite a good job of it, painting her stubby little nails silver and then putting a dab of red on each one that looks like a rose – sort of. But Sweetie's very hard to please.

'You're doing it all *wrong*, Sunset. It's all gone blobby and smudgy!' she wails.

'Well, of course it'll smudge if you won't keep still and wave your hands about like that,' I say.

'I'm going to get Claudia to do it *properly*,' says Sweetie, though we both know that Claudia thinks any kind of nail varnish on little girls is an awful idea.

I flop on my bed, wishing I had Destiny with me as my real sister. I wonder if I dare tell her about Wardrobe City. I'm sure she'd laugh her head off – though she did say she loved my doll's house.

I get up again and peer in at Wardrobe City. I badly want to join all my people. I imagine them behind the walls, chatting away – but when I open up the doll's house they are suddenly silent, morphing into chipped and grubby toys with unblinking beady eyes.

'Please come alive. Let me play too,' I whisper, but they don't so much as twitch.

I kneel there, biting my lip. 'I'll *make* you play,' I say, and I drag little Mrs Furry out of her soft bed. 'Come on, it's time you were up. We'll give you a quick wash. Hold out your paws. And hang on, we'd better spruce up your whiskers.'

She stays limp in my palm and my voice sounds silly and self-conscious. It's no use. I hide her back under her bedcovers and slam the doll's house shut.

I feel like crying. *Why* can't I believe it any more? I know I'm too old, but I don't want to be. I want to be little and cute like Sweetie, and free to play imaginary games all day long. Though the only game she really likes playing is pretending to be grown up, laughing and pouting and standing

179

with her hands on her hips, as if she's permanently strutting down a red carpet.

I hear Ace roaring in the playroom. At least he's happy being Tigerman. Dad is still doing his own roaring downstairs. Whatever can they have written about him?

My heart starts banging. Could Destiny and her mum have gone to the papers and told them that Dad is her father?

I've got to find out. Dad and Mum and Rose-May are all shouting in the big living room. I know better than to go in there.

I put my head round the kitchen door. Margaret is making coffee and arranging a plate of her home-made shortbread.

'Oh, Margaret, I *love* your shortbread,' I say, staring wistfully at the plate.

'Your mum says I mustn't give you any more snacks. She doesn't want you turning out tubby,' says Margaret – but she winks and pops a big wedge of shortbread into my open mouth.

I munch happily, unable to speak for several seconds.

'There! I hope my shortbread will shut them up too when I serve it. Going at it hammer and tongs, they are. What a fuss about a silly newspaper article. I didn't think it was anything to get het up about.'

'Have you got a copy of the paper, Margaret?'

'I *did* – but His Lordship came and ripped it to shreds, would you believe! As if that's going to help! And even if he rips up every copy he can find, it's still posted on the Internet, as any fool knows. And I hadn't even read half of the paper – and John always likes to do the crossword. Ha! There's been enough cross words just recently to last us a lifetime. I've had about enough of it.'

'Oh, don't leave, Margaret, please,' I beg – though all the staff leave sooner or later.

She gives me a wry little smile. 'It's you kids I feel sorry for,' she says.

That makes me shiver. Margaret sees, and looks anxious.

'Here, have another shortbread, pet,' she says. 'Now, you run along. Steer well clear of your mum and dad. I wish *I* could steer clear of them – and that Rose-May.'

I go out of the kitchen, mouth full of shortbread. I go back to my bedroom and switch on my computer. I type in Dad's name and the newspaper – and Margaret's right, there's the article! There's a headline in big letters: LAST DINOSAUR OF ROCK 'N' ROLL. I see a cartoon drawing of Dad as a dinosaur with a long wrinkled neck and a bandanna round a tiny reptilian head.

I start to read the article but it's quite difficult and boring, analysing the music scene, and going on about Dad way back at the start of his career, when the journalist was a big fan. But then it talks about him being a parody of himself nowadays, unwise enough to collude with the *Milky Star* film-makers. The journalist wonders if it was overwhelming vanity or simple stupidity that made Kilman make such a fool of himself. He talks about Dad's looks: his many wrinkles, his puny arms, his pot belly, his ridiculous bandanna failing to hide his receding hairline – on and on, relentlessly.

Then it talks about Dad's love life – his first family and his string of girlfriends. I pore over this part, looking for the name Kate Williams, but she's not mentioned. So many other women are though. Then, after many paragraphs, he starts writing about Mum, calling her the Page Three Popsie, not scared to show her claws if any other deluded girls start fawning over Danny.

So now the senile rock star has ceased his strutting. It's many years since we've heard that once-great gravel voice. Now he plays Happy Families in Hi! Magazine *with his kitten wife and three unfortunate kids with the standard outlandish names of celebrity offspring – Danny*

Kilman, the last dinosaur of Rock 'n' Roll.

I shut the page quickly and sit rocking in my chair, trying to make sense of it all. Why does the journalist hate Dad so much? Is he really a laughing stock? I always thought everyone adored my dad, but now everything's turned upside down. And why does he call Sweetie and Ace and me *unfortunate*?

The row goes on for most of the day. I creep downstairs every now and then to listen. Rose-May can usually calm Dad down but he's mad at her this time, shouting that it's all her fault.

'You'd better watch it, Danny,' Rose-May says. 'You can only push me so far.'

'Oh yeah? *You're* the one who'd better watch it. I could just get myself a new manager,' Dad yells.

'What makes you think anyone else would take you on?' Rose-May shouts, and she slams out of the room.

Then the row gets worse because it's just Mum and Dad. It rumbles on and off throughout the evening. Then there's a shouting match in the hall because Dad's going out again.

'*Where* are you going, Danny? You're going to see *her*, aren't you?' Mum shrieks.

'Shut up, you jealous cow,' Dad says.

'Why should I be jealous of you? *You're* the sad old fart that's past it,' Mum yells.

There's a horrible slapping sound. I don't know if it's Dad hitting Mum or Mum hitting Dad. Maybe they're fighting each other. I'm sitting with Claudia and Sweetie and Ace now, and she's trying to make us play a silly old game called Snakes and Ladders, but none of us can concentrate. We hear the shouting, we hear the slap, and we sit frozen, as if the snakes have wriggled right off the board and are writhing towards us, their forked tongues flickering.

'You needn't think I'll wait in for you, sobbing my heart out,' Mum cries. 'I don't give a stuff any more. *I'm* going out and having fun.'

We hear her rushing up to her bedroom and then clopping back downstairs in high heels.

They both slam out and drive off in separate cars.

'This is the absolute pits!' says Claudia, shaking her head.

'I want Mummy,' says Sweetie.

'She's obviously gone out,' says Claudia.

'But she didn't say goodbye. I want to go with Mummy! I want her to buy me my party dress! I want to go to the *shops*!' Sweetie cries, distraught.

She tries to run into the hall but Claudia takes hold of her.

'Don't be silly, Sweetie. The shops will all be closed now,' she says, struggling with her. 'Come on, let's carry on playing Snakes and Ladders. Whose go is it to throw the dice?'

'I don't like Snakes and Ladders,' says Ace. 'The snakes are all staring at me. I'm Tigerman and I'm going to bite them into bits.'

He snatches up the board, spilling counters everywhere, and crams the edge into his mouth, biting hard – and then bursts into tears, because of course it hurts. Claudia tries to calm him. I try cuddling him, but he wriggles and screams. Sweetie is wailing for Mummy, so Ace yells that he wants *Daddy* Tigerman.

'Oh Lordy,' says Claudia. 'Look, it's no use going on at *me*. *I* want your mummy and daddy to come back. This happens to be my night off and I had plans to go out. I get a Saturday night off once in a blue moon, but they didn't even think of that when they both stormed out. They could have just *asked* me. It's so unfair.' She looks as if she's about to burst into tears herself.

'Never mind, Claudia. You go out. Sweetie and Ace will be just fine with me,' I say, patting her shoulder. 'I'll be the babysitter.'

'Oh, Sunset, don't be silly. You're much too young.'

185

'I'm *not* silly.' I was only trying to *help* – and I can control Sweetie and Ace better than she can.

But she's intent on being a martyr so I let her get on with the long tedious job of getting each child quiet, bathed, and into their own beds. I retire wounded to my room. I don't try to go to Wardrobe City. I sit on the end of my bed muttering, 'Why do they have to shout and cry all the time? *Why* do they, all of them – Dad, Mum, Sweetie, Ace, Claudia. Why can't they all shut up and leave me in *peace*?'

The mutter turns into a rhythm. I start whispering it over and over. Then I fetch a piece of my teddy-bear notepaper and try to write it down. I work out the words in a flash and sing them to myself until they make the right tune. I don't know how to write music but I put little arrows under the words, showing where the tune goes up and where it goes down, so that I'll remember it.

They shout and cry,
I wonder why
They moan and scream
While I dream.
I dream of peace
Where no one shouts,
No one tells lies

And no one cries.
I'm all alone
Where no one can moan,
No one can scream
In my land of dream.

Then I go right inside Wardrobe City, shut the doors so no one can hear me, and sing it. My voice is still a frog-croak so it doesn't sound right – but inside my head I can hear just how it should be. I clasp my arms round myself, thrilled. Claudia is shouting for me but I don't feel like answering her just yet. Then she starts hammering on the door, trying to wrench the city walls open.

'Go away, Claudia,' I say furiously.

'Well, come *out*. I couldn't find you anywhere. I thought you were lost. You're too old to play ridiculous tricks like this.'

'First I'm too young, then I'm too old,' I say, emerging sulkily.

'Whatever have you *got* in there?' Claudia asks, flinging the doors wide.

'Stop it, it's *private*.'

'Why have you got your doll's house inside your wardrobe with all the rest of that junk?' Claudia asks.

'It's not junk – how dare you! Look, it's *my*

wardrobe. I can put what I like inside it,' I say.

'I give up. You're the three weirdest children I've ever come across. I'm at the end of my tether!' Claudia says. 'Now get into bed, Sunset.'

'But it's nowhere near my bed time yet!'

'I don't *care*. Get undressed, clean your teeth and go to bed this instant. I'm sick of the lot of you.'

'Are you going to hand in your notice?'

'Yes I am!'

I don't know whether to beg her to stay or not. I don't really like her – but some of the nannies we've had have been much worse.

'Do you hate us, Claudia?' I ask.

'What? No, of course I don't *hate* you, Sunset! Don't look like that!'

I jump and put my hand up quickly. 'Was I showing my teeth?'

'No! There's nothing *wrong* with your teeth. Or you. Or Sweetie or Ace. It's not your fault.'

'Is it Mum and Dad's fault?'

Claudia hesitates. 'I shouldn't discuss your parents with you.'

'Oh, go on. I won't tell. And if you're leaving, what does it matter anyway?'

'Well – they're pretty impossible to work for. They don't act like normal human beings at all. All

188

this arguing! They don't even try to lower their voices. They seem to think they can do anything they want, just because they're so-called celebrities. They throw tantrums just like little children.'

'Well, you're the nanny. Maybe you should put them on the naughty step and not let them have any supper.'

Claudia stares at me, and then bursts out laughing. 'You're a funny girl, Sunset. I shall miss you.'

'So you really really really are leaving?'

'I'm sorry, but I've made up my mind. Now, I'd better go and check on the other two. You don't have to go to bed just yet, Sunset. Go back in your wardrobe if you want to!' She squeezes my shoulder and goes to the door.

'Claudia?'

'Mmm?'

'Claudia, if – if Mum and Dad split up—'

'Oh, darling, I don't think they'll do that. I know they quarrel dreadfully but I'm sure that's just their way.'

Claudia doesn't know about the girl texting Dad.

'Yes, but *if* they do – what will happen to us? Will we live with Mum or Dad?'

'I don't really know. Your mum, I suppose – though of course you'd still see your dad.'

189

'But *where* would we live? This is Dad's house, isn't it?'

'Well ... you mustn't worry about it, Sunset. You'll be fine. And your mum and dad will be fine too. And if by chance they do break up, they'll both still be your parents. They both love you very much indeed and will see you're properly looked after, I'm sure of it,' says Claudia, and she goes out.

She doesn't *sound* very sure. I worry about it half the night. I listen out for Mum, I listen out for Dad. What if neither of them come back? I start to wonder if that might actually work. Sweetie and Ace and I could still live in our house. I could take over and be their mother. We wouldn't need a real mother. We wouldn't need a nanny. If Margaret and John left too, I could do all the cooking. I know how to do baked beans on toast and baked potatoes and egg and bacon and fairy cakes already, and I'm sure I could learn lots of other recipes. I can't drive, of course, but we could walk to places, and maybe get the bus – that would be ever such fun, I've always longed to take a bus ride. And I wouldn't go to school – I so hate Ridgemount House. I'd study by myself at home and I wouldn't go to the dentist and I wouldn't get my teeth fixed, I'd just let them be all crooked and I *wouldn't care* ...

But then I start to feel guilty. I don't *really* want

to get rid of Mum and Dad, do I? What if they don't come back because I've been so wicked? What if they've both *died* and it's all my fault? I picture two separate car smashes, Mum with scarlet blood all over her white dress, Dad slumped lifeless with his bandanna slipping sideways, and it's so real I start shaking. I see Sweetie and Ace and me in black velvet, weeping by their twin graves, holding bunches of white roses, scattering petals . . .

But then I hear the front door, and that's one of them back safely, and two hours later I hear the door again, and I have two living parents once more. They don't appear till lunch time on Sunday. I don't think they're speaking to each other, but they're speaking to *us*, both of them fussing over us like crazy. Sweetie and Ace play up to this. Sweetie sits on Dad's knee as she toys with her roast potatoes, so Ace climbs up on Mum's lap and demands to be spoonfed.

'You're such a baby, Ace,' says Sweetie scornfully.

'I'm not a baby, I'm Tigerman, and I'm being fed my lumps of meat by my keeper lady,' says Ace, chewing. 'Mum, can we go to the zoo and see the real tigers?'

'Of course we can, poppet,' says Mum.

She's barely eating anything herself, and looks very pale.

'Oh, that's not fair, I *hate* the zoo. All the animals smell of poo,' Sweetie whines.

'Hey, that's a song, Sweetie. *I hate the zoo, the animals smell of poo!*' Dad sings it in a silly voice.

'Dad, *I* made up a song yesterday,' I say.

'Did you, Sunset? Don't fret, Sweetie, we're not going to the zoo.'

'Where are we going, Daddy?'

'*We're* going shopping because my best little girl needs a party dress.'

Sweetie squeals excitedly, and starts burbling away about the sort of outfit she's after.

Dad isn't the slightest bit interested in my song. Neither is Mum.

'You can't take Sweetie shopping for the dress, Danny. You haven't got a clue when it comes to the kids' clothes. I'll take Sweetie tomorrow.'

'She's got school tomorrow. I'm taking her now. You want to go shopping, don't you, little darling?'

'I love shopping,' says Sweetie, clapping her hands.

'I don't want to go shopping, I hate it!' says Ace.

'Well, you don't have to go shopping, little Tigerman,' says Mum, cuddling him. 'We're going to the zoo and we'll see lots of tigers, and the lions too, and all the funny little monkeys and the great fat elephant . . .'

I don't want to go to the zoo with Ace or shopping with Sweetie. I want to stay at home but I can't do that. Mum and Dad have given Claudia Sunday off instead of Saturday evening, and Margaret's gone off to her own home now she's served lunch. There's no one to look after me. I argue that I'm perfectly capable of looking after myself, but they won't listen.

'You go to the zoo, Sunset. You like animals,' says Dad.

'No, you'd better go with Dad if he's suddenly turned into Gok Wan. You need a new dress for Sweetie's party too,' says Mum.

'Neither of you want me to come, do you?' I say.

I'm just stating the obvious truth but it really annoys them.

'Stop being such a little drama queen, Sunset,' says Mum.

'Yes, don't go all stroppy with me, kiddo,' says Dad. 'I'm offering to take you shopping and get you a lovely dress, so what's with the silly face? *You* want to come, don't you, Sweetie?'

'Oh, yes, yes, yes, you're the kindest daddy in the whole world!' she says, kissing him.

So I have to trail along with them and it's a total nightmare. John drives us to Harrods. There's a place at the back where the doorman lets us park the Merc, and we go up to the girls' department. The assistants there all recognize Dad and make a fuss of him and coo over Sweetie, and I skulk around while she skips from one dress rail to another, gathering armfuls of clothes.

'Come on, Sunset, you get choosing too,' says Dad.

I try to gather my own selection, choosing blue and green and purple clothes because I like those colours, not really thinking about style or whether they go together.

Then we go into the changing rooms. Sweetie has her own assistant helping her in and out of all her clothes, though she can easily dress herself. They even offer to help *me*, but I back away in horror and mumble that I'll manage.

Sweetie looks adorable in every single one of her outfits: a deep violet silk dress, a white ruffled smock threaded with pink ribbons with matching tight pink jeans, a little blue and white shirt dress, and a rainbow dress with a full skirt and little yellow buttons like smiley suns. She prances in and out of the changing rooms showing Dad and all the other assistants, flouncing around and twirling like a little model on the catwalk. Dad claps his hands each time and says she looks beautiful. Well, she does.

I stand half in and half out of my clothes, staring at myself in the changing-room mirror, wanting to burst into tears.

'Come on, dear, let's see what you look like,' the assistant calls from the other side of the curtain.

I know all too well what I look like. The blue dress is too tight and makes my stomach stick out, the purple top and short skirt look ridiculous because I go in and out in the wrong places, and the green makes my skin look green too, as if I'm about to be sick.

The assistants smile anxiously. Dad frowns.

'Yeah, yeah, it's just they're not quite . . .' He flaps his hands. 'Maybe you'll have to wait for your mother to come with you, Sunset. She'll be able to pick something out for you.'

So I change back into my own clothes, humiliated, while Dad buys every single one of Sweetie's outfits because she looks adorable in all of them. I wander around the girls' department while they're getting them wrapped up. On a stand of fluffy pink and lilac accessories I see a tiny pair of black net mittens.

I pick them up. Then I rush back to the jeans section and find black ones – and then a black T-shirt.

'Dad! Oh, Dad, please can I have these?' I beg.

'Oh, Sunset! Look, we're all ready to go. Why couldn't you have tried them on earlier? What *are* they anyway? Isn't black a bit plain for a party?'

I take a deep breath. I tell the most sickening lie. 'I want to look like you, Dad. You know, that picture on the *Midnight* album. You look so cool.'

All the assistants coo at me this time, going '*Ahhh!*' in unison. Dad looks astonished – but pleased too.

'Don't be daft, Sunset,' he says, but he puts his arm round me and gives me a little hug. 'So you want to look like your old dad, eh? OK, run along and try them on, sweetheart.'

I run and do just that. Thank goodness the jeans are big enough and the T-shirt's not one of those skinny tight ones so it covers my tummy properly. I wriggle my fingers into my mittens, and then try pulling my hair up in a ponytail. As if I'd want to look like Dad! I look like Destiny, I really do. Like sisters.

The assistant's making me go and show Dad what I look like in the black clothes. Dad stares, acting a bit puzzled.

'Yeah, you're right, they suit you. But haven't you got another outfit just the same? I've seen you wearing those little net mittens, haven't I?'

Not *me*, Dad. Destiny. Your other daughter.

But I can't say it here, in front of half of Harrods.

Sweetie is scowling at me. 'That's not a party dress, Sunset. You're supposed to wear pretty stuff at my party.'

'*You'll* be the pretty one, Sweetie,' I say, not minding for once.

I wait till John's driven us home and Sweetie's gone charging off to try on her new clothes again. Mum and Ace are still out at the zoo. Dad is reaching for his mobile.

'Dad?' I reach up and give him a hug. 'Dad, thank you ever so much for buying my lovely new outfit,' I say.

Dad ruffles my hair. 'That's OK, sweetheart. You look good in it.'

'You *have* seen someone in black jeans with little black mittens.'

'Yeah, me, on the cover of *Midnight*, like you said. I wonder if I could ever go back to that goth look. Do you think I could still get away with it?'

'Yes, of course, Dad – but I didn't mean you. There was this girl at the premiere of *Milky Star*, remember?'

Dad frowns the moment I say the name Milky Star. 'Stupid little kids! They prance about on YouTube and suddenly they think they're stars. I thought I was doing them a favour, giving them a

197

helping hand, when all the time they were taking the mickey.'

'Dad, this girl . . . she was dressed like me, in my new clothes, black jeans and T-shirt and little mittens. She looks like me, but better—'

'Rose-May led me *right* up the garden path, but I'll show her. No one's making a monkey out of me.'

'Dad, listen, this girl in black with the mittens – *she's* your daughter, I know she is, and she's lovely, and if you'd just say you'd meet her – her and her mum – I know just how happy it would make them. *Please* say you'll meet them.'

'Will you *quit* this nonsense!' Dad takes hold of me, a hand on each of my cheeks so I'm forced to look right at him. '*I don't have any secret mystery kids!*'

'But she says—'

'I don't give a stuff what she says. There are hundreds of mad fans out there, and they all say I've fathered their wretched kids. It's just a scam, Sunset, a way to get their hands on my money. So stop playing these pathetic little games about sisters. You've only got one sister and that's Sweetie – and I wish to God you were more like her.'

9

DESTINY

Dear Sunset,
Everyone's getting all het up because it's the
talent contest TOMORROW!!! I kid on I'm not
the slightest bit bothered, but actually I'm just a
bit scared too. We do the contest to the whole

school in the afternoon, and it will be awful if they don't like me and shout, Off, off, off! so I don't even get to finish my song. There's a panel of schoolkids too, one from Year Three, one from Year Four, and two from Year Five, and I'm not sure they'll vote for me either because I'm not in any gang and the boys mostly don't like me at my school – not that the girls do either. They have to make comments on our performance. Imagine the fun they're going to have, making us feel like idiots. I shall just have to sing so well they'll give me a high score even if they hate me. I'm a bit worried about the Jack the Lads and the Superspeedos – they're two rival street-dance acts, and they're both looking quite sharp now. Mind you, they've had a LOT of help from Mrs Avery, our PE teacher, which isn't exactly fair. She's choreographed their entire acts. Well, I suppose Mr Roberts tried to help me a bit, giving me all these daft suggestions, wanting me to stand in a certain way and jiggle around when I start the chorus – honestly, totally cheesy ideas. I'm not taking any notice. I'm just going to sing it my way.

But it's not the school performance that's really getting to me, it's the contest in front of all the adults in the evening. There's going to be

a panel of teachers judging that. My mum's coming and she's so excited about it, much more worked up than I am. We've been allocated two tickets – I suppose it's one for our mums and one for our dads. Imagine if our dad came to the show!
Love from Destiny

I put the letter in an envelope, write the address and seal it – and then undo it all over again because I'm fussing about that last sentence. I meant it as a joke, but what if Sunset takes it seriously? What if she thinks I'm hinting to her to get Danny to come? *Was* I hinting? Oh wow, it would be so incredible seeing him there in the audience. Mr Roberts would *wet* himself. 'Are you . . . *Danny Kilman?*' he'd go, and Danny would toss his long hair and shrug and say, 'Yeah, just come to hear my kid sing.' Actually I'm not sure I could sing a single note with Danny in the audience. Think of all the other kids too! After the show I'd take Danny and say, 'Right, Dad, I'd like you to meet my friends,' and he'd say hi to Jack Myers and Angel and all the rest, and they'd practically pass out on the spot.

Like any of this could ever happen! He didn't seem the slightest bit interested in Mum and me –

he just ignored us, couldn't even crack a smile. He doesn't sound that friendly a father to Sunset. And her mum's *horrible*. Perhaps Sunset's not so lucky after all. I do like her though, ever so. I cross out the dad bit on my crumpled letter and scribble instead, *I wish you could come and hear me sing, Sunset. Pity we live so far away from each other.*

And now it's the day of the concert, I know it the moment I wake before I even open my eyes. My heart starts thudding. I tell myself I'm mad to get into a state over a silly little school concert. As if I care about this school or anyone in it. But I care about my mum and I care about me, and this is our song, and I have to make it special. My throat dries and I clutch my neck anxiously, wondering if it's sore, whether I've got some cough or cold bug and won't be able to sing. I get up and go in the bathroom and clean my teeth, gargling for a bit, and then I try out my voice as I have a quick bath, and it's fine – perhaps a bit husky, but it'll do.

I get dressed in my usual burgundy rubbish school uniform, but I pack my black outfit and my beautiful leather jacket, carefully wrapped up in a soft towel in a laundry bag. Mum's back early from her cleaning and catches me before I leave for school.

'Hey, babe, how are you doing?' she says, dashing in. 'All set for your big day?'

Then she catches sight of my bulging bag. 'What's that?'

'Well, I can't sing in my uniform, Mum.'

'Yeah, I know, but . . .' She opens the bag. 'Oh, Destiny, not your *jacket*! You can't take that to school.'

'I'll look after it, Mum. Believe me, I'm not going to let it out of my sight. But I *need* that jacket. I have to sing in it.'

'But if one of them kids gets their mucky little fingers on it—'

'Just let them try! I'm wearing it this afternoon – and you'll see me in it this evening.'

'I can't wait, babes! I'm so proud of you. Singing in front of a packed audience, just like your dad! I'm so thrilled you've got Danny's talent.'

'I don't want to take after Dad, I want to take after *you*,' I say, giving her a hug.

She feels so thin – and she's *burning*.

'Mum, you're so hot! You haven't got a temperature, have you?'

'What? No, of course not. I'm just a bit worked up, that's all,' says Mum.

I look at her worriedly. She's got dark circles under her eyes. I don't think she's sleeping properly. Her eyes look so big, as if they're about to pop right out of her head. She looks permanently anxious now. I wish I could stop her being so worried all the time.

'If I really do take after Danny then I'm going to be a big rock star, right – and do you know what I'm going to do?' I say, cuddling her.

'What's that, babe? Are you going to buy a lovely big mansion like Danny's?'

'Yep, and guess who's going to live in it with me?'

'Who's that, darling?'

'*You*, silly! You'll live like a queen. You'll have a whole suite of rooms, and one of those four-poster beds you like, *much* better than that one Steve got you, with wonderful velvet curtains and real silk sheets, and you can sleep in every morning because you won't *ever* have to do any work again – no cleaning, no sad old folk, no drunks down the pub – you can just lie back like a lady of leisure.'

'Oh, darling, that would be lovely,' says Mum. 'But just now I've got my old dears to change and feed and water – and you've got school. Good luck this afternoon, Destiny. You sock it to them! And for pity's sake, look after that jacket!'

This is harder than I'd thought. I lumber the laundry bag all the way to school – going the long way round, of course – and because I'm not as nippy as usual I arrive a minute or two after the bell has gone. It doesn't really *matter*. The teachers are mostly glad you've turned up at all – but as luck would have it, Mr Juniper is hovering at the door, officiously recording in the late book.

Mr Juniper is a tall weedy guy fresh out of training college. Maybe it was a training college for Serious Young Offenders, because he's sooo strict. He yells at everyone, getting so worked up that froth forms on his lips and you have to stand back or you'll get sprayed. He's always dishing out detentions, trying to make you stay after school. You just know he would so love it if teachers were allowed to whack us with a cane like they did in the old days.

'You! What's your name?' he shouts, starting to froth already.

'Destiny.'

'Destiny?' He pulls a ridiculous face. 'You are not telling me that's your *name*?'

'Yes. Is that a problem?' I say. How dare he patronize me just because I've got an unusual name.

'Don't you use that tone with me! Destiny what?'

'Destiny Williams.'

'Well, Destiny Williams, you're now down in my late book. You will lose a form point.'

I don't give a stuff about form points but this infuriates me even so.

'I'm only a *minute* late, Mr Juniper!'

He consults his watch. 'Five minutes and thirty seconds,' he says.

'Well, half of that time I've been here at school talking to you.'

'Stop answering me back in that impertinent way! You'll get a detention if you're not careful. Now on your way to your classroom, quick sharp.'

I walk off briskly, dragging my burden.

'What are you doing with that ridiculous bag?' he shouts after me. 'That's not a proper school bag.'

'It's my clothes for the concert this afternoon.'

'Well, you can't possibly drag them around with you all day. Unpack them and hang them up in the cloakroom.'

I stare at him. 'Are you *mad*?' I say it without thinking.

He holds me up for *another* five minutes, ticking me off for insolence and saying I've got to do a half-hour's detention in his classroom after school this afternoon – though he *knows* I've got to whizz home after the school performance to get my tea before coming back for the evening one. Still, it's a waste of breath arguing with him. I just stand there, letting him witter on, until some other poor kid slopes in even later and he starts picking on him instead.

I make out I'm off to put my bag on my peg in the cloakroom – but as soon as Mr Juniper's back is turned I charge off with it down the corridor. As if I'm leaving my leather jacket there! Someone would nick it in five seconds. And I'm not going to bother to go to his poxy classroom after school either. He'll probably forget all about his detention – and too bad if he doesn't.

I manage to get myself and my bag into the classroom without Mr Roberts taking too much notice – he's in full flow, giving everyone performance tips for this afternoon. But then he starts walking up and down between the aisles – and trips right over my bag. He peers down at it.

'Are you taking in laundry, Destiny?'

'Oh, ha ha. It's my *costume*, Mr Roberts,' I say.

'Well, put it in the PE store cupboard. That's where everyone else is keeping their kit,' says Mr Roberts.

'I can't do that, Mr Roberts,' I say.

'Can't – or won't?' says Mr Roberts.

'Both,' I say.

Mr Roberts stands over me, folding his arms. The whole classroom goes eerily quiet. Mr Roberts is obviously pretty tense about the talent contest – and now, here I am, winding him up.

He clears his throat theatrically. 'Here we both are in the classroom, Destiny. I have a simple question for you. Am I your fellow pupil? In which case you can choose to do what I say, according to your general obliging nature or common sense. *Am I a pupil in this classroom, Destiny?*'

'No, Mr Roberts.'

'What am I, then?'

Various answers spring to mind, but I'm not entirely daft.

'You're my teacher, Mr Roberts.'

'That's right! So therefore *I* tell you what to do – and you obey. Is that correct?'

I hesitate. 'Generally, sir.'

'No, no, Destiny. You obey *at all times*. So take your cumbersome laundry bag to the PE store cupboard and *leave it there.*'

I don't move.

'Pronto!'

I don't know what to do. Mr Roberts isn't an officious twit like Mr Juniper. You can usually talk to him and explain stuff.

'Mr Roberts, I *can't*. It's too precious.'

'So what exactly *is* this costume, Destiny? Cloth of gold?'

'It's – it's my jeans and stuff,' I say, not wanting to say outright.

Some of the kids start sniggering.

'Oh, precious jeans,' says Mr Roberts. 'Hand sewn with Swarovski crystals, perhaps?'

Now everyone's laughing at me.

'Let's have a look at these little sparklers,' says Mr Roberts, and he dives into my bag before I can stop him.

He brings out the old towel. The classroom collapses. Mr Roberts shakes the towel as if he's a bullfighter, really hamming it up – and the leather jacket falls out. He picks it up in astonishment. *Everyone's* astonished.

'Wow! Look at Destiny's jacket!'

'That leather – it looks as soft as butter.'

'Look at all those zippy bits.'

'Where did she *get* it?'

'It must be worth *hundreds*.'

'I bet her mum nicked it!'

'My mum didn't nick it, so you shut your face, Angel,' I yell. 'It was given to me as a *present*, see.'

'Yeah, pull the other one!'

'You're talking rubbish, Destiny. A present!'

'It *was* a present. You shut up!' I shout.

'Now calm down, Destiny,' says Mr Roberts. He's folding my jacket up again, trying to put it back inside my towel, but doing it all wrong so that the sleeves are wrinkling up.

'Let me do it,' I say. 'It's my present. A friend gave it to me.'

'Don't be so daft, Destiny,' says Angel. 'You haven't *got* any friends.'

'You don't know anything about me! I have so got a very *special* friend, only I'm not going to tell you anything about her because it's none of your business, see.'

'Hey, hey, let's stop all the argy-bargy. We're all losing the plot here,' says Mr Roberts. 'Settle down, all of you.'

He leans over me. 'It's a beautiful jacket, Destiny,' he says very softly. 'I can see why you're so worried about it. A *sensible* girl would never take such a clearly expensive jacket into school with her – but I can see why you long to wear it for the talent contest. A *sensible* teacher would send you all the way home with it – and a *really strict* teacher wouldn't let you take part in the contest for refusing to do as you're told. But I'm not always sensible and I don't seem to have it in me to be strict. *However*, I can't keep falling over that bag, and now the others have seen the jacket they'll be all over you to try it on, and before you know where you are it will be ripped to shreds. So how about running it along to the school secretary's office? Mrs Hazel keeps her room locked whenever she's

210

out of it. I'm sure she'll look after it for you until after lunch. Is that a deal?' He holds out his hand and I shake it very gratefully.

'You're a very, very *kind* teacher, Mr Roberts,' I say.

I take the jacket in its bag to Mrs Hazel and tell her Mr Roberts said I had to leave it with her. She keeps all the money and the medication locked up. Her office is like Fort Knox.

She doesn't look too happy about it. 'Tell Mr Roberts my room isn't a left-luggage office, Destiny. I don't want it cluttered up with any more bags, thank you very much.'

But I know my jacket is safe now.

I still can't manage to concentrate on school work, and eating lunch is an ordeal. I manage five baked beans and one chip and know I'll throw up if I have any more. Most of the boys still shovel stuff down, but outside in the playground, where both boy dance groups are rehearsing their somersaults and backflips, Rocky throws up all down himself like a disgusting fountain. Mr Roberts sends him off to be hosed down and shakes his head at all of us.

'Why don't you all *relax*, guys. No more rehearsing. Just chill out until the bell goes – and then quietly collect your stuff from Mrs Avery, get changed, and come backstage in the hall. There's no need to get so worked up. You're all going to do splendidly.'

They go off in little groups. I wander off by myself, walking round and round the playground. I pretend Sunset is walking round with me. We're linked arm in arm, and she's telling me I'm going to sing *Destiny* perfectly. 'Better than Dad!' she says, and we both laugh.

Then the bell rings and – oh God – it's *time*! I whizz off to Mrs Hazel and collect my stuff, and then I change in the girls' toilets. The mirror by the wash basins is too high up to see all of me, but if I leap up I can see as far down as my waist. The jacket looks wonderful. I feel like I've got Sunset's arms round me, giving me a hug.

I rush off to the hall, and then force myself to stop and breathe deeply before joining the others. I mustn't show I'm nervous. I need to look *cool*!

It's pandemonium behind the stage, kids running around everywhere, boys doing backflips, girls step-shuffle-tapping, Fareed dropping all his cards, Mrs Avery frantically sewing up someone's skirt, Mr Roberts red in the face, great damp patches under his arms.

Lots of the kids nudge each other when they see me.

'Look at Destiny!'

'*Love* the jacket!'

'Wow, doesn't she look different?'

Angel tugs my jacket. 'What you wearing them silly mittens for? And why all black? You look like you're going to a funeral.'

'It'll be yours if you don't take your clammy hands off my jacket,' I say, twitching away from her.

Jack Myers is still staring at me. Is he going to have a go too? He comes up close, sticking his hands in the back pockets of his jeans. 'You look great, Destiny,' he says.

I blink at him, wondering if this is a wind-up.

'I think you're a fantastic singer too. I bet you win the contest,' he says.

I stare at him. 'Thanks, Jack,' I say.

We're still staring. We've run out of words. Jack eventually nods and goes over to the rest of his gang.

'You can take that smirk off your face,' says Angel. 'He's just saying that. He knows *he'll* win. He's the most popular boy in the whole school. Everyone will vote for him.' She pauses. 'Or me.'

I shrug. 'As if I care,' I say. 'It's just a silly little school concert.'

Yes, it is. But I care, I care *enormously*. Jack might be popular – maybe *I* even like him a little

213

bit – but I don't think he and his gang are very good dancers all the same.

The hall fills up with all the kids. If I peep out of the wings I can see the panel of judges sitting on a bench right in front of the stage. At Mr Roberts's suggestion they've all got dressed up. Both the boys are in white T-shirts, trying for the Simon Cowell look, and the girls are in their big sisters' posh frocks. One of them is even wearing a blonde wig.

Mr Roberts goes bustling onto the stage. He's put on an embarrassingly weird shiny brocade jacket, but at least it hides his damp shirt.

'Hello, everyone. Welcome to *Bilefield's Got Talent!*' he bellows into his mike. He introduces the boys and girls on the judging panel. I can tell by the cheers that both boys are in the Flatboys gang – *big* mistake.

'Now for our first act – the Jack the Lads!' says Mr Roberts.

Jack and his mates bounce onstage, all style and swagger. Jack spits on his hands like he means business and the others spit in unison, making everyone laugh, even the Speedos. Then Mrs Avery puts on their loud music and they start their dance. You can tell they've rehearsed a bit. They've put in several extra moves, including a pretend

214

fight, but they haven't worked hard enough at it. Jack trips several times, and one of his lads falls on his bum when he tries a backflip. They're all a bit rubbish at keeping time with the music and they don't end properly – they just look at each other and then try to stop when Jack does, petering out so that at first no one realizes they've finished, so no one claps. There's an awkward pause – and then sudden cheers and applause, mixed with loud booing and hissing from the Speedo boys.

Then the panel have their say. Both boys and the girl in the blonde wig insist the Jack the Lads are fantastic. The littlest girl from Year Three looks puzzled and mumbles that she didn't think they were that great. She doesn't live on the Bilefield Estate so she's not associated with either gang. When she votes she gives the Jack the Lads five out of ten, and then looks worried when the audience hiss her. The other three judges each give the Jack the Lads *ten*. It's crazy – a performance should be perfect to warrant ten out of ten – but half the audience approves noisily, while the other half yells abuse.

Mr Roberts has a hard job quietening everyone down to announce the next act, Girls Very Soft. As their name suggests, they sing very softly at first, but then get louder and louder until they're belting it out at the end of their song. I don't know whose idea it was, but it works well. They dance well too, though their routine is a bit basic. The *other* half of the audience cheers loudly this time. Someone whispers that Simone is the girlfriend of one of the Speedos. The little girl on the panel *loves* their act and gives them an eight, but Blonde Wig and the boys say they are prissy rubbish and give them *two*.

Fareed and Hannah are hopeless. Poor Fareed keeps dropping his cards and Hannah rushes round in a fluster trying to pick them up and drops them all over again. Someone shouts, 'Off!' and then nearly everyone starts chanting, 'Off, off, off!' though Mr Roberts has specifically said everyone can complete their performance. I can't understand why Fareed and Hannah *don't* clear off because they're both all hot and sweaty now, and Fareed is fumbling every trick. Mr Roberts must have told him to remember to smile at his audience because he grins madly the entire time, baring all his teeth. When the *next* trick goes completely wrong, his smile is still fixed on his face. Someone bursts out laughing – and then everyone is laughing, and someone else starts clapping. When Fareed's toy rabbit finally falls right out his top hat, everyone collapses and then cheers.

Fareed isn't a Flatboy or a Speedo and so the voting is bizarre. One of the boys gives him nought, but the other boy gives him nine because he still can't stop laughing. The two girls give him five, so weirdly his final score is higher than Girls Very Soft.

The girl dancers call themselves the Dancing Queens. They're all wearing shocking pink T-shirts and little black shorts and those fake tiaras that light up in their hair. All the boys whistle, whether Flatboy or Speedo. Their dancing isn't really all that great, they just repeat the same sequence of steps again and again, but they get huge cheers from the Speedos because one of them has a brother in their gang – so the Flatboys on the panel meanly mark them with a three, though Blonde Wig is fairer this time and gives them a six, because she's clearly impressed by their costumes, and the little girl gives them ten.

The girls' play drags on for so long that everyone gets fidgety, especially when half of them forget their words and keep nudging each other and whispering. Someone starts up the 'Off, off, off!' chant, and soon everyone's shouting it. Two of the girls run off in tears, but two of them act it out to the bitter end. I think one of the girls is a Flatboy sister, but even so their scores are terrible because the play's so boring.

Then it's Angel's turn – and she's certainly not boring. She's wearing a skimpy top and very tight shiny white leggings and she struts onstage, grinning and wiggling her hips to this very sexy music. I see Mr Roberts tense, wringing his hands, clearly wondering what on earth Angel's going to do next. She does a few simple cartwheels, arches her back and walks across the stage on her hands and feet, and then spins on her bottom for a bit. Angel has a very *big* bottom so this is easy-peasy for her. It's not really a brilliant acrobatic routine at all, but when she finishes there's a *roar* of applause.

Angel is no one's sister, but she hangs out with the Flatboys. She gets two tens from the boys and a nine from Blonde Wig – and even the little girl gives her an eight. Angel's in the lead and she knows it. She punches the air and looks thrilled. When she swaggers offstage she gives me a little poke in the chest. She doesn't say a word, but it's obvious what she means: *Beat that!*

Raymond comes after her, and he's truly brilliant, leaping about all over the stage and twirling his arms and legs, but because he's wearing leggings the boys yell stupid comments at him and he gets a rubbish score. It's so unfair – Jeff and Ritchie come next with a silly comic ballet routine. They just lumber around and make silly gestures, but they're given higher marks than poor Raymond.

Everyone's getting fed up now, chatting away, so Mr Roberts has to raise his voice and bellow to announce the Superspeedos. They all have a red Superman sign clumsily inked on their T-shirts, but thank goodness they *don't* wear red underpants over their trousers. They still look a little silly, but their routine is quite clever, all of them managing backflips more or less simultaneously, and it's clear they've rehearsed far more than Jack and his lads. They do a lot of leaping, swooping movements too, making out they're flying, and then they end in a row with arms spread, grinning. I'd give them an eight or a nine – they're definitely the best act yet apart from poor Raymond – but those hateful Flatboys give them *one* each. Blonde Wig wavers a little and gives them five, and the younger girl gives them a ten, but they're not even in the top three and it's so unfair. They all look gutted and I don't blame them, but I haven't got time to think about that now because Mr Roberts is announcing *me*.

'Please put your hands together and welcome the last lovely contestant for *Bilefield's Got Talent*, Miss Destiny Williams, who will delight us with her namesake song, *Destiny*, made famous by Mr Danny Kilman. I give you *Destiny*!'

Oh God. I walk right out onstage, and there's everyone staring back at me. Some of them clap half-heartedly, all of them staring at my black outfit. I get hot inside my beautiful leather jacket. I'm scared I'm sweating onto the sleeves. I see them all whispering and giggling. I do my best to blot them all out. I open my mouth and start singing.

'*You are my Destiny . . .*'

The words and the music take over. I'm just a voice, and it soars around the hall. I finish and there's a pause, as if they're all stunned. Then there's clapping. Some kids are clapping loudly, even cheering – but some are silent, not knowing what to make of me. I'm the new girl. They aren't sure if I'm in the Flatboy camp or the Speedos. And if I'm neither, how can they vote for me?

The two Flatboys confer – and both give me two. Blonde Wig gives me three. The little girl looks bewildered and gives me nine, but of course it's not enough to get me anywhere. I don't even do as well as Fareed. I come second to bottom, just above the girls in the play.

10

SUNSET

'*Please* may I open my presents?' Sweetie begs.

'Not yet, darling. You have to wait till your party, when the magazine people come,' says Mum.

'Oh for God's sake, let the kid open a few of her presents. What harm will it do?' says Dad. He's up very early, specially for Sweetie's birthday.

'Rose-May will kill us. She's had all the presents professionally wrapped to go with the party theme.'

'What *is* my party theme, Mum?' Sweetie asks, jumping up and down, looking so cute in her white embroidered top and pink jeans.

'Let's just say it's specially for you, darling,' says Mum. 'Now, we're all going to be busy-busy-busy getting the big living room transformed – the party planners should be arriving any minute. I want you children right out of the way until well after lunch time. Danny, I don't suppose you could take them out somewhere? Maybe Kingtown?'

'Oh *yes*, that would be the best birthday treat ever!' says Sweetie, bouncing on Dad's lap.

'I'd love that too, Sweet Pea, you know I would, it would be the greatest fun in the whole world, but I've got to nip up to London this morning—'

'Oh, Danny, it's Sweetie's *birthday*!' says Mum.

'Yeah, yeah, and I'm not going to miss a moment of it, don't you worry. But I need to see some of the lads – there's talk about this benefit concert and they want me to take part.'

'Which lads?' Mum asks suspiciously.

Dad taps his nose. 'What's it to you, hmm? You get on playing parties and I'll get on with doing the work that pays all the bills, OK?'

He slopes off, leaving Mum clenching her fists.

'Right. Well, *I* can't take you out, darlings – I have to sort out the party planners and rush to get my hair and nails done. So I'll need my car, and it looks like Dad's taking his – so maybe you can ask John to drive you and the children somewhere, Claudia?'

It turns out that John's already off running errands and won't be back until after lunch.

'This is just too bad,' says Mum, sighing. 'Well, you'll just have to keep the children amused up in their rooms, Claudia.'

'That's not a very good birthday treat,' says Sweetie, drooping.

'Well, there's nothing I can do about it, darling. I was relying on your daddy, but of course that was a *big* mistake,' Mum starts. 'He's so selfish he doesn't mind who he lets down – even you, Sweetie.'

Sweetie puts her thumb in her mouth.

'Don't suck your thumb, you'll ruin your teeth!' Mum snaps.

'I can still take the children out,' Claudia says quickly. 'We'll take the bus to Kingtown.'

'A bus!' Sweetie cries, spitting out her thumb. 'Oh, a *bus*!' She twirls around as if Claudia has offered her a ride in a fairy-tale chariot.

'A bus, a bus, a bus, we're going on a bus!' Ace screams, capering about.

'Now don't get the children too over-excited, for heaven's sake,' says Mum. 'Just keep them quiet and calm, especially Sweetie. She's going to need to be on tip-top form this afternoon. She's got to cope with a really big photo shoot. There can't be any tears or tantrums.'

'I'll do my best to make sure Sweetie enjoys her birthday,' Claudia says coldly.

'That wretched woman!' she mutters to herself as we go out the gate, Claudia, Sweetie, Ace and me.

'Mum gets awfully worked up before we have a magazine shoot,' I say.

'Why does she think it's a good idea to turn her own daughter's birthday into a commercial bear-garden?' says Claudia.

'Bear-garden!' Ace repeats. 'Where are the bears in the garden? I'm Tigerman and I want to play with the bears, but they might have big claws.'

'You roar at them and they'll run away,' I say.

Ace roars at every hedge and tree and picket fence along the road. Sweetie skips along beside him, pointing her toes.

'It's ridiculous,' Claudia grumbles to me. 'Imagine making the poor little mite wait till the photographer's there before she can open her presents! And did you know Margaret's been told to make two birthday cakes just in case they can't get all the photos they need of her blowing out the candles and cutting the cake the first time round.'

'I *like* having two cakes,' Sweetie calls.

'And then apparently there are going to be all these completely strange children coming, not Sweetie's real friends from school, but celebrity children. I'm willing to bet Sweetie's never even met half of them before.'

'I know. I had that happen to me for one of my birthdays when I was little, and it was awful. I didn't know what to say to anyone, and I had to play all these awful games, and there was a clown doing silly tricks and he scared me. I'm so glad Mum doesn't make me have birthday parties now.'

'You're silly, Sunset,' says Sweetie. 'I love having birthday parties. I want to play *lots* of games. Mummy says the birthday girl always has to win. I shall wear my violet dress and Mum says I'll have real rosebuds in my hair.' She skips round and round us, her hair flying out in a golden cloud.

'Will you have flowers in *your* hair, Sunset?' Claudia asks.

'Maybe thistles and dandelions?' I joke. 'No fear!'

I like the way the words sounds, like a bouquet

for a witch's child. I start making up a little song as we walk down the road towards the busy hill and the bus stop.

Thistles and dandelions,
They are my flowers.
Burdock and tangleweed,
Blackberries sour,
Rosehips and crab apples,
They are my fruit.
Rabbit foot, snakeskin
And eye of newt,
Duck's beak and antler
Ground up for a spell.
I am the witch's child
But I wish you well.

It takes me a while to get all the lines right, and I haven't got a pen and paper so I have to keep mumbling it over and over as we wait at the bus stop. The music comes easily – it's strange and eerie, and every fourth line I drag out the words with a little wavery bit at the end.

I'm almost as excited about the bus ride as Sweetie and Ace. I've only been on a bus twice before, and even though I'm ten *I* want to sit upstairs at the front and pretend to drive the bus.

I sit beside Claudia, humming my new song very softly to myself.

Sweetie and Ace sit on the other front seat, jumping up and down with their hands on the front rail, little knuckles white, though Claudia keeps begging them to sit down nicely. She's vaguely nodding to my tune.

'Is that one of your dad's songs?' she asks.

'No, it's mine,' I say proudly.

'Sing it,' says Claudia.

'I can't. I'm rubbish at singing.'

'Go on, have a go.'

So I kind of whisper it. Claudia listens carefully.

'Did you make that up all by yourself?'

'Well, sort of,' I say, blushing. 'I think I copied "eye of newt" from Shakespeare, and we once had to read a poem called "Goblin Fruit" in drama, and I copied from that just a little bit.'

'It's very good,' Claudia says quickly. 'Perhaps you should sing it to your dad?'

'He wouldn't be interested,' I say.

'Sunset, he's your *dad*. He'll be proud of you,' says Claudia, though she doesn't sound totally sure.

'Is your dad proud of you, Claudia?' I ask.

Claudia smiles. 'Oh yes, my dad's a silly old sausage. I was never one of the brain boxes at my school, but I won a prize for thoughtfulness when I was about your age, Sunset, and when I marched up to collect my certificate there was this terrific hooting sound and it was silly old Daddy blubbing. Can you imagine!'

I'm trying my hardest to imagine it.

'What about your mum? Is she proud of you too?'

I hope I'm not being terribly tactless. I don't think Claudia's mum could possibly be proud of her. She isn't at all pretty and she has a habit of wrinkling her nose to hitch her glasses up. I would have thought she'd be forever on at Claudia to get a decent haircut and use more make-up on her shiny face and switch to contact lenses.

'Oh, Mummy's a lamb,' says Claudia, still smiling. 'She always *says* she's proud of me, though heaven knows why, because I always make rather a bish of things. She calls me her extra-special favourite daughter – but she says that to both my sisters too, she's so sweet.'

I think about last prize day when I won the English prize. Dad didn't come. He said those kinds of affairs gave him the fidgets. Mum *did* come, and she said, 'Well done' – but she also nagged on and on about the way I'd walked up to the front of the hall. 'Plod plod plod, like a ploughman,' she said. 'Maybe we ought to send you back to ballet.'

I try to see myself reflected in the bus window. I'm wearing my new black T-shirt and jeans and my lacy mittens. I thought at first when I put them on this morning that I might look a little bit cool, but now I'm not so sure.

When we get to Kingtown Sweetie wants to go straight to the shops, so we let her, because it is her birthday. There's one of those make-a-bear places in the big shopping centre. Sweetie isn't that interested – she'd sooner go to the shop that sells all the glittery jewellery and make-up – but the manager is standing near the doorway and comes rushing out.

'Are these Danny Kilman's children?' she asks Claudia, sounding awestruck. She must be a keen reader of *Hi! Magazine*. 'Oh, my! Would they like a complimentary bear each?'

'That's very kind, but no thank you,' Claudia starts politely.

'Oh, please, please, *please*, Claudia, I'd *love* a bear,' Sweetie begs, switching on the charm simply because it's second nature now.

'I want a Tiger! I'm Tigerman and I want a toy tiger!' says Ace.

'Ace, stop it. You mustn't ask for things,' I say,

but I want one of these teddy bears too, even though I know I'm much too old.

We all look pleadingly at Claudia, who looks anxious but eventually gives in. We take a long time choosing our bears and their outfits. Sweetie dithers for a while, exclaiming, while the manager clucks and coos in her wake. She eventually chooses a very flushed pink bear in a magenta ballet frock. Ace sticks in tiger mode and chooses his new stripy friend blue pyjamas and a dressing gown. I can't decide. All the teddies look so cute and floppy and helpless. I pick one and then another and then a third, gazing at them intently, trying to guess their personalities.

'Oh, for heaven's sake, Sunset!' says Claudia.

I get flustered and plump for a panda, though when she's stuffed I'm not sure I really like her after all. Her head's slightly on one side as if she's sneering at me and her body's too big and bouncy. I'd like her to wear black jeans and a black T-shirt but they don't make them. I have to compromise with a white blouse and blue denim dungarees.

'Why did you pick a little boy panda, Sunset?' Sweetie asks.

'It's a *girl*,' I hiss – but she doesn't look like one any more.

'There now,' says Claudia. 'Say thank you very much, children.'

But we're not finished yet. We have to stand by the shop sign holding out our bears and smiling while the manager whips out her camera. Claudia fusses, not at all sure she should allow this, but she can't make us give back the teddies now they are made up and personalized, so she's stuck.

'Smile, please. Say cheese,' says the manager.

'That's what little mice eat. My Rosie bear says *honey*,' says Sweetie.

'My Tiger bear doesn't say anything, he just roars and roars,' says Ace.

'What does your panda say, dear?' the manager says kindly to me, so I'm not left out.

I shrug, horribly embarrassed, because I'm too old to play this game. My panda casts her beady eyes on me contemptuously, refusing to say a word.

We pose for further photos and then Sweetie drags me off to the sparkly accessory shop. She hopes the manager there will also tell us to take our pick of the goodies on sale, but if she recognizes us she's not letting on. Sweetie rushes from one stand to another, marvelling at earrings, lilac nail polish, pearly lipsticks, neon pink feather boas, dinky purses, cute key-rings and sparkly tiaras. She's in Sweetie Heaven.

'Don't get too excited, Sweetie, I haven't got my wallet with me,' Claudia fibs.

'Don't worry, Claudia, *I've* got money,' says Sweetie, delving into the pockets of her smock. She produces a twenty-pound note in each hand! 'Daddy gave me some birthday spending money.'

'Oh my Lord,' says Claudia, rolling her eyes. 'You're six years old, Sweetie, and he's given you *forty* pounds to fritter away?'

'Where's *my* spending money?' Ace wails, sitting down and trying to tug his Tiger free from its packaging.

'Don't undo that, Ace, for pity's sake. Stand up, you're getting in everyone's way.'

'It's not your birthday, Ace, it's *my* birthday, and Daddy says birthday girls get lots of treats,' says Sweetie, sticking a tiara on her head and flinging a feather boa round her neck.

Claudia winces but doesn't argue. She catches my eye as Sweetie darts around the shop. 'I told a teeny fib about my wallet, Sunset,' she whispers. 'Do you want to choose a little something for yourself?'

'I'm not really into all this sparkly stuff,' I say. 'But thanks anyway, Claudia.'

'I tell you what. We'll go to Paperchase when Sweetie's done and buy you a special little notebook to write your songs in,' says Claudia. 'Would you like that?'

'Oh! Yes *please*,' I say.

'That's not *fair*!' Ace complains bitterly. 'Sweetie's getting heaps of girly stuff and Sunset's getting notebooks and I'm getting *nothing*.'

'For heaven's sake, you've just been given your lovely toy tiger.'

'He's *tired*!' says Ace, yanking him right out of the cardboard box. 'He's in his jim-jams and he's yawn-yawn-yawning and he wants to go to *sleep*. Night-night!' He sprawls on the floor right in the doorway, where everyone has to step over him, his Tiger bear clutched to his chest – just as Sweetie reaches for a diamanté necklace and pulls the whole jewellery stand down on top of her.

'Oh, *why* did I ever think I wanted to be a wretched nanny?' says Claudia, nearly in tears.

She tries to set the stand to rights, while I yank Ace up out of the way and tell him that it's getting-up time now, and pour Tigerman and his pet a pretend glass of Tiger juice for breakfast.

We get out of the shop at last, Sweetie bedecked in all her new finery. Ace wants real juice now, so we go to a café and have a healthy juice each, and then several deliciously *un*healthy doughnuts. We have to go to the ladies' on the top floor to wipe all the sugar off Ace's mouth (and his Tiger bear's paws). There's a toyshop nearby and so we have to spend a long time in there too. I start to worry that Claudia's forgotten about my notebook, but after we've found a tiny toy bus for Ace and a little pocket doll for Sweetie, Claudia nods at me.

'Right, Sunset. *Now* we're going to Paperchase.'

I *love* Paperchase with all its brightly coloured stationery. I want to spend hours gently stroking each notebook in turn, carefully flipping through the pristine pages, happily deliberating, but Ace and Sweetie are bored now and I have to pick my notebook in double-quick time. I choose a little blue velvety one with blank pages so I can draw little pictures to illustrate my songs. When Claudia buys it for me I can't quite manage to give her a hug and a kiss because I'm too shy, but I squeeze her hand very tightly to show her how happy I am.

'There now!' she says cheerfully.

'Can we go home for my party now?' Sweetie asks.

Claudia looks at her watch. 'No, darling, not quite yet,' she says. 'Shall we go for a nice walk along the river?'

'Yes, Tigerboy and I want to go swimming!' says Ace.

Claudia changes tack quickly, realizing this is not a good idea at all. 'No, *I* know, let's find a playground,' she says.

This idea takes us all by surprise. I know what a playground is, of course – children play on the swings in picture books – but I didn't think they still existed. Sweetie and Ace get really excited.

'A playground, a playground!' says Sweetie. 'I want to go to the Fairy Palace!'

'No, I want to go on Space Mountain. I know I'm big enough,' says Ace.

'No, no, it's not like Disneyland,' I say quickly.

It's not *remotely* like Disneyland. When Claudia eventually finds us a playground, it's small and grey and dismal, with little tyre swings and a tame short slide and a tiny roundabout. A little gaggle of kids about my age wearing hoodies and tracksuits are lolling on the roundabout or draped, tummy-down, on the swings. They peer over at us, particularly Sweetie in her tiara and feather boa.

'There isn't any fairy palace!' Sweetie says, pouting. 'This isn't a pretty place at all.'

The kids splutter with laughter.

'Tigerboy and I want to go on a tyre, but *they're* there,' says Ace. 'So we shall roar at them and frighten them away, won't we?' He gives a very *timid* roar, more of a mouse-squeak.

They laugh louder. 'Who *are* these nutters?' one says.

'Maybe we'd better try and find another playground,' says Claudia, trying to take Sweetie and Ace by the hand. Ace pulls away.

'Want to go on the *tyre*,' he says desperately.

'Well . . . perhaps one little go,' says Claudia. 'You look after Sweetie, Sunset.'

'Sweetie! Sunset! What bonkers names!'

Sweetie nestles close to me, bewildered. She's so used to everyone making a fuss of her. She's never really played with ordinary children. None of us have. I'm scared too. I'm especially terrified they'll notice I'm holding a cardboard box containing a pathetic panda. I shall die if they start mocking me.

'Now now,' says Claudia, marching up to the children. 'How about letting this little boy have a go on the swings?'

'Now now, now now,' they echo, mocking her posh accent.

I ought to go and stick up for her – but then they'd pick on *me*. Besides, I have to look after Sweetie.

'You let me have a swing!' says Ace bravely. 'I'm Tigerman and I can bite you.'

'You're Tiggernutter, you sad little whatsit,' says one kid.

He doesn't actually *say* whatsit – he uses a very rude word indeed.

'Stop that swearing! Don't be so mean, he's only a little boy,' says Claudia.

'Are you their mum then, Posh Knickers?' says another kid.

'I'm their nanny,' Claudia says, and they all hoot.

'A nanny! A nanny for a bunch of ninnies,' says one.

'Let me have a turn on the tyre,' says Ace. He thinks hard. *'Please.'* He tries to grab the chain, but they unpick his hands and give him a shove. It's only a very *little* shove, but Ace is a very little boy. He lands on his bottom.

His mouth gapes wide in astonishment. He looks like a bewildered baby bird. I can't bear it.

'Stay there and don't move!' I say to Sweetie, shoving my panda into her arms alongside her Rosie bear.

I run over to Ace, who is now howling. Claudia's trying to pick him up and carry him off, but he's struggling.

'Want to go on the *tyre!*' he bellows.

I dither helplessly.

'Watch out, here's another nutter. Who does she think she is wearing them daft black mittens?'

I *know* who I think I am in my new black outfit. I'm dressed like my sister Destiny. So why can't I try to act like her too?

'Bog off, you lot, and let him have two minutes' swing – go on,' I say fiercely.

'Who's going to make us?' says one girl.

'*I'm* going to make you,' I say, and I seize hold of her swing. 'Get off or I'll knock you off!'

'All right, all right,' she says, and she jumps off the tyre!

I am so amazed I just stand there, stunned. I didn't think she'd move for a minute. I thought she'd yell back, maybe even fight me.

'Here's the wretched swing,' she says, and shoves it at me.

It gives me a hard whack in the ribs but I don't let myself flinch. I grab the tyre. 'Here, Ace,' I say triumphantly. 'Come and have a swing.'

He hurtles forward, still whimpering. I lift him onto the tyre.

'There now. Hang on tightly,' I say, and give him a little push.

He squeals triumphantly, while I stand proudly pushing him backwards and forwards. Claudia and Sweetie stand watching, amazed. The hoodie kids are all watching too. One of the other girls edges off her swing.

'Here, your little sister can have a swing too,' she says.

'Do you want a swing, Sweetie?' I call, but she shakes her head, clinging to Claudia.

'Why are you called them daft names?' the girl asks.

'Because we've got daft parents,' I say. 'It's not our fault.'

'I've got a friend called Marley-Joy – that's almost as bad,' she says.

'I've got a friend called Destiny,' I say, 'but I like that as a name.'

We're chatting as if *we're* almost friends. I give Ace another nine or ten pushes, and then slow him down.

'Come on, we'll go on the slide now,' I say, hauling him off. 'Thanks for letting him have a swing.'

They nod at me, and I strut back with Ace to Claudia, feeling ten feet tall.

'We'll just let Ace have a little slide,' I say. 'Do you want a slide too, Sweetie? It's all right, I'll look after you.'

I give them both a slide. Ace hurtles down happily. Sweetie is much more timid, worrying that the slide isn't quite clean and she'll stain her new pink trousers. I sigh at her. The girl I spoke to sighs too, raising her eyebrows at me. When we go, I wave to her and she waves back.

'Well!' says Claudia. 'Get you, Sunset!'

Yes, get me, get me, get me! I understand why Ace wants to wear his Tigerman suit all the time. I want to wear my Destiny outfit for ever.

I hope Claudia will tell Mum how I coped with all the kids in the playground – but Mum is too busy to listen to any of us. The house is buzzing with people running in and out of the big living room.

'Can I see my party yet?' Sweetie begs, but she still has to wait.

'Not just yet, my pet, we've got to get you ready first! What's with the tacky tiara, Sweetie, and all the other bits? My word, you all look a raggle-taggle bunch – but we'll soon get you sorted, and there's a stylist who will see to your hair. Come on, upstairs, quick as a wink.'

'Oh, please, Mummy, just one peep! I want to see my presents.'

'No, darling, you need to get dressed up for the magazine people first. You want to wear your pretty party frock, don't you? Come on, all of you, I've got everything laid out in my room, and you all need to have a good wash first. Claudia, you come and help. What are these *boxes*? Did you buy the

240

kids these teddies? Haven't they got enough already?'

'They were a gift from the shop people. They recognized the children.'

'Well, I hope you didn't let the kids be photographed. They'll use them as freebie adverts for their bears. Rose-May needs to sanction any commercial endorsements,' says Mum.

Claudia swallows.

'We went to a playground too, Mum,' I say quickly.

'Yes, there were some nasty children who laughed at me,' says Sweetie.

'They didn't want me to have a swing, Mum, but Sunset made them,' says Ace.

'Yes, Sunset was very brave,' says Claudia.

'Why on earth did you take them to a playground?' Mum snaps, whisking Sweetie's smock off her head. 'That was asking for trouble. Come on, Sweetie, darling. Oh dear, look at your hair, all over tangles. Never mind, that stylist's good. He'll give you princess curls in no time.'

Mum starts unbuttoning Ace. 'Well, get a move on, Sunset! Get undressed.'

'But I don't need to, Mum. I'm not the slightest bit dirty, look – I'm all ready.'

'Why are you *always* deliberately awkward,

Sunset?' she hisses. 'Get those awful cheap jeans off at once – and that top, and those ridiculous mittens.'

I clench my fists. 'No. These are my favourite clothes,' I say.

'You can't wear them to Sweetie's party.'

'But I like them. I feel comfy in them. And it doesn't matter what *I* wear. It's Sweetie's party, not mine.'

'You'll be in most of the photographs. I'm not having you spoil them all wearing that dreadful black outfit. I've bought you a new dress. And you, Sweetie, darling.'

'But Dad bought me my violet dress,' says Sweetie anxiously.

'Yes, I know, and you look lovely in it, but I want my little birthday girl to look utterly knockout fantastic, so just you wait and see the dress Mummy's got for you, angel.'

'What have you got for me, Mum?' Ace asks.

'Oh, I've got you a pretty party dress too, little man,' says Mum, tweaking his nose. 'A *pink* party dress.'

Ace squeals and shudders, joining in the joke.

It's not a joke for me. I can't *believe* the dress Mum's bought for me. It's an ankle-length frilly floral pink-and-white garment with puff sleeves. It looks even worse on me, long and billowing, but uncomfortably tight across my chest.

'There! It gives you a bit of a figure,' says Mum.

'I can't wear it, Mum! I look like a shepherdess. Give me a crook and a toy lamb and I'll look like blooming Bo Peep. Claudia, make Mum see I look *awful.*'

Claudia is busy helping Ace into some bizarre pageboy outfit, but she cranes her head round his flailing arms and kicking legs to look at me. 'Oh, Sunset!' she says sympathetically. 'I say, Suzy, Sunset will be much happier if she wears her black jeans – you know what girls are like at her age.'

'It's not about *Sunset* being happy, Claudia. It's Sweetie's party and we've got *Hi! Magazine* coming, plus twenty-five children and an entertainer and the caterers, and it's going to be an eight-page feature and everything has to look perfect, so I'll thank both you and Sunset to shut up and get *on* with things.'

'Twenty-five children?' Claudia says weakly. 'I'm not expected to look after them all, am I?'

'Oh, they'll have their mothers or their own nannies with them,' says Mum, pulling Sweetie's frock over her head. Then she stands back, clasping her hands. 'Oh, Sweetie, you look a picture!'

Sweetie does look truly beautiful. Her dress is

243

long too, white silk, with tiny pink roses embroidered on the bodice, and a froth of pale pink petticoat lace showing at the hem.

'Oh, Mummy, I really do look like a princess!' says Sweetie, seeing herself in the mirror.

'Yes, you do, my little darling. Now, I've got you new little silver sandals – see? Slip them on. Then we'll get your hair sorted.'

'Can I wear my tiara too?'

'I think *not*, angel cake. I've got your little posy of real pink rosebuds. We'll thread a few through your hair. It'll look beautiful,' says Mum.

I have to have my hair styled too by this elegant young man in black T-shirt and jeans. It's so unfair. Why can he wear them and not me? He makes my hair look almost lovely, easing out all the frizz and arranging it in loose waves, but I see him looking at my frilly frock with raised eyebrows and I go hot all over. He even fixes Ace's hair, making it cutely fluffy, sticking up like a little duckling. He's especially good with Sweetie. He calls her Birthday Princess and bows to her, then combs out her long gold curls. He fixes little sprays of rosebuds here and there and then gives a little cry of delight.

'Oh, Birthday Princess, you look utterly gorgeous, so fragrant and flowery and fabulous,' he says, making funny kissing noises at her.

'Oh, Sweetie!' Mum says, her eyes brimming with proud tears. She blinks hard, not wanting to make her mascara streak. 'Now, darling, I want you to stay still as still and keep looking this gorgeous until *Hi!* get their cameras set up and all your little friends arrive.'

'These "little friends",' Claudia whispers to me. 'Are they the children of really famous celebrities? Little Madonnas and Beckhams?'

'No! Not *really* famous. They'll be the children of other artists from Dad's record label, or any other likely children that Rose-May finds at a model agency,' I say bitterly. 'Like that awful party I had when I was younger.'

It was so awful I ran away and hid in Wardrobe City – but Sweetie is made of sterner stuff. She smiles sweetly at all the horrible *Hi!* people and stands at the front door greeting each little guest with a happy hug. Mum insists that I take each child by the hand and lead them into the big living room.

It's been totally transformed while we were out in Kingtown. It's been turned into Sweetieland. All the sofas and chairs are draped in white velvet and scattered with big bright cushions in the shape of huge sweets. Rainbow fairy lights hang from the white walls and climb new white curtains. The carpet's scattered with great white rugs. There are red and yellow and green and purple and orange jars everywhere, full to the brim with sweets. A chocolate fountain bubbles in one corner, and a lemonade waterfall trickles in another. There's a silver present tree decked out with real sweets and more fairy lights, and there's an enormous pile of silver parcels all around, wrapped with multi-coloured ribbon: Sweetie's birthday presents. The entertainer's wearing a black-and-white striped suit and calls himself Mr Humbug. He has two assistant 'fairies' in different shades of yellow: Miss Barley Sugar and Miss Lemon Drop.

'Oh my God, I can't *believe* this!' Claudia whispers to me. 'It's so utterly over the top it's sickening!'

'The party guests will be sick if they eat all the sweets,' I say. 'I don't think those white rugs are a good idea at all!'

Mum and Dad are sitting together on one of the sofas, all dressed up too. Dad's wearing a big floppy white satin shirt, black leather trousers and black and silver boots. Mum is in a tightly fitting silver dress with a red lollipop necklace and red patent shoes. They are sitting hand in hand, smiling at each other, especially when the camera flashes. Ace is suddenly acting shy, sitting on Dad's knee, mumbling about Tigerman. Sweetie is totally composed, skipping backwards and forwards in her silver sandals, her dress whirling to show her pink petticoats. All the newly arrived little girls are gazing at her enviously.

There are two small girls I vaguely recognize, Emerald and Diamond, the daughters of one of the Dollycat Singers, and there's Jessie and Lucie-Anne, twins belonging to a soap star who's recently made a record. Mum and Rose-May have worked together to assemble lots of little girls who look right: they're all small and blonde with flouncy dresses, though none quite as petite and pretty and ultra-flouncy as the birthday princess. They are like a bevy of small bridesmaids, and Sweetie is quite definitely the bride.

They are nearly all here now, so the photographer takes several group photos. Then there are grisly family portraits on the long sofa, Sweetie sitting up very straight between Mum and Dad, smiling serenely, while Ace flops about at their feet. I edge to the furthest corner of the sofa, mouth set in a rigid smile, my lips pressed together so I don't expose my teeth.

'Cuddle up to Mum and Dad, darling,' says the photographer, but I take no notice. Mum doesn't make me. Perhaps she's thinking it will be easier to lop me off the photo that way.

Mr Humbug is playing an accordion, singing little-girly songs, and Miss Barley Sugar and Miss Lemon Drop are playing a *Tie a Yellow Ribbon* game with everyone. Sweetie isn't concentrating, desperate to open her presents.

The photographer takes lots of shots of her kneeling by the present tree, holding this parcel and that, taking particular notice of the largest presents in their sparkly paper, bedecked with yards of ribbon. One is as tall as Sweetie, the other even taller.

Mum decides we can't wait any longer for the last guest, and Sweetie is allowed to start feverishly unwrapping. There are dolls and teddies and picture books and jewellery from all the little girls. Margaret and John give her a cake-making set with a little apron. Barkie gives her a big box of chocolates. Rose-May gives her a silver bracelet with dinky charms. Claudia gives her a big box of crayons and a drawing book. Sweetie doesn't look very interested so I hope I might be able to purloin them. She barely gives my present a second look either – it's a big book of fairy tales with lots of coloured pictures of palaces and golden-haired princesses. Ace gives her a toy tractor and starts playing with it himself.

Sweetie opens Mum's present next: it's a beautiful life-size doll with real fair hair, eerily like Sweetie's, and she's wearing a matching party dress.

'There, darling! She's been specially made to be your little twin! Isn't she lovely? You can comb her hair and change her clothes. See how many outfits she's got! I ordered her from a lady over in America – she usually makes these dollies for grown-up ladies, but I knew just how much you'd care for her and treasure her. You will, won't you, Sweetie?'

'Oh, *yes*, Mummy, she's the most wonderful doll in the world!' says Sweetie.

She poses beautifully with her, kissing the doll's forehead, stroking her hair, holding out both their dresses, while the photographer flashes and clicks. She even lets all the other little girls have a turn holding her, walking her up and down.

Then it's Mum's turn to be photographed. There they are, three golden-haired smiling beauties, like a puzzle in a child's comic: *Which one is the doll?*

I'm smiling too, but I can't help remembering *my* sixth birthday. Why didn't *I* get a wondrous life-size replica doll? Well, it's obvious why. Imagine a great gawky doll with frizzy hair and gappy teeth. Who would want a doll like that?

Now Sweetie's about to open the last and biggest parcel, Dad's present. It's far too heavy for her to lift. Dad has to help her undo all the wrapping. A pink edge pokes out, and then little glass jars on a shelf. It's a shop, Sweetie's own sweetshop. It says so in fancy lettering on the shop sign. It's big enough for Sweetie to clamber behind the counter and sit on a little pink stool. There are tiny old-fashioned scales on the counter so she can weigh all the sweets, and a cash register where she can keep her money. This is pretend, but all the sweets in the jars are real: fruit drops all colours of the rainbow, peppermints, chocolate toffees, wine gums, dolly mixtures . . .

'Oh, Daddy, it's such a glorious present!' says Sweetie, clapping her hands. 'You must come to my shop and be my first customer!'

Dad looks thrilled, but he glances at Rose-May, wondering if it's right for his image to be photographed squatting down buying sweets from his little girl. Rose-May nods approvingly, so Dad plays his part while the photographers flash all over again. Then Sweetie has to serve all the other little girls, acting so charmingly, like a real little birthday princess.

I can hear Mum and Dad whispering.

'You might have *told* me!'

'I did, I did, I *said* I was getting her a shop.'

'Yes, but you didn't say a sweetshop, not with real sweets. She'll make herself sick if we're not careful – *and* rot her perfect little teeth.'

'For God's sake, Suzy, it was your idea to have an entire sweet-themed *party* – look around you, there are sweets *galore*.'

'Yes, but they're just decorations. The kids aren't scoffing the lot.'

'Lighten up, can't you? Let Sweetie *enjoy* her present. Why make such a fuss just because she likes it more than that big dolly?'

'She *loves* that doll. She'll be like a real heirloom for Sweetie.'

The photographer is calling for a family picture in front of the sweetshop.

'Come on, Danny and Suzy,' Rose-May says, shaking her head at them as if they're naughty toddlers. She's smiling brightly, with strange emphasis, to set them an example: let's have Happy Faces for the birthday photo.

Dad smiles, Mum smiles, and they hasten obediently over to Sweetie and her shop. Ace is there too, delving into the jars, sucking and licking each sample.

The photographer beckons to me to be part of the Happy Family, but I'm saved by the bell. The last little guest has arrived at long last. I run down the hall to open the door and usher her in.

Then I stand frozen, open-mouthed, forgetting to hide my teeth. It's a very little girl with bunches, younger than Sweetie, only three or four years old – a plain little girl blinking at me anxiously, clutching a grubby cuddle blanket over her nose so that it hides her face like a hijab. The young woman with her tugs at the blanket impatiently.

'Come on, Pandora, time to put blankie away now, we're at the party.'

'No, no, Auntie Liz, I *need* blankie,' Pandora protests.

I know this auntie. She's blonde and ultra-skinny in her tight jeans and tiny top. She's got a little girl's bobbed hair and darkly shaded eyes with thick lashes and a very big mouth shining bright red. It's Big Mouth, the girl in the *Milky Star* film, turned up like the Bad Fairy at Sleeping Beauty's party.

She smiles at me with those terrifying lips and moves forward.

'Hello. I think you're Sunset, Danny's elder daughter? Your dad invited us to the party. This is my little niece, Pandora. Sorry we're so late – we lost her wretched blanket . . .'

She steps indoors in her strappy high heels, dragging Pandora after her. I'm not quick enough to stop them. I stand stupidly dithering when I should push them back outside and slam the door in their faces, because I know what will happen, I know, I know. I follow them helplessly down the hall, watch as they go to join the party, Liz Big Mouth pulling Pandora along, and then they're in the room and I hover at the door, holding my breath.

I see Dad look up and give a little nod, I see Claudia hold out her hand reassuringly to Pandora, I see the photographer flashing away, I see Mum smiling, kneeling beside Sweetie, and I think for a moment it will be all right. Pandora will be absorbed into the crowd of little girls, and Big Mouth will blend in with the gaggle of mums and nannies drinking champagne at the other end of the room. But then Mum's head jerks. She's staring at them. She stands up, her face flushing a startling red.

'Suzy,' Rose-May says quickly, looking at the photographer and the journalist from *Hi!*

I don't think Mum even hears her. 'Who invited you?' she hisses.

Big Mouth stands still, looking over at Dad.

'Get out!' Mum screams, and everyone jumps.

Some of the little girls start crying. 'Get *out* – and take that mousy little brat with you!'

Pandora cries too, sobbing into her blanket, and I follow as they're both hustled down the hall.

'Don't cry, Pandora, it's not your fault!' I gabble.

I see the little pile of our new bears discarded on the stairs and grab my panda. 'Here, have this for a going-home present,' I say.

I thrust it into her arms as she's tugged off down the drive.

11

DESTINY

'Where's my little singing star?' Mum calls as she opens the front door.

I don't answer.

'Destiny?' She comes into the living room, and then stops. 'Destiny, what is it?'

'Nothing, I'm fine,' I mumble.

'Well, come on, you silly girl, don't just sit there all hunched up. Give me a hug! Aren't you pleased I'm home so early? Louella was an angel, said she'd see to my last two ladies.'

I stand awkwardly and let her put her arms round me. I don't want her to hold me. I'm scared she'll start me crying. I can see she's dying to ask about this afternoon's contest – but doesn't quite like to now she can see there's obviously something wrong.

'Tell me, sweetheart,' Mum says quietly. She suddenly jerks. 'Oh God, your leather jacket's OK? No one's nicked it?'

'It's there, on the back of the chair.'

'So what's up?'

'*Nothing's* up.'

'Are you feeling a bit nervous about tonight's concert? Don't worry, darling. The moment you step onstage and start singing you'll feel wonderful.'

'No I won't.'

'Well, *I'll* feel wonderful, watching you.'

'You won't. Because I'm not singing tonight.'

'What?'

'Oh, Mum, don't look like that. I'm not singing. It's no big deal, so let's shut up about the stupid concert and have tea.' I go into the kitchen and put the kettle on.

'Who says you're not singing?'

'Me.'

'Did you sing this afternoon?'

'Yep.'

'And?'

'And nothing.'

'Oh, sweetheart, did you forget your words?'

I give her a look.

'I can't stand this, Destiny! Will you just tell me what happened? Did your voice go funny? Did you just dry up? Tell me, darling.'

I lay out two mugs, two plates. Mum's put a white cardboard box on the worktop. I look inside. There's a slice of pink cream gâteau with a strawberry on the top. It's from the posh French pâtisserie near the market. We've often looked in the window and played the game of choosing which cake we like best. I chop and change, but nearly always choose the strawberry gâteau.

I stare at it. The strawberry blurs, the cake wavers. I'm crying, though I vowed I wouldn't.

'I didn't win the talent contest, Mum,' I whisper.

'Well, never mind, darling. As if it matters,' says Mum bravely. 'Who won then?'

'This girl Angel.'

'That's a lovely name.'

'She's so not a lovely girl.'

'But she's a good singer?'

'She didn't sing, she did a dance.'

'So, did you come second?'

'Nope. I didn't come anywhere. And it's not *fair*,' I cry, like a total baby. 'I sang OK, Mum, I know I did, but none of the kids gave me good marks because I'm still the new girl and I'm not in the right gang and they don't like me.' I'm crying in great ugly gulps, my nose running. I cover my face with the shame of it.

'Oh, darling, I'm so sorry. That's awful! And ridiculous. So you think they deliberately voted against you? Couldn't Mr Roberts sort them out? What sort of a hopeless wuss is he, unable to get the upper hand with a bunch of children? And what sort of spiteful, mean-spirited kids are they, deliberately marking you down?' Mum's working herself up into a state, making the tea but banging the mugs down hard.

'Well, I don't know for *certain* that was why they didn't give me good marks. Maybe I just sang like rubbish.'

'That's nonsense talk, you're a wonderful singer.'

'Yeah, but you're my mum – of course you're going to think that.'

'Everyone's going to think it this evening when they hear you.'

'No one's going to hear me because I'm not taking part. There's no point. It'll happen all over again. And it'll be awful. They were all nudging each other and laughing and Angel said horrible stuff and—'

'And that's why you're going to go to this evening's concert with your head held high. You're going to sing your little heart out. I don't give a stuff if they vote you first or last. You'll still have sung your special song. I want you to sing it for me, Destiny. It means so much. Please.' Mum's looking at me with her big staring eyes and squeezing my hands tight and I can't possibly wriggle away from her.

'*Please*,' she says again. 'I don't ask you for much, darling. We both know I mostly let you do what you like. But just this once I'm begging you.'

'Oh, Mum. Stop it. All *right*.'

'There!' says Mum triumphantly, wiping my face, dabbing at my nose as if I'm a toddler again.

'*Mum!*'

'Now, let's sit down and have a cup of tea and you eat your gâteau. Don't you dare say you're not hungry, it cost a blooming fortune.'

'Only if you have half.'

'I'll have a bit. Then I've got to go and have a quick bath and get changed. Do you think my best blue top will be all right or it is a bit too low cut for school?'

'Mum, it's no big deal. It's a crappy school concert and *I'm* going to be crap and it'll be torture for both of us. I wouldn't bother with your blue top. I'd go for a bin bag. Wear it over your head so no one realizes you're related to the girl who's a rubbish singer.'

Mum wears her blue top – but it *is* too low cut. She used to wear it with a special push-up bra and it looked really sexy, but now she doesn't seem to have much chest left to push up. Her collarbones stick out and you can see the start of her ribs. She's wearing a belt on her best jeans, but they're still much too baggy, practically hanging off her.

'Mum, just how much weight *have* you lost?'

'A few pounds.'

'Don't give me that. It looks like a few *stone*.'

'Of course it's not. Stop staring at me like that, you make me feel a freak. I've always been thin – it's natural for me,' says Mum.

'Not this thin. Mum, I think you should go to a doctor.'

'Why, for heaven's sake? I'm fighting fit, full of energy, holding down all three jobs. There's absolutely nothing wrong with me.' Mum's saying it too quickly, her words jerky. She's frightened too.

'Mum, this is the deal,' I say, taking hold of her by her poor bony shoulders. 'I'll make another total fool of myself and sing in this poxy contest if you'll go to the doctor.'

'But I told you, there's nothing wrong. And even if there is, what can he do about it?'

'He can give you pills – or special treatment – or take you into hospital and give you an operation,' I say. My own voice is wobbling now.

'Yes, well, I'm not going into any hospital, thanks very much. How would we cope?' says Mum.

I suddenly get it. I realize why she's suddenly so keen for me to meet Danny, why she's palled up with Louella. She's been worrying what will happen to me if she's really ill. If . . . if . . .

'You're going to the doctor tomorrow, promise? And whatever it is, we'll manage, we'll get you better – do you hear me, Mum?' I say. 'It's a bargain, right? Or I won't do the concert. You've got by far the best deal, because I've got to hang around backstage for two whole hours while the others perform, and then I've got the total public humiliation of all the judges rubbishing me. You've just got to nip down the medical centre and see someone for ten minutes. So, shall we shake on it?'

I hold out my hand and Mum shakes it. Then we hug each other hard because we're both so scared. I don't even care about the concert now. All I care about is Mum. It's like I've sensed there's something wrong for months. I've woken up and worried at night. I used to have bad dreams as a little kid, scared there was a man hiding in the wardrobe. Sometimes I'd lie there and fancy I could hear him breathing – but in the morning I'd forget all about him and go into the wardrobe for my coat and shoes without a second thought. This illness of Mum's is just like that man in the wardrobe. I've been keeping him at bay for weeks – but now I've opened the door and there he is, grinning horribly, with a big knife in his hand, aiming it at Mum.

I hang onto her arm as we walk to school. She takes the quickest way through the estate and I don't know what to do. She doesn't realize what the Flatboys and the Speedos can be like. If I tell her she'll only worry about me even more. At least we're together – and if any boy dares do anything to mum I'll kill him, I swear I will.

Speedo boys are lurking in a stairwell, Flatboys are spitting off a top balcony, but none of them take any notice of us. The flats are too busy, mums and a few dads and lots of grannies with gaggles of little brothers and sisters, are all making their way purposefully towards the school.

Mum nudges me. 'Your audience, babe!'

'Don't!'

I see Angel strutting along with a whole posse of family and friends – aunties, cousins, all sorts – she must have traded for extra tickets.

'That big girl waved at you. Is she your friend?' Mum asks.

'No, more like my deadly enemy. That's Angel.'

'Oh. Her,' says Mum, sniffing loyally.

I spot Jack Myers coming out of his flat with a couple of the Jack the Lads. They hurry on ahead of their mums – but Jack stops when he sees me.

'Hi, Destiny,' he said.

I mumble 'Hi' back.

'You nervous?'

'Nope.'

'Me neither.'

We stay silent. Mum's glancing from me to Jack and back again, her eyes big.

Jack clears his throat. 'It wasn't fair this afternoon,' he says. 'You were robbed.'

'Angel was good.'

'Yeah, but you were heaps better,' says Jack.

'Anyway, good luck tonight.' He nods and then hurries on to join his mates.

'Wish him luck too!' Mum hisses.

'Good luck, Jack!' I shout.

He turns back, grinning, and gives me a wave.

'Who was that?' Mum asks. 'Another total deadly enemy?'

'Well, I thought he was. But he was quite nice, wasn't he? He's in a street-dance act. Maybe he'll win tonight – he's ever so popular.'

'Just you wait and see,' says Mum.

It's so weird going into school with her. There's a big banner over the main door: *Bilefield's Got Talent – Tonight's the Night, the Grand Final!!!*

Mrs Avery is in the hall, giving out programmes and showing people where to sit. I stare at her, astonished. I'm used to seeing her in T-shirts and tracky bottoms and trainers – but tonight she's wearing a tight sparkly red dress with really high heels. She looks amazing, not *at all* like a teacher.

'Hello, Destiny,' she says.

'You look so *different*, Mrs Avery!'

'I'm on the judging panel tonight. Mr Roberts insisted we all dress up a bit,' she says, pulling a face.

'Oh no, is he wearing that jacket again?' I ask.

'Destiny, don't be so cheeky!' says Mum.

Mrs Avery giggles. 'You got it, it's the brocade jacket jobby again. Anyway, you'd better nip back-stage. Good luck!'

I suddenly don't want to leave Mum. She squeezes my hand and mouths *I love you* at me. I mouth it back to her, and then go out of the hall again and in through the backstage door. It's crammed full, of course, but no one's doing back-flips or practising dance routines. Mr Roberts has them all sitting down cross-legged. He's sitting cross-legged himself, looking like the Buddha.

'Come and join us, Destiny. We are eliminating our nerves by doing yoga – well, an approximation. You'll twist your legs back to front if you try to get into the lotus position without proper training. Sit with a nice straight back, hands loose, and breathe i-i-i-n, and then very gently and slowly ou-u-u-ut. Close your eyes and visualize a quiet happy place – maybe the seaside or a country field, or maybe just your own bed, and—'

'Can we breathe again, Mr Roberts?' Hannah gasps.

'Yes, Hannah, the trick is to keep on breathing, even when I don't remind you. There now, my little class of calm children, I want you to *enjoy* the contest tonight. Things went a little haywire this afternoon. I rather think it was all my fault. I didn't pick a particularly balanced panel and they clearly let their tribal loyalties overcome their artistic appreciation—'

'What are you on about, Mr Roberts?' asks one of the Superspeedos.

'Very well, I'll put it another way. You was robbed. This afternoon's panel weren't voting fairly. I'm sure we were all surprised by some of the scores.'

'Are you saying I shouldn't have won?' says Angel, sticking her chin in the air.

'No, Angel Cake, I'm absolutely thrilled that you won, and you fully deserve your prize.'

She got a little silver pin-badge with WINNER! engraved on it in tiny letters. She's wearing it on her top now. She keeps pointing to it and smirking.

'Have you got another one of them pin-badges for tonight's winner?' Jack asks.

'I might just have one hidden about my person,' says Mr Roberts. 'I wish I had one for all of you, because I think you're *all* winners. You've all tried very hard and performed to the best of your ability in very difficult circumstances, so give yourselves a pat on the back. Not too vigorously in this confined space – I was speaking metaphorically. I want you to go onstage tonight and do yourselves justice. Let's hope tonight's panel will vote fearlessly and with common sense.'

'Who are the panel, Mr Roberts?'

'Is it our parents?'

'Yes, pick my mum, then I'll get all the votes!'

'It's not parents, for obvious reasons. The panel are utterly impartial, specially selected teachers.'

'That's not fair! All the teachers hate me, so no one will vote for me!'

'The voting will *strictly* reflect ability, hard work and talent this time, or I shall have one of my famous hissy fits,' says Mr Roberts. 'Now calm down again, all of you. Breathe i-i-i-n and ou-u-u-ut . . .'

I can't. I'm all tensed up. Will the new panel really vote fairly? If so, Raymond should win, or the Superspeedos – or *me*.

Mrs Avery's on the voting panel, and she's funny and fair and she was quite nice to me just now.

'I know it's Mrs Avery on the panel – but who are the other teachers, Mr Roberts?' I ask.

'Mr Juniper.'

Oh no, oh no, oh no. He'll take one look at me and give me nought out of ten. I've somehow accidentally-on-purpose forgotten to report to him for my detention. I'd hoped it had gone out of his mind – and yet here I'll be, singing straight at him.

'Then there's Miss Evans.'

Some of the boys wolf-whistle. Miss Evans is very young and very pretty and very girly. She'll vote for Girls Very Soft or the Dancing Queens. I'm not her style at all.

'And the last member of our excellent panel is Mrs Riley.'

Everyone goes 'Ahhh!' Mrs Riley is the most popular teacher in the whole school. She teaches the little kids in Year Three. She's plump and cosy with a very gentle voice. Everyone adores her – even Louella's terrible twins think she's lovely. She's especially good at coping with bad boys, so she'll like the Jack the Lads or the Superspeedos. She didn't ever teach me so I won't mean anything to her.

I'm going to lose all over again. Maybe I'll come bottom this time. I don't think I can do it. I might as well walk out now, take myself off and save my breath. The others would jeer at me and say I'd lost my bottle. No, I'll say I just can't be bothered. I'll yawn and act like I'm bored and have got better things to do – I'll be the girl who's too cool to compete.

I stand up and start strolling out casually.

'Where are you going, Destiny?' asks Mr Roberts.

'I'm just going to . . . to nip to the toilet, Mr Roberts,' I say. 'Back in a minute.'

He lets me go – and I'm *off*, it's as easy as that. I walk out of the door and down the corridor. I can carry on walking right out of the school. I needn't ever come back. We break up in a few days. I'm free as a bird. Yes, I can sprout beautiful leathery wings from the back of my jacket and fly away . . .

There are parents still crowding into the hall, talking to each other, laughing and waving and gossiping. I look through the door – I can't stop myself – and see my mum right at the front, all by herself, staring up at the stage as if I'm already on it. She's got her hands clasped, almost as if she's praying.

Who am I kidding? I've got to sing for my mum. It doesn't matter if they don't give me a good score. They can throw rocks and rotten tomatoes at me, and do their best to boo me right off the stage, but I'll stand there and sing my socks off for my mum.

I go to the toilet and then hurry back. Mr Roberts gives me a little nod. I sit down obediently and cross my legs and do his daft breathing exercises, i-i-i-n and ou-u-u-ut – and then it's *time*.

'Good luck, everyone,' says Mr Roberts, and I see the beads of sweat on his forehead and realize he's really nervous too.

Then he dashes onstage and there's a burst of applause. We're meant to stay sitting still as mice waiting for our turns, but we all crowd into the wings, wanting to see what's going on.

'Hello, hello, hello. Good evening, ladies and gentleman. Welcome to *Bilefield's Got Talent*,' Mr Roberts shouts into the microphone, bouncing about the stage. 'I am Mr Roberts, I teach Year Six, and my goodness me, they are all *tremendously* talented. You are in for a night to remember and no mistake. Our preposterously gifted pupils will perform, and our tremendous panel of hand-picked teachers will comment and give marks accordingly. Let me introduce Mrs Avery, Mr Juniper, Miss Evans and Mrs Riley. Thank you very much. Now, let our show begin. I'd like you to put your hands together and give a warm welcome to . . . the Jack the Lads.'

Jack takes a deep breath and then bounds onstage, all his lads following. Mrs Avery can't do the music as she's on the panel. It's Mrs Linley who's been left in charge, and she's not quite as practised. She starts the music too quickly, before everyone's in place. Jack's so keyed up he starts at once, spitting on his hands and stamping his feet, but the lads are two beats behind and can't catch up. But it's actually *better* like that – Jack does a backflip, they look, they copy; Jack does a handstand, ditto. It's got more pace and rhythm to it than when they're all trying to keep together. The fight is funnier too. Jack pretends to punch, then all the others swing their arms and start up another fight. At the end, when they usually just peter out and stop, Jack trips. Is it deliberate? He falls flat on his face – and down go all the other boys like dominoes. There's a *huge* round of applause, and the panel join in.

'These boys have improved tremendously,' says Mrs Avery. 'They've obviously worked very hard on their routine. I thought tonight's performance was brilliant.'

'If you'd only put the energy and determination you've shown in your dancing into your schoolwork you'd all be top of the class. Well done, lads,' says Mr Juniper.

'Wow!' says Miss Evans. 'You were amazing, boys!'

'Good for you, Jack the Lads. You always made me chuckle when you were in my class, Jack, even though you were so naughty – and you're still making me chuckle now. Well done, all of you,' says Mrs Riley.

'Your scores, please, ladies and gentleman,' says Mr Roberts.

Mrs Avery gives them *ten*, Mr Juniper eight, and Miss Evans and Mrs Riley give them both nine. So that's it then. The Jack the Lads have got thirty-six. Only one less than Angel scored this afternoon, I think they'll win this evening – and although this hurts, I'm truly pleased for Jack. I grin at him when he comes panting backstage, still terribly out of breath.

'Well done!' I whisper.

'I thought I made a right prune of myself,' he whispers back. 'I didn't mean to fall over. It didn't half hurt too! But it seemed to work, didn't it?'

'You know it did,' I say. 'I think you'll win.'

'Rubbish. You will,' says Jack.

'You're *both* talking rubbish. *I'm* going to win again,' says Angel.

'Shh!' says Mrs Linley as she puts on the music for Girls Very Soft. They're very good, but a bit boring. We all know their little step-shuffle routine and join in backstage, though Mrs Linley glares at us and gestures to us to sit down. The panel all make positive comments and the girls end up with twenty-eight, not a bad score at all.

Then it's Fareed and Hannah. They *still* haven't got the hang of half the tricks. The audience don't laugh so much, trying to be kind, so their act doesn't work so well until right at the end, when the toy rabbit gets stuck in Fareed's hat. He struggles, tapping it hopefully, biting his lip.

'Look, it's in there *somewhere*, Fareed,' Hannah hisses. She scrabbles inside the hat and yanks it out. There's a sudden burst of helpless laughter as she waves the poor mangled toy in the air, its ears drooping, and they both end up with a big round of applause though they don't score high.

The Dancing Queens are good – well, they *look* good in their pink T-shirts and little black shorts and flashing tiaras, and one of their mums has made them up with silver eyeshadow and pink lipstick, and sprayed pink streaks in their hair. Mr Juniper goes pink himself watching them and gives them a nine. Miss Evans likes them too, but Mrs Avery isn't quite so keen, and Mrs Riley says they're all lovely girls but she wishes their act wasn't quite so . . . sophisticated. Wait till she sees Angel!

Then there's Natalie and her friends doing the play. Mr Roberts went over it with them after school and he's helped them cut half of it – but it still seems ultra long-winded and very silly and shouty. When they finish at last, someone in the audience gives a *huge* cheer. It's probably Natalie's dad. The teachers don't rate them at all, though Mrs Riley says they've all clearly tried extra hard and it was a brave attempt.

'And now, ladies and gentlemen, I give you Miss Angel Thomas, this afternoon's overall winner. Give her a big hand,' Mr Roberts bellows.

Angel elbows her way past us, wiggling her big bottom. There's enthusiastic applause as she stands on the stage. She grins and waves her hands, mouthing *More, more!* milking it for all she's worth. Maybe Angel's going to win *again*.

She does her cartwheels, she performs her little crab act, she spins on her bottom with such gusto it's a wonder she doesn't rub a big hole in her leggings. She finishes differently this time, doing rather wobbly splits, but this gets her more applause.

'Well done, Angel, that's certainly an incredible dance routine,' says Mrs Avery. 'No wonder you won this afternoon.'

Angel positively glows – but Mrs Avery only gives her a seven, as does Mr Juniper, Miss Evans gives her an eight and Mrs Riley a six – so she *hasn't* won this time. She gives us all a shove as she comes backstage, absolutely furious.

So Jack's still in the lead – but now it's Raymond's dance, and he is so brilliant. He whirls around and leaps up in the air, twiddling his feet, his head up, his arms out, the whole line of him perfect poised. No one whistles or yells silly things at him this time, everyone watches, totally rapt, and when he's finished everyone claps like crazy. Mrs Avery stands up to clap him, smiling all over her face.

'Well *done*, Raymond. We're so lucky to have such a brilliant dancer at our school. I wouldn't be at all surprised if we're flocking to watch you in a real dance company in a few years' time,' she says – and she gives him ten.

Mr Juniper gives him nine, and Miss Evans and Mrs Riley give him nine too.

So that's it then. Raymond's won, with thirty-seven points. At least he deserves to come first. I clap him as he bounces backstage, and Jack pats him on the back – though Angel glowers.

'It's not fair if Raymond wins,' she whines. 'He's been going to his poncy dancing classes for years and years. Of course he's going to know more twiddly steps than any of us.'

'Shut up, Angel,' says Jack. 'He's better than us, full stop. And we don't know whether he *has* won yet.'

'There's only rubbish acts left,' Angel hisses. 'Them two stupid boys mucking about, then the Speedos doing their little swoopy dance, and Destiny caterwauling. *They're* not going to win, are they?'

'Just ignore her,' Jack mutters, though I think she's right.

Jeff and Ritchie certainly aren't any competition, though they *look* funny now because someone's lent them tutus and they've certainly got bottle to go out onstage wearing those fluffy white sticky-out skirts. They still haven't worked out a proper routine. They just flounce about and teeter on the tips of their trainers. It's funny for a few seconds but quickly gets tedious – and the teachers vote accordingly.

'Now we have another astonishing dance routine. Ladies and gentlemen, I'm delighted to introduce the very talented Superspeedos,' says Mr Roberts.

My stomach starts churning. I'm next, I'm next, I'm next. My throat tightens and I'm not sure I can even speak, let alone sing. I watch the Superspeedos sweeping through their routine. Jack fidgets by my side, watching them anxiously too. He doesn't seem to mind Raymond beating him, but I know he'll hate it if the Superspeedos get a better score than the Jack the Lads. There's very loud applause at the end, and Mrs Avery goes on and on about their hard work and how they've proved practice makes perfect. Jack groans, especially when she gives them another ten. Mr

Juniper gives them an eight, and Miss Evans and Mrs Riley both go for a nine – so that's thirty-six, exactly the same score as the Jack the Lads.

Jack breathes out and grins.

'Our last act on *Bilefield's Got Talent* is a little lady with an astonishingly large voice. Please give a warm welcome to Miss Destiny Williams,' Mr Roberts shouts.

Jack reaches out and squeezes my hand. 'Good luck!'

I stumble out of the wings and onto the stage. It's exactly the same stage as this afternoon, so why does it seem so much bigger? There's a spotlight on me, half blinding me so I can't see the audience. I can't even see Mum right at the front. She's part of the dark blur – but she's out there, I know she is, and I can't let her down. I detach the mike from its stand and wait till the audience are quiet.

'I'm singing this for my mum,' I say into the mike. It's so powerful it makes me jump hearing my voice boom out so. 'It's her favourite song. So this is for you, Mum.'

There's a few '*Ahhh*'s, a few groans and several nervous giggles. Mrs Avery, Mr Juniper, Miss Evans and Mrs Riley are all sitting in front of me, looking expectant. Mr Roberts is at the side of the stage, looking a little worried now.

'Take your time, Destiny,' he whispers.

I've taken my time. I open my mouth and start singing.

'You are my Destiny . . .'

My enhanced voice fills the large hall. It feels so big and powerful I picture it spilling out, flooding the corridors, bursting out of the windows, rushing in a torrent along the roads until the whole town is awash with the sound. Maybe far, far away in Robin Hill, Sunset and our dad are listening, hand in hand.

I sing each word, thinking of it as a deeply personal message for me, not just a simple love song. I feel it in every part of me. I ache with it, and after the last long note I'm wrung out, exhausted, near tears. There's a long silence. I take a couple of steps towards the wings, wanting to hide – but then the clapping starts. Such clapping! I'm dazed by the noise. All four teachers are on their feet, clapping. *Mr Roberts* is clapping! And down there in the audience there's Mum. I can see her now the lights have gone up a bit. She's standing up and cheering – oh God, the embarrassment – but there's lots of people standing. It's all right, they're all showing me they like me – so why have I got tears running down my face?

Mrs Avery's dabbing at her own eyes. 'Oh,

Destiny, that was marvellous. I've been lucky enough to hear you sing before, and I knew you had a lovely voice, but that was just incredible!' she says.

Then it's Mr Juniper's turn. Surely he'll still hate me.

'I think your voice is awe-inspiring, Destiny. It's practically rendered me speechless. However, I've got *just* enough breath to remind you that we have a little detention date, so see me on Monday after school!' He's trying to look fierce, but he's laughing – everyone's laughing.

'You've got a thrilling voice, Destiny. I could listen to you for ever,' Miss Evans gushes.

'It's hard to believe such a big powerful sound could come out of such a slight girl! You've given us the performance of a lifetime, Destiny,' says Mrs Riley.

'Wonderful comments, Destiny,' says Mr Roberts. 'You're clearly going to get a high score – but you've got Raymond's excellent thirty-seven to beat. Teachers, may I have your scores, please.'

They hold up their cards. *Ten, ten, ten, ten!* I can't believe it! I've got a ten from each of them, even Mr Juniper, so I've got forty, maximum marks, and *I've won*! Poor Raymond – but lucky, lucky, lucky me. I've won the contest, I've won it for Mum!

I want to rush down into the audience and hug her, but I have to stay up here on the stage while Mr Roberts presents me with a WINNER pin-badge – a *gold* one this time.

'A gold star for a gold-star performance!' he says, shaking my hand vigorously.

His own hands are wringing wet, but what does it matter? He's a lovely teacher, they're all lovely teachers, even Mr Juniper. Mr Roberts calls everyone out onstage to line up and take a final bow. Jack comes leaping out and gives me a big hug in front of everyone!

Then the contest is finished, but it's not all over: there are refreshments – juice and tea and little bits of cheese on Ritz crackers – and we can go and mingle with our parents.

Mum's already got a cup of tea when I get to her, and we hug so hard we nearly spill it all over her best blue top.

'Oh, Destiny, you sang it so wonderfully!' she says.

Lots of parents come up and congratulate us both, even Angel's mum, though Angel herself glares at me and says that silver is ultra-cool and gold is just tacky bling.

Miss Lewis, our IT coordinator, comes up with her big camera. 'I've been recording the show for the school archives. I can easily burn you a DVD of the show if you'd like it, Mrs Williams,' she says.

'Yes please, that would be wonderful!' says Mum.

I raise an eyebrow at her. 'We haven't got a DVD player, Mum!'

'Yes, but I can always borrow someone else's, can't I?' she says. 'I want to relive every single moment.'

I don't need a DVD to remind me of my performance. I'll remember every split second of it for the rest of my life. It plays inside my head all evening – and long after Mum's asleep I relive it. It's wonderful that I've won. It's amazing that all four teachers gave me ten out of ten, even Mr Juniper who never gives full marks to anyone. It's great that I beat Angel and that Jack gave me a hug. It's fantastic that Mr Roberts said when I was going home that he was really proud of me. But the *best* thing of all was standing there onstage, my voice soaring, nailing every note.

I lie wide awake, not wanting to go to sleep, savouring it all. But I obviously sleep at some stage because I wake with a start in sunlight. Mum's standing over me with a breakfast tray.

'Hi, sleepyhead,' she says. 'I thought I'd better wake you. It's gone eleven!'

'Oh goodness! I bet you've been up for hours, Mum,' I say sleepily.

'Just done a bit of tidying. You know me, I'm hopeless at lying-in even on my day off. I was thinking, Destiny – shall we have a little day out to celebrate? We could go into Manchester, look round the shops, maybe go on the big wheel? Or we could maybe catch a train to the seaside. It's a lovely day.'

'It's a bit late, isn't it, Mum?'

'Well, we've got all day. We can please ourselves, little singing star,' says Mum, playfully pinning my gold star on my pyjama top.

I look at it proudly, letting my finger outline its five little points, wondering whether I'd sooner go to the shops or the seaside. Though weren't we going to do something else on Saturday? I puzzle in my head – and then remember with a start.

'Oh, Mum, we're going to the doctor's!'

'What?' Mum acts like she doesn't understand for a moment. 'Oh, for heaven's sake, Destiny, I don't want to spoil a lovely free Saturday going to the doctor's. I'm fit as a fiddle anyway, there's no point.'

'Mum, you promised!'

'Yes, all right, I *will* go. I'll make an appointment for next week – will that make you happy?'

'You're going this morning!'

'I can't, I haven't got an appointment, silly.'

'You should have rung up and made one earlier! I should have woken up and made you. Oh, Mum, how could I have forgotten?' I take two bites of toast, a big gulp of tea, and then get out of bed.

'What are you doing? You haven't finished your breakfast!'

'I'm going to get washed and dressed and then I'm going to drag you to the clinic and see if they'll make room for you somehow.'

'You're acting daft, Destiny. I told you, I'll go next week. Don't let's waste this lovely day trailing off to the medical centre, especially as I'm one hundred per cent certain they won't see me anyway.'

I think Mum's probably right, but I can't give in. I look down at my little badge, horrified that I could have been so caught up in my own success that I forgot all about my mum's health. I can see plain as anything now that she's ill. She's not just thin, she's not just anxious. It's as if she's got something inside her and it's burning her up.

'You're coming with me,' I say.

'I'm not going to that clinic, not this morning.'

'You're coming, even if I have to pick you up and carry you there,' I say. I make a sudden grab at her and lift her right off the ground. There's so little of her now it's like picking up a six-year-old.

'Put me *down*, you mad girl,' says Mum, struggling. 'Ouch – you're hurting!'

I look down. My pin-badge has scratched her chest. It's only a little scratch but it looks alarmingly red on her white skin.

'Oh, Mum, I'm sorry,' I say, setting her down gently.

'It's all right, I'm fine,' she says.

'No you're not, and you know it. You're just scared of going to the clinic and seeing a doctor.'

'Well, is it any wonder?' Mum says. 'Suppose I *am* ill, seriously ill – what do we do then? Suppose there's nothing the doctors can do to make me better?'

She's nearly crying now and I put my arm round her.

'You mustn't be frightened. There'll be heaps of things they can do. They'll get you better in no time. They'll just need to find the right pills,' I parrot.

I'm trying to be comforting, but inside I'm terrified. What if they really *can't* make Mum better? What if it's cancer? What if she's dying? How can I ever live without my mum?

I get washed and dressed in double-quick time

and then we set off for the clinic. We go by the shortest route, through the estate. As if I'm scared of silly boys in gangs now. I've got far worse things to worry about.

The word *clinic* makes you imagine a gleaming building with nurses bustling around in white uniforms and patients sitting subdued, silently waiting their turn to see the doctor. *This* clinic is an ugly little prefab, with graffiti sprayed all over the walls. Inside it's pandemonium: little kids running up and down, people shouting, and one receptionist looking like she's going to burst into tears.

'Let's go home,' says Mum. 'I can't be doing with all this. I feel a bit woozy.'

'Exactly. That's why you're here,' I say, hanging onto her hand. I tug her up to the receptionist. 'Can my mum have an appointment for this morning, please?'

'What? No, the clinic's nearly over, and we're completely booked up. She'll have to come back on Monday,' she says dismissively.

'OK, I'll come back Monday,' says Mum. She's got beads of sweat on her forehead. 'Come on, Destiny. It's so hot in here. I need to get some air. It's all right. I'll come back on Monday, like she says.'

But I know she won't come back, she's far too

afraid. She'll go to work and I won't be there to make her.

'I'm so sorry, but this is an emergency,' I say.

'All our emergency appointments are taken. She'll have to come back on *Monday*,' says the receptionist, getting impatient.

'Destiny, I'm going all swimmy,' Mum gasps, and then she falls to the floor, crumpling up at my feet.

'Mum, Mum – oh, Mum!' I crouch beside her, slipping my arm round her, putting her head on my lap. 'Oh, Mum, please wake up. Please be all right. Please don't die!'

Mum's big staring eyes open slowly. 'What happened?' she whispers.

The receptionist has run for the doctor, the families have quietened, apart from one small child who's crying.

'I think you just fainted, Mum,' I say.

The doctor is a thin Asian man with a gentle face. He's kneeling beside Mum, taking her pulse.

'Can you examine my mum today and tell us what's wrong?' I beg.

'Of course I can. Right this minute. We'll just see if you can stand up now,' he says to Mum, carefully helping her.

He leads her off into his consulting room. I try to follow but the receptionist catches hold of me.

'No, you wait there. The doctor needs to see your mother in private.'

So I have to sit down and wait, with everyone else glaring at me because Mum's inadvertently pushed in front of all of them. I pick up a tattered magazine worn furry from thumbing, but I can't concentrate. I stare at the clock and try to imagine what's going on with Mum. She's been in with the doctor for five minutes – then ten. What's he doing to her?

Someone's muttering angrily that they have to get to work for their lunch-time shift and now they're going to be late. The little kid is still crying, a dismal wail that goes on and on. Its mother doesn't try to pick it up or even wipe its nose. Someone else stands up and stomps out, giving up on their appointment. Mum's been in there fifteen minutes – *twenty*.

I stand up and start along the corridor.

'Where are you going?' the receptionist calls.

'I'm going to find my mum. She's been gone so long. She might have fainted again. She needs me,' I say.

But just then the consulting-room door opens, and there's Mum, chalk-white and trembling.

'Oh, Mum!'

'I'm OK,' she mutters quickly. She turns back.

'Thank you so much, Doctor. I'll go to the hospital on Monday then, first thing.'

'The hospital!' I gasp.

The room starts spinning, and I wonder if I'm going to faint too.

'It's all right, Destiny. It's for blood tests. But it's not what you think. Come on, darling, let's get out of here, and then I'll tell you,' says Mum, pulling me.

We stand outside the little concrete clinic and Mum holds me by both hands.

'I'm truly OK, darling. I don't know why I fainted like that. I suppose I got horribly worked up inside. I must have made such a fool of myself. Did my skirt ride up when I fell?'

'No, you did it all very gracefully, but I thought for one minute you were *dead*. Mum, why have you got to have blood tests at the hospital? Are they testing you for cancer?'

'No. That's what I've thought I had, all these months. I was losing so much weight and feeling so weird all the time. But it's nothing like that. The doctor thinks there's something wrong with my thyroid gland,' says Mum.

'What's that? Is it serious?'

'Well, I was crazy to leave it so long, just because I was so scared. The doctor thinks this over-active thyroid is why I've got so thin, and why I feel so worked up and anxious all the time. It even affects your eyes, makes them go all funny, just like mine. But they can cure it, Destiny. When they've tested how much thyroid hormone is in my blood they can give me special medicine and it will sort itself out. He's promised they can make me completely better. Oh, I can't believe it. I've been so worried, but it's all right. *We're* all right, you and me, babe. We're going to be fine.'

12

SUNSET

We stagger through the rest of Sweetie's party
somehow. Half the little girls keep peering anxiously at Mum, wondering if she's suddenly going
to shout at them too. Mum herself stays bright red.
Even her chest is painfully mottled. She smiles

whenever the camera points her way, she sings *Happy Birthday* to Sweetie when the cake's brought in, and she even chats to the mums and nannies while Mr Humbug organizes party games – but her fists are clenched. She doesn't chat to Dad. She doesn't even look in his direction.

Dad is trying to seem ultra-cool and relaxed, lolling around and laughing with Sweetie or mock-wrestling with Ace – but he's not looking at Mum. He keeps getting texts on his phone and going off into a corner to look at them.

Rose-May talks earnestly to the *Hi!* journalist, maybe begging her not to write about the banished birthday guest. Sweetie carries on with her party valiantly but her laughter is high-pitched, and when she fails to win a party game she bursts into tears.

'Oh, Sweetie, you mustn't cry on your birthday! It's only a silly game!' Mum says, though she promised Sweetie she'd win every single game. 'Now come along, you don't want to have red eyes and a blotchy face in the photos, do you?'

Sweetie stops crying almost immediately, and even gives the little girl who won a big kiss, but she spends the rest of her party with her thumb in her mouth. People start to leave, though the birthday food is mostly untouched and Mr

Humbug is only halfway through his party repertoire.

We carry on grimly until the last guest is gone. Mr Humbug and Miss Barley Sugar and Miss Lemon Drop get paid and go. The *Hi! Magazine* people pack up all their equipment and go too. The party planners roll up the white drapes and the rugs and gather the jars of sweets and the fairy lights. Rose-May leaves, shaking her head. The party's over.

Then it starts.

Mum walks up to Dad and slaps him hard on the face. Claudia takes hold of Sweetie and Ace and hustles them out of the room. She hasn't got a spare hand for me. She calls me but I ignore her, standing at the door.

'Don't you dare slap me around, Suzy! Do that again and I'll slap you straight back, right in the chops.'

'How dare you invite that little tart to Sweetie's party!'

'Liz is a *friend*. I've got a perfect right to invite who the hell I want to my kid's party.'

'Who was that child? Is she yours too?'

'*What?* Are you crazy? Liz is only a kid herself. She brought her little niece – poor little moppet, she's probably traumatized, you yelling at her like that. I've had just about enough of your jealous tantrums, Suzy.'

'And I've had enough of your lies and your girlfriends. I'm sick of all this sneaking around, all these whispers and texts and secret meetings. If you want her so much, why don't you clear out and go off with her?'

'All right – I'll do just that,' says Dad.

He stands up and walks to the door. I try to catch hold of him, crying, but he brushes me to one side, barely looking at me. He walks right out of the house.

Mum sits on the sofa, thumping the cushions with her fists, tears spilling down her red cheeks.

'Oh, Mum,' I say, but when I try to put my arms round her she wrenches away from me. 'Don't cry, Mum. He'll come back,' I say, over and over.

I'm sure he'll come back. Maybe he'll stay out overnight again, but he'll be back in the morning.

But he doesn't come back, not for the whole of Sunday. He's not back on Monday. Claudia says we still have to go to school. Mum doesn't say anything at all. She just stays in bed most of the time, crying.

I don't tell anyone at school. I wear my black T-shirt and jeans and mittens day after day. I wash them out at night and hang them over the towel rail in my bathroom. I don't concentrate in class. I compose new songs instead. I am especially pleased with *In My Black Clothes*.

I am in my black clothes,
I wear the colour of death.
I sob, I sigh, I wonder why
I go on drawing breath.
Nobody loves me, nobody cares,
I wander the world alone.
I cannot eat, I cannot drink,
Cannot talk on the phone.
I hold my tongue and close my eyes,
I shut my mouth up tight.
I am in my black clothes –
Won't someone see my plight?

I write it down in my school jotter and then tear it out, ready to stick in my blue velvet notebook tonight. But the song flutters out as I trudge to the classroom door when the lunch-time bell goes, and my teacher, Lucy, picks it up. Oh no, oh no, oh no.

She glances at it and then stares at me. She's looking anxious. 'What's this, Sunset?'

'Nothing, Lucy,' I say stupidly.

'Did *you* write this? It's very disturbing.'

I see Sheba nudge Lila.

'Wonky Gob's written a dirty poem!' she says delightedly.

'Read it out, Lucy!' Sheba begs.

'Go on, give us a treat,' says Lilac.

Lucy holds my page up. *Oh God, please don't let her read it aloud. They will all laugh at me and I will die.*

'I can't read it out, it's too private,' says Lucy

This makes them giggle even more.

'Lucy means it's too rude.'

'Get old Wonky Gob! I didn't think she had it in her.'

'I think it would be a good idea if you both went and had your lunch,' says Lucy.

The teachers don't believe in direct commands, but Lucy gets her point across and they drift off. I try to go too, but she calls me back.

'Sunset, I think we need a little talk. Come and sit down, dear.'

'Please could I have my song back?' I mumble.

'Yes. Yes, of course. So it's a song, is it? How does the tune go?'

I shrug my shoulders, though I've worked it out in my head. It's very high and insistently rhythmic, a bit like a religious chant.

'It's very *good*,' Lucy says.

I can't help feeling pleased, even though this is so humiliating.

'But it's very, very sad. Do you *feel* very, very sad, Sunset?'

'No, I'm fine,' I say.

She's still looking worried. 'I know you haven't got many friends at school just yet,' she says tentatively.

'I don't *want* friends,' I lie. 'I like to be by myself.'

'But it can be very lonely sometimes. And I know you say you're fine, but you *seem* sad. I could suggest to a couple of girls that they be specially kind to you for a few days—'

'Not Sheba and Lilac!'

'No, I don't think that would be a good idea,' Lucy concedes. 'But two of the others, maybe?'

'No. Please. I'm totally fine,' I say, agonized.

'How are things at home?' Lucy asks, trying another tack.

'They're fine too,' I lie. 'Please can I go and have my lunch now, Lucy?'

I get away from her, unable to bear the thought of telling her that my dad's walked out and my mum keeps crying and I don't know what to do. She finds out anyway, because the head of the Infants has a word with Claudia. Poor Sweetie has wet herself in class and is terribly upset about it. They've put her in dry knickers and given her a little plastic carrier bag containing the wet ones. It's like Sweetie's banner of shame and she's scarlet in the face. Ace is hot and flustered too – he's been in a fight.

'So I had to tell the teacher that things were . . . very disturbed . . . at home. I didn't want Ace to get into trouble when it isn't really his fault,' says Claudia. 'He's just upset. I'm sure he didn't really mean to bite that other little boy.'

'Yes I did,' says Ace. 'I'm Tigerman and I go round biting all the bad people.'

He roars and pretends to bite Sweetie. She'd normally simply give him a shove, but she shrinks away from him now, looking woebegone. I try to give her a cuddle, but she hunches up, thumb in her mouth. She kicks the bag with her wet knickers to the other side of the car.

'Not near me! I don't like smelly wet knickers!' Ace yells meanly, because they're inside the bag and don't smell at all.

Sweetie bursts into tears.

'Don't cry, Sweetie,' I say. 'Anyone can have an accident. Ace wets himself heaps of times, you know that.'

'No I don't!' Ace roars.

'He's only little so it doesn't count,' Sweetie sobs mournfully.

'Darling, it truly doesn't matter,' says Claudia. 'Goodness, I've wet my wretched knickers in my time.'

'But not in front of everyone,' says Sweetie. 'I didn't even know it was going to happen. I was feeling sad because we were all talking about our daddies, and then *whoosh*, it just came out! They all saw because it made a puddle and they *laughed* at me. You won't tell Mummy, will you, Claudia?'

'Well, perhaps Mummy needs to know you've had an unhappy day, darling,' says Claudia uneasily.

We drive along the road towards our house. There are a couple of photographers waiting as Claudia struggles to get the car through the security gates. They click and flash at us through the windows, though Claudia shouts at them angrily. Ace pulls faces at them through the window but Sweetie shrinks away in terror.

'They'll see I've got the wrong knickers on! They'll guess I've wet myself! Oh help me, help me, they're *looking*!' she whimpers.

'Don't be silly, Sweetie, they can't possibly tell,' I say, wondering what the paps are doing back outside our house. They haven't waited there for years. Perhaps Dad's come back and Mum was waiting on the doorstep with open arms, and they've photographed the reunion, and now Mum and Dad have fallen in love all over again and are already planning to renew their wedding vows?

I don't think so. There's no sign of Dad indoors. Mum is up now, stamping around the house, closing all the curtains so the photographers can't get any pictures with long-range cameras.

'They know already,' she says, calling them very rude names. She's got a glass of wine in her hand, carrying it wherever she goes. She keeps spilling it and then refilling it. She gives Sweetie a kiss and ruffles Ace's hair distractedly but barely listens when Claudia tells her about school.

'Never mind, never mind. I've got more important things to worry about now,' says Mum. 'Take the children off for their tea, Claudia, for God's sake. I've got a splitting headache.'

'If you keep on drinking like that you'll only make it worse,' Claudia mutters as she drags Sweetie and Ace away upstairs for a wash.

I go over to Mum, who's now lying on the sofa, her hand over her eyes. I sit down on the sofa beside her.

'Sunset! You're pulling the cushion lopsided. Please go and have your tea.'

'I could massage your poor head, Mum, and try to make it better. Look, like this.' I touch her gently on the temple but she swats my hand away.

'I know you mean well, Sunset, but for pity's sake, *leave me alone.*'

So I stand up and slope off. I notice a little torn-up scattering of newspaper in the corner. It's just little bits so it's impossible to piece together, but I know what to do now. Up in my room I google Dad's name and the tabloid on my computer, and a photo of Dad flashes onto the screen – Dad and Big Mouth.

Dad is wearing a ridiculous cowboy hat tipped at a silly angle. He's got one hand up making a peace sign. His other arm is round Big Mouth's shoulders. She's staring up at him, her mouth very big and black in the photo. She's wearing tiny shorts that wouldn't even fit Sweetie, and very high heels. The caption reads: *Danny Kilman and his new friend Lizzi Shaw leaving Beaches nightclub at 2 a.m. Danny and Lizzi met on the set of their new film* Milky Star. *Danny insists they're just good mates – but they were seen getting very close and personal in the VIP section of Beaches earlier in the evening. Tut tut, Danny! Up to your old ways?*

I put my hand over Lizzi Big Mouth, blotting her out. I stare hard at Dad.

'You *can't* just go off with her, Dad,' I whisper.

'What about Mum and Sweetie and Ace and me?'

Dad stares back, making his silly sign, tipping his hat, not caring. Is this it? Isn't he *ever* coming back?

It doesn't look like it. He stays away all week. Every day when I Google the tabloids there are new pictures of Dad and Lizzi reeling out of different clubs and restaurants, climbing into cars, even buying bags of sweets and chocolates in a late-night shop like a pair of greedy children.

Dear Destiny,
I wonder if you've seen the photos of our father
in the papers? It is so awful. He has gone off
with this horrible actress, Lizzi. She is only
eight years older than me. She is young enough
to be Dad's daughter too. No, she could be his
GRAND-daughter. You should be glad Dad's not
part of your life. I hate him. But I also miss
him. It's so awful that he seems to have
forgotten us altogether. Mum keeps crying, and
don't tell anyone but she's drinking all the time
too, and last night she was sick on the stairs.
She told our housekeeper, Margaret, that it was
Ace who'd been sick, which was really mean, but
Margaret didn't believe her and they had a big
row.

It is so horrible here now. Everyone is so cross and unhappy. Sweetie has all these wonderful new toys – a doll as big as herself and a shop with real sweets, but she doesn't play with them much – and Ace keeps breaking all HIS toys.

I'm too old for toys of course. Well, I did try to play with my doll's house – you know, the one I keep in my wardrobe. I rearranged all the furniture and tried making new clothes for all the little teddies and people, but then I got fed up. What I mostly do now is write songs. They're not very good – in fact they're total rubbish, but I like doing it. There's one sad one I think you might like. It's called 'In My Black Clothes'. I've written it out for you on a separate sheet. I copied you. I wear black clothes now. I hope you don't mind.

I do hope your concert went well. I wish I could have been there too. I am so glad you're my sister.
Love from Sunset

Destiny wrote back to me immediately.

Dear Sunset,
I can't believe Danny could do this. Mum says she's sure it's just a temporary mad fling and

302

he'll soon see he's made a BIG mistake and come running back. Yes, we've seen the photos in the paper and can't understand it. This Lizzi isn't even very pretty. Your mum is heaps prettier (and if I'm saying this it must be true, because I've no reason to like your mum seeing as she was so rude to me and MY mum.)

Mum says Danny is a family man at heart and wouldn't ever walk out on you permanently. I said he didn't mind walking out on US, but Mum says that's not fair, he didn't even know I existed until that day at the premiere of Milky Star. Well, he does now, and yet he still doesn't seem at ALL interested – quite the opposite in fact, so I hate him too sometimes. I think he's MAD. Mum bought Hi! Magazine this week, and we've pored over it for hours. Danny and your mum look so HAPPY together. We can't believe they can have split up so soon. We've worked it out – it must have been that very night. What a terrible thing to have happened on Sweetie's birthday! We couldn't believe the photos of all the presents, the huge doll and the shop, and Sweetie looked so lovely in her posh party dress. I wish there'd been more photos of YOU. You're just on the edge in the family picture and I can't spot you at all in the rest of the party photos. I'll tell you something silly my mum did. She cut out a photo of me and stuck it beside you in the little gap on the sofa, like I was really part of the family too.

I have been soooo worried about my mum. She got so thin and ill and was acting a bit crazy at times, but we've found out she's got HYPERTHYROIDISM (I looked it up in a medical book in the library) and she's been to the hospital to get her blood tested and now she's on a special medication called THIONAMIDE and it's going to make her better.

I dedicated my song to her when I sang at the talent contest. The afternoon concert was a bit rubbish because the kids on the panel didn't reckon me, but I WON the evening contest. And I don't want to boast but I got four tens, the top mark!!!

I'm enclosing a DVD of the concert. I'm right at the end. You might want to fast-forward lots of it, but the leader in the first act, the dark good-looking boy, he's called Jack and he's started to hang out with me. He comes calling for me in the morning and walks me through the estate to school, and then sometimes he comes back with me after school and I make

him some tea and stuff. He's not like a
BOYFRIEND, just a friend. If you want to check
out my worst enemy, watch out for the girl in
shiny white leggings (yuck!) in the middle of the
DVD, doing this weird acrobatic dance.

I think you're amazing writing your own
songs!!! 'In My Black Clothes' is soooo good. I've
learned all the words. Maybe I could sing it
some day?!? I wouldn't have the first idea how
to write a song. You've obviously inherited
Danny's talent, though you probably won't like
me saying that just at the moment. I do hope
things are back to normal when you get this
letter. Mum sends her love to you, and like I
said before, she says she's sure Danny will come
back soon.
Love from Destiny xxx

Dad comes back on Saturday afternoon, when
he's been gone exactly a week and we've broken up
from school. Claudia's out buying stuff at the off-
licence for Mum. Sweetie hears his car outside and
goes running to the door.

'Daddy, Daddy, my Daddy!' she cries.

Mum runs to the door too, we all do, but when
we see the car at the front of the driveway we stop.
There's Dad getting out, wearing that cowboy hat,

already holding out his arms to Sweetie – but there's someone else in the car. *He's brought Lizzi Big Mouth with him.*

Mum cries out, grabs Sweetie and Ace, pulls them inside and slams the front door shut. 'How *dare* he bring her here again!' she says.

'Mummy, please, let me go to see Daddy!' Sweetie says frantically.

'No, absolutely *not*. I'm not having you kids contaminated by that little tramp,' says Mum, and she bolts the door.

It's ridiculous: there's Sweetie and Ace screaming to get out and Dad thumping on the door to get in. I'm shivering in the hallway, not sure what I want, just wishing we were a proper family again. I wouldn't even mind if we were all pretending, the way we do for a photo shoot.

It's so silly anyway, because Dad simply strides right round the house to the back door by the kitchen and Margaret lets him in right away. So here he is, coming back up the hallway, and Mum can't stop Sweetie and Ace running to him and giving him a huge hug, their arms and legs wrapped right round him like little monkeys. I hang back, but Dad looks over Sweetie's shoulders and says, 'How about a hug from my big girl?' I burst into tears and rush to him too.

306

All this time Mum is screaming, 'Get out, get out, I'm not having that girl in my house!'

'Whose house?' says Dad. '*My* house, Suzy. Now get a grip – she's not coming in, not just now. Stop the silly noise, you're upsetting the kids.'

'How dare you say that when you're the one who's broken their hearts, not coming to see them for a whole *week*.'

'Well, I'm here now. Where's the nanny? I want their little cases packed. I'm having them for the weekend. You'd like that, wouldn't you, kids?'

'No you don't! You can't just waltz in and whisk them off like this. I don't even know where you're staying.'

'I'm at the Lane Hotel. I've got a suite. The kids will love it. Wait till you see the bathtub, Sweetie, it's just like a swimming pool!'

'Is she staying there too, that little tramp?'

'Stop calling her names, Suzy, it's pathetic. Yes, as a matter of fact she is staying there. So what?'

'Then they're not going, I won't have it! What are you *playing* at, Danny? I'm your *wife*.'

'Look, let's not go into this now. I'm trying to think of what's best for the children. I'm going to be renting a place soon, somewhere with a garden so the kids can run around – and we're

307

going to need to have serious talks about *this* house eventually.'

'What? You're trying to steal the children away – and now you're taking the *house*?'

'Let's just take this one step at a time. We'll get everything sorted fair and square. I'm perfectly willing to provide for you and the kids. I'll be truly generous, no worries, but you know I've lost a lot of money because of the recession. Things will pick up once I get the new album launched—'

'There isn't going to *be* a new album! Your career's over, you wizened old fool. You're just a laughing stock now,' Mum shouts.

'Right, that's it. I'm not hanging about to be insulted. Come on, kids. Never mind your stuff, we can always buy you new clothes. We're going.'

'Oh no you're not! There's guys with cameras outside. What will it look like, you dragging three screaming kids away from their mother – you with your Mr Nice Guy Family Man image nowadays. What would your precious Rose-May say to that?'

'Look, Suzy, grow up. What's the point of making this so ugly? See what you're doing to the kids? You'd better watch it. You've clearly had a drink or two – or ten. If you don't clean up your act you'll find I'll fight you for custody of the kids. I've got myself a very good lawyer. You'd better start cooperating. The kids are coming with me now, and if you have hysterics in front of the paps you'll simply be helping my case. I'll bring them back tomorrow afternoon. Come on now, kids.'

He lifts Sweetie in one arm, Ace in the other, and starts walking.

'Don't you go too, Sunset,' Mum says, hanging onto me.

I hover helplessly, not knowing what to do. My heart's pounding and I feel sick. Mum's asked me to stay, she needs me – but Sweetie and Ace need me too. Dad doesn't have a clue how to look after children. They won't be able to manage without me.

'I'll have to go, Mum. Don't worry, I'll look after Sweetie and Ace,' I say. 'I'm not taking sides, I love you both. Please don't be cross with me, Mum . . .'

But she turns away from me and won't say good-bye to any of us, not even Sweetie.

Then we're bundled into the back of the car and we hurtle out of the gates, Dad telling us to duck down. He laughs as he speeds away, waving his cowboy hat and then plonking it on Lizzi Big Mouth's head. She laughs with him and then looks round at us.

'Hey, kids!' she says, waving her fingers in the air.

We stare at her. We don't wave back.

'Who are you?' Sweetie asks indistinctly, her thumb in her mouth.

'I'm Lizzi, sweetheart. I'm your dad's girlfriend,' she says.

'I'm Sweetie, not sweetheart. And *I'm* Daddy's girlfriend,' says Sweetie.

Dad roars with laughter. Lizzi Big Mouth laughs too, her horrible lips wide open, as if she could swallow us up in one gulp.

'You're my little sweetheart, Sweetie. Liz can be my *big* one,' says Dad.

'What about Sunset?' says Sweetie. '*She's* your big girl, not *her*.'

'Oi, little Miss Sulky Chops, I'm not *her*, I'm Lizzi,' she says. She pulls a face at Sweetie, then raises her eyebrows at me.

'Hi, Sunset. You were very kind to my little niece – unlike *some* members of your family. Thanks for giving her that panda. It was sweet of you.'

I don't want her to feel I'm sweet. I don't reply. I hold Sweetie's hand and Ace's grubby paw in solidarity. Ace shuffles nearer to me.

'I don't like her,' he whispers, not quietly enough.

I don't either, I mouth.

'I'm Tigerman and I'm going to *bite* her,' he says.

Then he looks down at himself, stricken. 'I want my Tigerman costume!'

'Oh, Dad, Ace needs his Tigerman outfit. He'll never settle without it. Can we go back for it?' I say.

'Don't be silly, Sunset.'

'But it'll only take five minutes—'

'I'm not going through all that palaver with the paps and your mother screaming her head off. I've told you, we'll stop off somewhere and buy you all new clothes, OK? And stop taking that tone with Liz, all of you. I want you to be very, very nice to her, because she's a very, very nice girl, OK?'

Of course it isn't OK. She's not the slightest bit nice. She's stolen our dad and she doesn't seem to care. Ace starts crying and Sweetie starts fidgeting. I hope she's not going to wet herself again. I'm starting to feel horribly sick. One way or another it seems likely we're going to make a mess of Dad's upholstery.

He drives us to Harrods again, trying to turn it into a treat. At least we can all go to the bathroom. Lizzi Big Mouth comes into the ladies' with us. She doesn't try to supervise Ace or Sweetie. She just stares at herself in the mirror and applies another shiny dark coat of lipstick to her big mouth.

'You wear too much lipstick,' says Sweetie.

'That's your opinion but you're just a silly little girl,' says Big Mouth.

'I'll tell Daddy you said that,' says Sweetie.

'Tell away, darling. See if I care,' she says.

She's so sure of herself. She doesn't even flatter Dad when she's with him. She just shrugs when he asks her to help us find new clothes, and says, '*I* don't know what little kids like. *You* kit them out. It was your idea to have them with us for the weekend.'

Dad calls an assistant over quickly and Lizzi wanders off humming, messing around with the clothes on the rails, not the slightest bit interested.

Sweetie perks up now and starts to organize a new top and trousers and frilly nightie for herself, and then decides she simply *has* to have some little suede boots with heels. They don't make them as small as Sweetie's size but she wants them anyway, saying she'll stuff socks in the toes.

I know what I want too. It's easy: a new black T-shirt, black jeans and even new lacy mittens because the first ones are starting to tear. I'd like black pyjamas too but I can't find any. I have to make do with navy blue.

Ace is much more difficult to please. The assistant tries hard with him, offering him army khaki or bright scarlet, but he's not interested in ordinary clothes. He wants a Tigerman costume and we can't find one anywhere. He starts crying and he won't stop.

'For God's *sake*, Ace, what's the matter with you?' Dad shouts.

He picks out a T-shirt, shorts and pyjamas for Ace, not bothering to let him choose. Ace is in despair. I pick him up and he sobs into my neck. I have a sudden idea.

'Dad, can we go to the toy department?'

'The *toy* department? You kids, you're always after something. Aren't you getting a bit old for toys, Sunset?'

'It's not for me, Dad. I've thought of something we could get Ace. I promise it's only little, not at all expensive.'

'Ace doesn't deserve anything – he's acting like a spoiled brat,' says Dad, but he gives in.

Lizzi huffs and sighs when he says we're going to the toy department, but she acts like she loves it when we get there. She and Dad muck around with the teddies, making them bob about and talk to each other. It is seriously embarrassing, but I ignore them and search hard, holding Sweetie's hand and lumbering Ace along on my hip. Then I find what I'm looking for: face paints!

'Here you are, Ace, this will do the trick!' I say.

He stops grizzling to peer at the tin. 'That's make-up!' he says. 'That's not for boys.'

'No, no, it's magic sticks of paint for your face. I'm going to paint you. I'm going to use the orange stick and the black stick, with maybe the pink stick for the nose – and guess who you'll be?'

Ace shuffles uncertainly. 'I don't know.'

'Of *course* you know. You'll be Tigerman!' I look at Sweetie. 'And I'll paint you too, with blue shadow for your eyes and red lipstick, and you'll be a fairy-tale princess.'

I take them back to Dad, both smiling. I want him to say, 'Thank you so much for calming them down, Sunset. You're so good with your brother and sister. What would I do without you?' But surprise surprise, he just smiles back at us and buys the face paints, saying mildly, 'What do you want them for?'

So I start to tell him, and he nods a bit, but I know he's not really listening, and then he's distracted anyway because two silly grannies start squealing and blushing like schoolgirls, begging him for his autograph. Big Mouth laughs at them, raising her eyebrows at us. She's more interested in the face paints.

'Oh, cool! I love face paints! I used to run the face-paint stall at my school fête. I love doing it.

Wait till we get back to the hotel, you three, and I'll make you all up.'

'They're *my* face paints. I want to do it,' I say childishly.

She shrugs. 'OK. No probs. You do it, Sunset.'

So when we get to Dad's hotel suite (which is *huge*, like an apartment, with so many flowers and ornaments and fancy bits I'm terrified Ace will knock them all over), I have a go at painting Ace's face like a tiger. It's much more difficult than I thought. I can't get the stripes to go right and he doesn't look fierce enough.

'You're Tigerman now, Ace. Oh goodness, I'm scared of you!' I say nevertheless, but he scowls at himself in the mirror, not convinced.

I try with Sweetie too, but the colours are too strong and she doesn't look like a fairy princess at all. She looks like a pantomime dame. Her chin quivers when she sees herself.

'Maybe it was a silly idea,' I mutter. 'I'll wash it all off.'

'Have a wash in my big bath,' says Dad.

It's an enormous bath made of blue marble. The water comes out of the silver dolphin taps already blue too! There are all sorts of soaps and shampoos and bubblebaths. I wish I could lie back in the bath all by myself and pretend to be a movie star, but

I'm stuck with Sweetie and Ace. I don't even take all my clothes off to get in the bath because I'm worried Dad or Big Mouth will come in. Sweetie and Ace strip off and splash around and pretend to swim and cheer up considerably. I'm anxious when a lot of the face paint is wiped off on the snowy white towels, but Big Mouth Liz shrugs again when she sees.

'We'll get housekeeping to bring us more,' she says.

She's eyeing up her face in the mirror, putting on more lipstick. I bet she gets that all over the towels too.

'Could you do my face so it looks *properly* like a princess?' Sweetie asks her.

I'm taken aback by her betrayal. Liz paints her a *beautiful* princess face, with little blue and lilac flowers on her cheeks, silver stars round her eyes, and a tiny blue butterfly shimmering on her forehead. Sweetie is delighted, running around in just a towel to show Dad. He bows to her and acts as if he's blinded by her beauty. Then it's Ace's turn. Big Mouth turns him into a magnificent Tigerman. She can do all the stripes the right way. She can even manage whiskers, and she makes him look comically fierce. I remember how she held Ace in her arms at the premiere of *Milky Star*. It's only a few weeks ago but it seems like years now, so much has happened since.

It's all Big Mouth's fault that our family's been ripped apart and made so unhappy. I think about Mum at home and how miserable she'll be. She'll drink much too much and I won't be there to help her up to bed.

I glare at Lizzi when she asks me if I'd like my face painted too. 'No, thank you,' I say coldly – though I'd actually love to see what I look like with flowers and stars and butterflies on my face.

'OK, I'll make your dad up then,' she says.

I think Dad will make a fuss but he sits obediently on the bathroom stool and lets her paint his face. He's actually chuckling, enjoying himself. She turns him into a vampire, making his face very white, with dark rings round his eyes and blood trickling from the corner of his mouth. He looks pretty scary, and Sweetie and Ace squeal in delighted horror. Dad chases them round the suite pretending he's going to bite them, and they charge about, shrieking.

'Dad, Dad, you're getting them too excited,' I say. 'They won't settle at bedtime.'

Big Mouth looks at me. 'How old are you, Sunset, seventy? Why can't you lighten up and let everyone have a bit of fun?'

She's not the one who gets woken up in the middle of the night with Ace screaming that the vampire's going to get him and bite him to bits. I have to rush Sweetie to the toilet too because she feels sick. Dad ordered room service for our dinner and let us choose anything we wanted. Sweetie chose three puddings – Ice-cream Delight, Chocolate Heaven and Lemon Yum-yum. They're not at all delightful or heavenly or yummy when they splash into the toilet. Sweetie needs a lot of mopping up and cuddling afterwards.

None of us sleep properly after that. We huddle up together in this king-size bed in the second bedroom. The pillows are too fat and the sheets are too tight and the room is too hot. We turn and fidget and fuss in our unfamiliar new nightclothes. Eventually I lie on my back and put my arms round both of them and they go to sleep at last. I stay wide awake, getting pins and needles in both arms. I try to pass the time by writing a song in my head, but I'm too tired and uncomfortable and feeling pretty sick myself. I ordered a salad thing from room service because I wanted to seem sophisticated. It came with black olives and terribly smelly fishy things that looked like worms. When I eventually fall asleep I dream about them wriggling inside my tummy.

We wake up late, but Dad and Big Mouth are

318

not up yet, sleeping on and on and on, their bed-room door firmly closed. I take Sweetie and Ace to the bathroom and we all get washed and put on our new clothes. We forgot to buy any underwear or socks, so we have to make do with yesterday's.

We go into the great big living room and I work out how to switch on the huge television so we're OK for a while, but we're all getting very hungry now, especially Sweetie, who lost all her puddings. I don't quite dare order room service, but I find a big fridge full of drinks and snacks, so we have a very odd breakfast of Coke and peanuts and Pringles and chocolate. Sweetie feels a bit sick again afterwards, and the Coke makes Ace burp a lot. He keeps on doing it just to be annoying.

'I'm *bored*,' he says. 'I'm going to wake Daddy.'

'No. You can't. You know you can't wake him in the mornings. Besides, *she'll* be there.'

'I don't like her,' says Sweetie.

'You did yesterday when she painted your face.'

'No I didn't! I was just pretending because I wanted to look pretty. I don't *really* like her one bit,' she says.

'I don't like her either,' says Ace. 'Mum's much nicer. Why does Dad like her better than Mum?'

'Oh, you're too little to understand these things,' I say, though I don't really understand why either.

When Dad and Big Mouth get up at long, long, long last, we have a room service breakfast with them, though it's more or less lunch time now. Dad says he wants to take us all out. Ace asks to go to the zoo to see the tigers, even though he's been to the zoo and seen for himself that there aren't any tigers there.

'I know another zoo – a good zoo, specially for children,' says Big Mouth. 'There aren't any tigers – there are mostly little furry animals like monkeys – but you can get right up close to the meerkats. You know what meerkats are, Ace?' She does a sudden amazing meerkat impression, sticking her neck right up and quivering her nose, looking so comically like a meerkat that we all burst out laughing.

So we decide to go to this zoo in Battersea Park. Dad keeps on ruffling Big Mouth's hair, pretending to feed her titbits and calling her 'my little meerkat' – which is totally sickening. But she's right, the zoo is lovely, and we can wriggle down a tunnel and put our heads up right inside the meerkat enclosure. Their little beady eyes stare back at us as if *we're* the funny animals.

Ace likes the pot-bellied pigs too, though I have to hang onto him hard to stop him hurtling over the fence to get in with them. Sweetie likes the yellow squirrel monkeys. I prefer the little mice, who have their own big mouse house with proper furniture. I wonder about Wardrobe City and think how incredible it would be if I had real mice running round all its rooms, standing at the stove, jumping on the sofa, curling up on the bed. I wonder if I could secretly get just two little mice, though maybe not a boy and a girl because then they'd mate and there'd be lots of babies.

I look at Dad and Big Mouth. He's walking with his arm round her, cuddling her close. What if *they* have a baby? When Big Mouth stops and bends over the fence to stroke a big white rabbit (showing a great deal of her legs), I tug Dad's hand, pulling him a few paces away.

'Dad – Dad, can I ask you something?'

'What's that, darling?' says Dad. He's acting very relaxed and smiley – lots of people are recognizing him and he grins and nods all the time.

'Dad, do you love Lizzi?'

He looks at me in sudden surprise. 'Did your mum tell you to ask me that?'

'No!'

Dad laughs. 'Well, it's *her* favourite question too.' He waves in a courtly fashion to a bald grand-dad who gives him an eager thumbs-up sign and plays an air-guitar in homage.

'So – *do* you?'

Dad sighs a little. '*I* don't know. Give me a break, Sunset.'

'But I need to know, Dad. Are you really in love with her and planning to stay with her for ever – or are you going to come back to us?'

'I tell you, I don't *know*. I just want to have a bit of fun, for God's sake. Is that too much to ask? Your mum's doing my head in, Sunset. She does her nut if I so much as twitch when a pretty woman walks by. I can't stay cooped up at home for ever. I'm used to walking on the wild side, being on the road, a different gig every night . . .'

I stare at Dad. He hasn't done a tour for donkey's years. He hasn't had a new album to promote. So what is he going on about? He's playing pretend games with Lizzi, kidding himself he's young again. It's like he's stepped into his own Wardrobe City.

Dad puts out his hand gently and touches my mouth.

'What? Was I showing my teeth?' I ask anxiously.

'No, no, kiddo, you were nibbling your lip. Don't worry so about your wretched teeth, Sunset. Your mum's just got a hang-up about them. I used to have exactly the same gnashers till I had them fixed.'

I stop. 'Dad – Destiny, this girl who could be your daughter, remember – *she's* got funny teeth too.'

But I've lost him now.

'Give it a rest, girl. I can't cope with any more daughters, real or imagined.'

He goes to join Big Mouth, giving her an embarrassing pat on the bottom.

I look round for Sweetie and Ace and can't see them. We have ten minutes of terror, running round the whole zoo before we find them back by the squirrel monkeys.

'You two are a pair of monkeys. I need to put *you* in a cage,' says Dad, picking them both up and giving them a cuddle.

Big Mouth watches, yawning. I wonder if she'd like to settle down and have children with Dad – or does she just want to have fun too? She's looking at her watch.

'Hey, Danny, don't forget we're going out tonight. Hadn't we better take the kids back?'

We're held up in traffic and don't get back home till nearly seven. Mum opens the door, her face white, her eyes red.

'Oh, thank God!' she cries, and gives us all big hugs and kisses, even me. Then she turns to Dad. 'How dare you deliberately torture me? You said you'd bring them back this afternoon. I've been ready and waiting for them since two o'clock. I've been phoning you frantically, leaving so many messages, which you didn't even have the decency to answer!'

'Hey, hey, calm *down*. I had my phone switched off. We were chilling out, enjoying ourselves, weren't we, kids?'

'Yes, I want a pot-bellied pig for a pet, Mum!' says Ace. 'They make such funny noises. Listen!' He grunts and snorts with gusto.

'And I want a squirrel monkey,' says Sweetie. 'Oh, Mummy, they're so sweet and lovely and funny.'

They're jumping up and down happily telling Mum. They're too little to see that this is a big mistake. It's just winding her up terribly – and yet she's the one we're going to be left with. Then Dad says goodbye and they both start crying. Ace gets cross and starts trying to kick Dad.

'You bad bad daddy, you mustn't go!' he yells.

Sweetie sobs too, sounding heartbroken. 'Oh, Daddy, don't go. Please, please, please don't go. I love you so much, I need you. *Please* stay, Daddy, *please*!'

Dad suddenly seems near tears himself, hugging Sweetie, burying his head in her golden hair, whispering in her ear. I hug him too and he pulls me close.

'There's my good brave big girl. I love you, Sunset.'

'I love you too, Dad.' I can hardly get the words out because there's such a lump in my throat.

'Look after your sister and brother for me, won't you, darling?'

'Yes, I will, Dad, don't worry,' I promise – and then he goes.

It's so unexpectedly awful waving goodbye to him that I cry a little too. Claudia comes rushing downstairs and puts her arms round us.

'Look, I'll thank you to keep out of things, Claudia. They need their mother now,' says Mum, taking us into the big living room.

Sweetie's shop is still there, waiting to be carried up to her playroom. Sweetie goes over to it forlornly, still sniffing. She measures out a portion of sweets on her scales. Ace takes a sweet and eats it, then another. The enormous Sweetie doll sits all by herself in an armchair, neglected.

Mum sinks onto the long sofa, her head in her hands, clearly feeling rejected.

'Oh, Mum, we've missed you so,' I say awkwardly.

'Don't be ridiculous, Sunset. You've all clearly

had a wonderful time with your daddy,' Mum sniffs.

'Sweetie and Ace liked the zoo – but most of the time they were wretched,' I say. 'We none of us slept properly.'

'I didn't like my pjs, they were too tight,' says Ace, eating another sweet.

'Those clothes you've got on are too tight too, darling. Did Dad buy them for you? Honestly, fancy not being able to choose the right size for your own son! I see you've got new clothes too, Sweetie. Why didn't Dad bother to buy you anything, Sunset? Why does he always leave you out?'

'They *are* new, Mum. I wanted more of the same,' I say, but she's not listening now. She wants to hear about everything we did, demanding a minute-by-minute account.

'And I suppose *she* was with you all the time? Do you like her? I bet she's fun, isn't she? Did you do lovely things with Lizzi?'

Sweetie puts her thumb in her mouth. Ace eats two sweets. Even they can see this is a leading question.

'Take your thumb out of your mouth, Sweetie, you'll ruin your teeth. What about you, Ace? Do you like Daddy's new friend?'

'She's funny when she pretends to be a meerkat,'

326

says Ace, stuffing a whole handful of sweets into his mouth. 'But I don't like her either.'

'Ace! Stop being such a little pig!'

'I'm a pot-bellied pig, snort snort,' says Ace, laughing and dribbling horribly. 'And I'm ever so hungry.'

'I'm a bit hungry too, Mummy,' says Sweetie.

'Didn't Daddy give you any tea?'

Sweetie thinks for a moment. 'I don't think we even had *lunch*.'

Mum explodes at this. She starts telling *me* off for not making sure the little ones were fed. I try to explain that we nibbled from the mini bar and then had a large cooked breakfast at half past twelve, but Mum isn't interested in explanations.

'You must be starving, you poor babies,' she says, opening her arms wide and giving Sweetie and Ace a big cuddle. 'You must have some tea at once.'

'Can you ask Margaret to make us pancakes, Mum?' asks Ace.

'Oh yes, Mummy, I love Margaret's pancakes!' says Sweetie.

'Well, I'm sure you can have pancakes, my darlings, if that's what you want. Claudia, Claudia!'

Claudia comes practically running. I think she might have been listening in the hall.

'Make the children pancakes for their tea,' says Mum curtly.

'Oh, I want Margaret's pancakes with special jam and cream, and she writes my name on the top with strawberry syrup,' says Ace.

'Margaret is never around on Sunday evenings, Ace, you know that,' I say.

I go to help poor Claudia in the kitchen.

'Margaret isn't around, full stop,' she says.

'What do you mean?'

'She's walked out – with John. They packed up early this morning, told your mother when she surfaced and cleared off. I rather think they've had a little chat with your dad. He wants John to keep on driving him around – and he'll need a cook as soon as he gets a new place.'

'Oh, Claudia,' I say, stricken. 'Promise you won't go too.'

'Sunset, I've made plans, remember? I did tell you.'

'Yes, but that was different. Dad was still here and everything was OK, sort of. Please don't go just yet!'

'Do you have any clue how to make pancakes? I know you put batter in a frying pan, but how do you *make* the batter . . .? Try not to worry so, Sunset. I promise I'll stay as long as I can.'

But Claudia leaves in a few days. It's not her fault. Mum gets really worked up and angry when the post comes one morning because Dad's solicitor sends her a letter all about childcare arrangements during their separation.

'I'm not going to go along with this tosh,' says Mum, crumpling up the letter and throwing it in the bin.

It's already overflowing with tissues and takeaways and lots of bottles. Our daily cleaning lady, Danka, seems to have stopped coming too. The house has got really messy without her, and the kitchen is horrible, with stuff spilled all over the floor. Poor Bessie the cat is very upset because her litter tray is really, really dirty and she doesn't like to use it like that. I have to pinch my nose and tip the horrible litter into a big plastic bag. I try to do a bit of mopping too, but I just seem to smear everything around instead of cleaning.

I go to the wastebin now, wanting to see the letter.

'For God's sake, Sunset, don't start scavenging round the bins,' says Mum. 'What can you possibly want in there?'

'I want to know if Dad still wants to see us,' I mumble.

'Well, of course he does. He's demanding this and that, wanting to see the three of you every weekend, laying down the law about it – just so he can parade you around with that floosie for the benefit of all the paps. Well, he's not a fit parent. He can't clothe you, he can't even remember to feed you, so I'm not having it. It's a load of nonsense anyway. He could never be bothered to so much as play with you when he was living here. Why all the big fuss about his rights as a father the minute he walks out? What sort of a father is he, anyway? He doesn't give a damn about any of us. When has he ever done anything for you, Sunset? He just brushes you away and says, "Not now, babe," if you so much as try to talk to him.'

This is so horribly true that I put my hand to my face, trying not to cry. Claudia's trying to unload and repack the dishwasher. Mum's crammed it ridiculously full, with saucepans bashing against glasses. She's already broken several of the stems, and Claudia is fishing shards of glass out as she goes.

'Really, Suzy, you should be more careful. This is highly dangerous,' she says, wrapping the glass in newspaper. She turns to me. 'Your dad might be busy sometimes but he still loves you very much,' she says.

Mum gets even angrier. 'Don't you tell me off in that silly fancy voice! I'm the one who tells you what to do. And don't try to fill Sunset up with that rubbish about her dad. He *doesn't* love her very much. She's a total embarrassment to him.'

I feel as if the glass shard is sticking in my stomach.

'That's the most terrible, unfair and *awful* thing to say to your own child,' says Claudia. 'Your mother's being incredibly unkind because she's upset, Sunset. Of course your father loves you. Don't listen to her.'

'Excuse me? How dare you take that attitude with me!' Mum shrieks. 'You're just the wretched nanny.'

'You seem to have turned me into the chief cook and bottle-washer now,' says Claudia. 'But yes, I am the nanny, and I have your children's interests at heart.'

'You just want to turn them against me, like everyone else,' says Mum. 'And I'm not standing for it. You can get out of here now. Come on, pack your bags and go.'

'I'll very happily go, but not till you've made arrangements to have the children properly looked after.'

'How dare you dictate to me! You'll pack and be out of here in half an hour or I'll call the police! I don't need you or anyone else to look after my children. I can look after them myself.'

So Claudia goes, though she weeps when she says goodbye.

'I'm so very sorry, Sunset. I wish I could stay – but if I insist it will only make her worse. I'm sure she'll calm down a bit when I'm gone. And I've got your father's mobile number. I'll let him know the situation. Apart from anything else, I'm actually owed a lot of money, but that doesn't really matter. You're the ones who matter, you and Sweetie and Ace. Your parents don't deserve you – *especially* you, Sunset. You're a sweet, warm, lovely, clever girl and don't you forget it. I'd be proud to have you as my daughter.'

I start crying then, and Sweetie and Ace join in. We're all three realizing too late that Claudia is the best nanny we've ever had. But she's off in a taxi and we're left alone in our huge house with Mum.

I don't know what to do. I want to run upstairs and hide in Wardrobe City – but here's Sweetie and Ace wailing beside me, and Mum flat out on the sofa howling too. So I go into the bathroom and wash my face. When I look at myself in the mirror I hear *Total embarrassment, total embarrassment*, but I say loudly, '*Shut up!*'

Then I wash Sweetie's face and brush her hair, which calms her down. It's harder with Ace, who screws up his face and screams, but I cup his chin with my palm and wipe all his tears and snot away. He's still sniffling when I've finished, but at least he's not messy.

'Now,' I say, 'I want you to be Tigerman today, Ace. I'll help you climb into your costume. And you, Sweetie, are going to be a fairy princess, so we'll put on your party dress.'

They both blink at me.

'Am I having another party?' Sweetie asks.

'We can have a party for you, if that's what you'd like,' I say.

'*I* want a party. It's not fair, Sweetie's just had one,' Ace starts whining already.

'It's your party too, a special Tigerman party. We'll have two *simultaneous* parties. That means two parties at the same time.'

'*Real* parties, with real food?' says Sweetie, who is used to my pretending.

'Yes, we can have real party food,' I promise grandly.

'Are you having a party too, Sunset?'

'No, I am the party *planner*,' I say, rubbing my black lacy hands together.

'Will there be guests?' Sweetie asks. 'Can I invite Daddy?'

I take a deep breath. 'No, the only guests have to be inside this house. You can invite Mum – and your new big dolly. And me. You'll have to make proper invitations. You've got new crayons and a drawing book, Sweetie. Go and find them and I'll show you both how to do invitation cards. You can draw a fairy princess on yours, Sweetie, and if you're kind enough to lend Ace your black and orange crayons, he can draw a Tigerman on his.'

I leave them lying on their tummies in their party gear, colouring in their invitations. Sweetie's frock is getting creased but I decide it doesn't matter. I don't think she'll ever be wearing it again.

I go down to find Mum. She's making angry calls on her mobile, tears still running down her cheeks.

'That stupid, useless agency,' she says. 'They're telling me there isn't anyone suitable currently available! I don't believe it! "Because of exceptional demand!" Well, of *course* there's demand, it's a temp agency. They tell me to try next week – *next week!* – when there won't be any point because we'll all have starved to death, and if we *are* still going strong we'll be ankle-deep in rubbish. And when they *do* deign to send a housekeeper and a nanny they want me to find "alternative means of payment". Do you know what that wicked father of yours has done? He's cancelled all my credit cards! Oh, Sunset, what are we going to do?'

'We'll manage, Mum, you and me.'

'Oh yeah, you're going to start paying the wages, are you?'

'We won't have to pay any wages, because *we* can do the cooking and the cleaning and look after Ace and Sweetie.'

'You're still only a silly little kid – and *I* don't have a clue when it comes to cooking and cleaning and stuff.'

'You must have cooked and cleaned before you got famous, when you lived in those flats.'

Mum hates being reminded that she grew up on a council estate. She glares at me. 'You don't know what you're talking about. We didn't do any cooking, we just went down the chippy, and as for cleaning, don't make me laugh! I was out of that filthy hole by the time I was sixteen, earning my own money as a model. Sunset, I was thinking, I might have had three kids but I reckon I could still do a bit of modelling, especially with my latest boob job. What do you reckon?'

I reckon she's crazy, but she's perked up a little

at the thought, so I go along with this idea. 'Yeah, of course you could, Mum. You're still ever so pretty. Though at the moment your mascara's gone a bit smudgy. Hold on a tick, I'll get a damp flannel and wipe it off. Or why don't you go and have a shower, do your hair, get yourself all glammed up, because Sweetie and Ace are having a party.'

'Are you crazy, Sunset? We've only just held the most disastrous party ever. Are you deliberately trying to drive me insane? Hello?' She taps my forehead hard with her long false nails. 'Is there anyone *in* there?'

That's it. I'm suddenly sick of her. I knock her hand away. I very nearly slap her face.

'Yes, there *is* someone in here, Mum. I'm Sunset and I'm a *person*. I've got feelings. I'm sick sick sick of everyone being horrible to me. I'm trying hard to look after everyone, even you. Sweetie and Ace were crying so I thought I'd distract them with the idea of a party, just a play one, and it's got them all cheered up. This is all so *scary* – can't you see that?'

'Don't you dare talk to me like that!'

'What are you going to do? Tell me to pack my bags like Claudia? Get a new daughter from the agency – a pretty one with perfect teeth? I know you don't really want me but you're stuck with me. So why can't you stop moaning and crying and getting cross with everyone and look after us. You're the mother!'

She looks astonished, as if Sweetie's doll on the chair has suddenly stood up on her own two plastic feet and shouted at her.

'All right, I'm the mother – but I wish I wasn't!' she says, and she runs out of the room.

I don't know where she's going or what she's going to do. I decide I don't care. I go into the kitchen and peer into the fridge, wondering what we can have for party food. Well, we can have ice cream for a start, and there's a big bowl of fruit. I can chop it up and make a fruit salad. We've got sliced bread so I can make sandwiches. Egg sandwiches! I can boil eggs, you just put them in a saucepan on the stove, for goodness' sake. Then I can mix them up with mayonnaise. What else? I find a big packet of crisps and a pack of chipolata sausages. We've got a grill. I can line the little sausages up and brown them, easy-peasy.

I make a start. It isn't quite as simple as I thought. My eyes have to swivel everywhere, making sure the sausages don't burn, and the eggs clank together in the pan and start cracking. My hands ache from chopping fruit and spreading bread. When the eggs and sausages are cooked and I'm waiting for them to cool down, I look around the kitchen to see if there's any way I can brighten it up. I've decided it's the most suitable place for the party venue. The big living room would just bring back painful memories, and it's better to avoid anywhere with carpets when Ace is eating.

I wish I had balloons. I make do with a handful of Sweetie's hair-ribbons, tying big bows round the kitchen drawer handles.

Then I dash upstairs to see how Sweetie and Ace are getting on. They've been surprisingly quiet. They're not in the playroom, though there are lots of invitations stacked across the floor. They've found potential guests too – Sweetie's Rosie teddy and two Bratz dolls, and Ace's Tiger bear and several little toy soldiers. They're lying higgledy-piggledy on the floor as if they've already *been* to a party and are now dead drunk.

I hear whispering and giggling. Sweetie and Ace are in my room. I rush across the landing and through the door. They've not just gone into my room. The wardrobe doors are wide open and the doll's house is open too: they're in Wardrobe City! They are holding Mrs Furry and Mr Fat Bruin and Chop Suey and Trotty in their hands, making them jump about and talk in little squeaky voices.

'What are you *doing*?' I cry.

Sweetie and Ace jump guiltily. They know Wardrobe City is strictly forbidden territory. A few weeks ago I would have screamed my head off, snatched up all my precious private friends and bundled Sweetie and Ace out of my room. But now it's so strange, I don't really mind particularly. Wardrobe City isn't real to me any more. It's just a lovely toy that I used to play with – and now Sweetie and Ace like playing with it too.

'Sorry, Sunset! We'll put all your people back,' says Sweetie quickly.

'It's OK. I think I'm going to let you two play with my doll's house now, if you're very careful – and only when I say so. Shall we ask this one, Mrs Furry, to the party?'

'Oh, yes, let's! She wants to come to my princess party,' says Sweetie.

'Mind you look after her carefully. She might feel very small and shy standing next to your Rosie bear.'

I put nearly all my people back in their favourite places. I search around, looking in little cupboards and under tiny beds.

'Where's Peanut?' I ask.

'Who's Peanut?' says Sweetie.

'She's a little pink Plasticine baby,' I say.

They look stricken, especially Ace.

'What have you done with Peanut?' I demand.

'Nothing,' says Ace hurriedly.

'I think she might have accidentally got squashed,' Sweetie says. 'So we made her into food for all the little teddies.'

'Poor little Peanut!' I say. 'So you've turned the rest of my family into cannibals?' I try to sound cross, but can't help giggling, and the other two join in.

We collect up all the toys, sitting them around the playroom, and then Sweetie and Ace hand out their invitations.

'Don't forget your big new doll downstairs, Sweetie,' I say. 'What are you going to call her?'

'I don't know. I can never think of the right names for people,' says Sweetie.

'Let's call her Princess Rosabelle,' I say.

'Oh, yes, that's a *lovely* name,' says Sweetie.

'I am the Princess Rosabelle,
I have a pretty name.
I have a pretty face as well,
I like this party game.'

I sing, making it up as I go along. I think for a moment.

'I shall dance with pointy feet
and I shall sing this song.
I will kiss my sister sweet,
Playing all night long.'

It's hardly a proper song, but Sweetie sings it happily over and over again. Ace wants a song too.

'Hear him roar,
Feel him bite,
See him gore,
Watch him fight.
Stripes on his face,
My Tigerman Ace.'

He likes my song, though he can't remember my words *or* sing the tune, so he just goes *'Roar!'* and *'Bite!'* and *'Fight!'*

'OK, let's start the party,' I say. 'Come downstairs with all your guests.'

While they're trying to prop every doll and teddy up on the kitchen benches, I make up the egg sandwiches and pop little toothpicks in the sausages and lay out all the food in pretty patterns on the plates. I don't know how many places to set for real people. I go to the kitchen door and call.

'Mum, we're about to start the parties. Are you coming?'

I don't really expect her to answer me. She's probably gone back to bed with a bottle. But then I hear her footsteps coming down the stairs, little clip-clops, which means she's wearing her high heels. When she comes into the kitchen we all gasp because she looks so gorgeous. She's wearing her very best silver sequin dress. It's very low cut and clings to her all the way down to her ankles, sparkling and shimmering in the kitchen spot-lights. She's washed her hair and then teased it so it's all light and fluffy, and she's put on new make-up, with special silvery eyeshadow. Her eyes are outlined with black like Cleopatra, and she's got beautiful rosy cheeks, but her lips are ghostly pale. She's not wearing any lipstick whatsoever.

'Oh, Mummy, you look *lovely*!' says Sweetie.

'You're beautiful, Mum!' says Ace.

'Oh, Mum, thank you for coming to the parties,' I say.

'I wouldn't miss the parties for the world,' says Mum.

She sits at one end of the table, I sit at the other end, and Sweetie and Ace wriggle on either bench, forever leaping up to catch a party guest in a state of collapse.

342

We eat the party food, Sweetie and Ace sharing it out liberally so I have to keep wiping furry snouts and plastic lips. Mum nibbles at one sandwich and a tiny portion of fruit salad, but we're used to her not eating much because of her diet. Sweetie and Ace tuck in enthusiastically.

'You're *very* good at party food, Sunset,' says Sweetie.

'Tigerman says *Yum yum yum*,' says Ace.

'You really shouldn't boil eggs and grill sausages, Sunset. You could burn yourself,' says Mum. 'But well done, darling. This is a lovely idea. We'll get on fine just ourselves, won't we, kids? We're all having tremendous fun, aren't we?'

We're not *really* having tremendous fun, any of us, but we're all four pretending as hard as we can.

We carry on day by day, trying hard to convince ourselves. On Saturday Dad comes knocking at the door, and when Mum won't answer he tries to get in – but she's bolted the back door as well as the front. Dad yells and taps at the windows. Sweetie and Ace cling to me, crying, not sure whether they want to rush out to Dad or stay safe with Mum. She's acting like Dad is ultra-scary and just wants to hurt us, and we know this is rubbish. Yet some-how it still feels as if we're under siege and Dad is the bad guy trying to break in and hurt us all. He tries phoning too, over and over again, until it sounds as if the whole house is ringing – but eventually he gives up and drives away.

Mum cheers. We don't know whether to cheer too or cry. Dad doesn't come back on Sunday. This makes Mum triumph again.

'There! If your dad *really* cared about you he'd be back first thing today. *I* wouldn't rest until I could see you all, my darlings,' she says.

She makes an extra fuss of us and suggests we have a DVD party all evening, with popcorn and chocolate and ice cream – and lots and lots of wine for her.

'No boring early-to-bedtime. We can stay up all night if that's what we want. Life is much more fun with your mum, isn't it!'

Mum falls asleep first, curled up on the sofa, wine glass still in her hand. She doesn't budge when I try to wake her up. I have to carry Sweetie and Ace up to bed myself, then find a blanket for Mum and put myself to bed too.

We all sleep in till gone ten the next morning. Mum doesn't wake up for ages, so I fix Sweetie and Ace and me some cereal and then, as school has finished, we *play* school. I sit them at the kitchen table with Princess Rosabelle and assorted toys and we do old-fashioned lessons. If any of the toys are naughty or flop about the bench, I give them a little shake or stand them in the naughty corner with a saucepan for a dunce's cap. Ace is deliberately naughty because he adores standing in the corner, the saucepan at a rakish angle over one eye.

The telephone keeps ringing and I don't know what to do. Mum has forbidden us to answer it – but she's still up in her room. She won't *know*. I think I really need to talk to Dad – he'll be so worried about us. I pick the phone up gingerly.

'Dad?' I whisper.

But it's not Dad, it's Rose-May.

'Hello, is that Suzy? Why in God's name haven't you been answering your phone? Anyway, thank heavens you've stopped playing silly beggars. Now listen to me, dear—'

'It's not Suzy. It's Sunset.'

'What?' Rose-May sighs impatiently. 'Could you please put your mother on the phone, Sunset?'

'I can't. She's not up yet.'

'Then go and wake her up, it's gone eleven!'

'Yes, but if I do I don't think she'll talk to you.'

'For goodness' *sake*, has the woman gone off her *head*? This isn't about Danny. It's about Sweetie.'

'Sweetie?'

Sweetie looks up from helping Princess

Rosabelle draw a P and an R on her paper as part of her English lesson. 'What?' she says.

'I need to talk to Suzy about Sweetie. It's urgent,' says Rose-May. 'Oh, for God's sake, I'll drive round. I'll be with you in an hour.'

She hangs up. Sweetie and Ace are staring at me.

'That was Rose-May,' I say. 'But we won't tell Mum, she might get mad.'

'Why did you say my name?' Sweetie asks.

'She says she wants to talk to Mum about you,' I say, bewildered.

'I haven't been naughty, have I?' Sweetie asks anxiously. 'I don't want Rose-May to tell me off. She gets quite cross sometimes.'

'She doesn't want to tell me off too, does she?' Ace asks.

'Rose-May isn't going to tell anyone off, you pair of sillies,' I say.

Sweetie puts her thumb in her mouth nevertheless. She looks very cute in her little bunny nightie, but if Rose-May is really coming round I'd better get us all washed and dressed.

'Come on, kids, upstairs,' I said. 'Bath time.'

Sweetie takes her thumb out and rubs her mouth. 'My teeth feel all funny, Sunset,' she says.

'I think they just need to be brushed,' I say.

I get us all ready. When I've towelled Sweetie and Ace dry, I let them put on the princess party dress and the Tigerman outfit, and I wear my black clothes.

Mum's stirring now, peering round the door at us, rubbing her eyes. 'Oh dear,' she mumbles, 'I have *such* a headache. Do you think you could make me a black coffee, Sunset?'

She's up and showered and dressed in half an hour, thank goodness. She's tied her hair up in a tartan ribbon and is wearing a little white vest top and skinny jeans. She looks practically Sweetie's age, not like a mum at all.

When she hears a car drive up outside she jumps up. 'Is it Danny?' she asks.

Then she sees it's Rose-May's pink car. 'Oh God, *her*! Is Danny with her? Oh, typical, getting his wretched manager to do the negotiating! Well, that stroppy cow can just bog off. She's not *my* manager. I don't have to listen to a word she says.'

Rose-May has her own remote to make the gate open, but she doesn't have a key to the door. She knocks briskly.

'Knock knock knock, but you can't come in,' Mum mumbles.

'Mum, hadn't we better just see what she wants?' I say.

347

'No, don't let's!' says Sweetie hurriedly.

'Suzy?' Rose-May is yelling through the letter-box. 'Suzy, will you please answer the door? I'm starting to lose patience.'

'As if I care,' says Mum.

'Suzy, this isn't about Danny – well, not directly. It isn't about you. I need to have a serious discussion about Sweetie.'

'I don't want a discussion,' says Sweetie.

'Suzy, can you hear me? There's a very good chance we can make Sweetie a huge television star. I know this has come at entirely the wrong time, and Danny has been totally out of order. I've certainly given him a piece of my mind. I have a feeling he's about to crawl back with his tail between his legs. *However*, like I said, this isn't about Danny, it's about Sweetie. This is the most exciting new television venture I've heard of in a long time.' Rose-May stops shouting and waits for a response.

Mum nibbles one of her false nails. She looks at Sweetie. Sweetie looks at her.

'Mummy, *am* I going to be a television star?' Sweetie asks. She says it matter-of-factly, as if she's been expecting this to happen sometime soon.

'I – I don't know, sweetheart,' says Mum. She looks at me. 'What do you think, Sunset? Do you think she's telling the truth? Or has Danny put her up to this?'

'Why don't we ask her in and find out?' I say. 'You let her in. I'll put the kettle on for a cup of tea.'

I make shooing motions to get Mum to go to the door. Sweetie is already tossing her hair out of her eyes and smoothing the creases in her dress. Ace is pouting.

'Why can't *I* be the television star?' he protests.

Come to think of it, why can't I? Though I don't really want to go on television – especially when Rose-May tells us all about it. She sits in an armchair, wearing a violet shirt and white trousers, looking very bright and businesslike. I've made the tea in a proper pot and set the tray carefully. I hope she'll smile at me and say, 'What a lovely cup of tea, Sunset. How clever of you.' She barely notices.

'The show's going to be called *Little Darlings*, going out early Saturday evening. It's going to be *huge*, just you wait and see! The premise is that they do a documentary on a celebrity family every week. They're going to be using your neighbour, the tennis guy, with his little daughter. They're choosing children who take after their famous fathers. No prizes for guessing which footballer they've chosen, with his eldest son. I knew right away that Danny and Sweetie were a perfect fit. That child's such a picture, it would be criminal not to use her.'

I try not to react, but Ace is less reticent.

'Use *me*, Rose-May,' he says. 'I want to be on television!'

'I'm sure we *will* see you on television one day, Ace – but you're a tad young just now. The children in the show have to be at least six, just so that no tiny tot is exploited in any way. It's perfect for Sweetie as she's only just had her birthday. My guess is she'll be the littlest and cutest.'

'What will she have to do? Just look little and cute?' I ask.

'Oh no, the child has to take after its parent. So here's the sixty-four-thousand-dollar question: can Sweetie sing? Just a little bit, lisp a few words, carry a tiny tune? It's not like they're expecting infant opera, but she will need to sing her little heart out.'

'I can sing,' says Sweetie. She stands up on the coffee table, spreads out her party dress and opens her mouth. She sings my Princess Rosabelle song in a very little voice, wavering at times – but she looks so sweet she gets away with it. Mum watches her proudly and claps wildly at the end. Rose-May nods.

'Yep. Just as I thought. She'll walk it. The programme starts with the filmed documentary of the famous pair in their family setting, and then they appear before a live audience in the studio. So Sweetie will do a little act with Danny, singing a duet. I'll try to come up with one of Danny's hits, something really simple. Then Sweetie will round things off with a solo. That Princess song might do – it's quite cute and suits her voice. Who sings it?'

'*I* sing it,' says Sweetie. 'Sunset made it up for me.'

'Really?' says Rose-May. She doesn't look as if she believes it. 'Not the words *and* the tune? It's your own original song, Sunset?'

I nod, going red.

'Well, perhaps *you* could be on television too.'

'I can't sing for toffee,' I say.

'Perhaps you could be in the documentary. We could film you making up the song – feature *both* Danny Kilman's daughters. Anyway, we have to get Sweetie approved first. I've told the producer all about her. She can come out here tomorrow – say at eleven? You can have Sweetie looking her absolute best by then.' Rose-May looks around the room, shaking her head. 'I know a magic cleaning firm. I'll give them a ring to see if they can rush round later and spruce things up a bit.'

Mum is still nibbling her nail. 'Will Danny have to be here too?' she asks.

'Well, naturally,' says Rose-May. 'And I know just what a grand act you two can put on. We need a total togetherness, family-love vibe for this programme. I'm trying to rationalize all the tacky coverage of the past weeks, saying that it's simply the tabloid press jumping to ridiculous conclusions. Danny was just kindly showing his new young co-star the high spots of London—'

Mum says a very rude word.

'Exactly,' says Rose-May. 'But it's going to be worth it for all of us if we do a good smooth PR job on the situation. I think you and Danny belong together, Suzy. If you stay together it helps Danny's career enormously. He's too old a guy to be rushing off with a teenager. It starts to seem downright unsavoury. The press have pointed this out gleefully but it's not too late to salvage the whole situation.'

'I don't know that I *want* to salvage the situation,' says Mum. 'Danny needn't think he can come crawling back to me just to make himself look good.'

'Fine, dear, if that's what you really want – but you still need him to be earning good money if he's going to be paying you alimony. And if you give

Sweetie this big showcase, I'm sure she'll hit the floor running and turn into a total child star. I'm not just thinking this country, I think she's got huge Disney potential – and I'd be very happy to manage her,' says Rose-May.

'Oh, say yes, Mummy! I *want* to be a star,' says Sweetie.

So of course she gets her own way. We're all up ultra-early the next morning, making sure the future child star is bathed and brushed and dressed up to the nines. Her own party frock is a little stained and crumpled now, but we swap it with Princess Rosabelle's identical outfit and it fits perfectly. My tummy gets butterflies at the thought of little Sweetie having to sing in front of this unknown producer, but she seems very cool about it, though she's sucking her thumb a lot.

Rose-May drives up with Dad. Thank goodness there's no sign of Lizzi Big Mouth lurking in the car. Dad's wearing his new cowboy hat. He strolls up to the door nonchalantly – but he's looking nervous. Mum opens the door. Our parents stand awkwardly together in the hallway.

'Oh, Mummy, oh Daddy!' says Sweetie, running from one to the other.

Ace grabs Dad round his knees and hugs him hard.

Mum and Dad are barely looking at each other. Oh no, please, please, please don't let them start yelling at each other. But they stay weirdly calm.

'Hey, Suze,' Dad mutters.

'Hi, Dan,' says Mum.

We all go into the big living room. The sweet-shop is still standing in the corner, reminding us all of the fateful party. Rose-May sits between Mum and Dad and makes bright general conversation. They all look proudly at Sweetie, who sits neatly on a cushion with her skirts spread out around her, like a little fairy-tale Goldilocks. She's got her thumb in her mouth.

'Take that thumb *out*, darling,' says Mum. 'You don't want to look like a baby, do you?'

'I'm a baby, Mum, look,' says Ace, rolling onto his back and kicking his feet in the air. He nearly knocks Dad's cowboy hat off his head.

'Watch it, son,' says Dad. He yawns and stretches. 'God, I'm tired.'

'You've clearly been having too many late nights,' says Mum bitterly.

'Oh God, don't start,' says Dad. 'Where's this producer woman then, Rose-May? We're all here at the crack of dawn because of her so-called busy schedule. So what's happened to her?'

She arrives ten minutes later. She's quite young

and wearing several T-shirts over each other and fashionably ripped jeans, with her sunglasses stuck in her hair like an Alice band. She's called Debs. She smiles at me politely when Rose-May introduces us, she chuckles at Ace – but her eyes totally light up when she sees Sweetie.

'Oh, she's *gorgeous*, Rose-May,' says Debs.

Sweetie smirks.

Debs squats down in front of her and starts chatting to her in a silly voice. 'Hello, my poppet. So you're Sweetie, are you? I love your dress.'

'It's really Princess Rosabelle's but I'm borrowing it,' says Sweetie.

'Oh, how cute,' says Debs uncertainly, thinking Sweetie is rambling.

Rose-May is acting like the hostess, offering tea or coffee, but looking hopelessly at Mum. She takes no notice so I stand up and say I'll go and make it. When I come back, trying very hard to balance everything on my tray. Rose-May and Debs are deep in conversation about Sweetie.

'She seems *very* young,' Debs says. 'Are you *sure* she's six?'

Rose-May assures her that Sweetie's definitely had her sixth birthday.

'It's just that we're asking rather a lot of a small child. The filming is very tight, and the majority of the programme will go out live on a Saturday night. I can't afford for anything to go wrong. Any tears or tantrums and the press will crucify me for torturing little kiddies and the programme will be axed. So I need rock-solid children, not little moppets who can easily lose it and go to pieces.'

'Sweetie's a little star in the making,' says Rose-May firmly. 'She doesn't know the meaning of the word temperament. Come on, Sweetie, sing your pretty song for Debs.'

Sweetie stands up, mumbling something indistinctly behind the thumb in her mouth.

'Take your thumb out, darling,' says Mum.

Sweetie takes her thumb out with a little plopping sound and then gasps. There's something sitting on top of her little pink thumb. It's a *tooth*!

Sweetie stares at it, shocked, and then puts her hand to her mouth. She feels the gap. Her eyes pop with horror. She starts crying, dribbling blood.

'Oh, Sweetie! Oh God, *no*!' says Mum. 'I *told* you not to keep sucking your thumb!'

'Hey, it's not her fault. All little kids lose their teeth,' says Dad.

'Come here, darling, give Mummy the tooth. Maybe we can get the dentist to fix it back in? Or perhaps we can get you a false tooth?' says Mum.

'Get a grip, Suzy, the child's *six*. And she looks sort of cute with a little gap.'

'I don't *want* a gap,' Sweetie howls. 'It feels horrid and there's all this *blood*!'

'It's only a little bit of blood and it'll wash away. It's OK, Sweetie, I lost my front tooth when I was your age, but you just grow new ones,' I say, putting my arm round her.

'I don't want new ones like yours, I want my *old* ones!' Sweetie roars.

Debs is sitting looking at Sweetie, then glancing at her watch. Rose-May sees this.

'Come along, Sweetie, let's forget about your silly old toothy-peg. You're going to sing for us now, aren't you, darling? You don't want to lose this big chance, do you, dear?'

Sweetie tries to stop crying. Mum whips her off to the bathroom to wash off the blood, but this is a big mistake. Sweetie sees herself in the mirror and starts screaming. It takes a long time to calm her down. Debs makes notes, takes a phone call, drinks her coffee. She shakes her head at Rose-May.

'I don't think this is going to work,' she says.

'Just give her a chance to calm down, Debs. Come on, she's only a little girl.'

'Mmm. *Too* little, like I said,' says Debs.

'Hear her sing, please. I'll go and get her now,' says Rose-May.

She brings Sweetie back. Sweetie is trying very hard indeed not to cry, but she's gulping and hiccuping, tears still rolling down her cheeks. Both her hands are clamped over her mouth, as if she's trying to keep the rest of her teeth secure.

'Sing, Sweetie, darling,' says Mum.

'Let's hear you, little princess,' says Dad.

'Come along now, Sweetie, we're waiting,' says Rose-May.

Sweetie gives the song a valiant shot, but it doesn't work. She sings with her head bent, in a tiny lispy voice that veers on and off the tune. Her voice peters out altogether halfway through and she starts sobbing.

'Try once more, Sweetie,' Mum begs.

Sweetie goes and buries her head in a cushion, beyond trying.

'Poor little pet,' says Debs. 'Don't cry, dear. I know you did your best.'

Sweetie cries harder because she knows she's blown it.

'Oh well,' says Debs, putting her phone and notebook in her bag.

Rose-May is looking at me. 'Of course, we could always try Sunset,' she says.

They all stare at me. I feel myself blushing scarlet.

'I couldn't!' I protest.

'Maybe you could,' says Rose-May. 'Of course, you've got an entirely different look to Sweetie – but we could work with it. Try a different approach, kind of tween grunge.'

Debs is eyeing me up and down appraisingly. 'Mmm,' she says.

'No,' I say. 'Absolutely not.'

'Now then, Sunset, don't be so negative,' says Mum. She looks at Debs. 'She lacks a little confidence, but I know she'd try hard, given a bit of encouragement. And her hair looks much better when it's styled properly.' She seized handfuls of my hair, trying it this way and that.

'Yes, but can she *sing*?' says Debs.

'No,' I say.

'Hold on now,' says Rose-May. 'Didn't you say you made up Sweetie's little princess song? So you *can* sing!'

'I can't,' I say. 'I truly can't. I would if I could, but I can't. Listen!'

I sing the first two lines of Princess Rosabelle to show them.

'Try clearing your throat and giving it another go,' says Rose-May.

'I *can't* sing, I'm always croaky,' I say.

Debs sighs. 'Never mind, dear. It can't be helped. And you never mind too, Sweetie!'

She's still traumatized, hunched up and hugging the cushion.

Debs shakes her head at Dad. 'Sorry, Danny, it looks like the programme isn't going to happen – unless you've got any other daughters tucked away.'

She's joking – but I jump up.

'Yes! Oh please, Debs, will you just watch this—'

'I'm sorry, Sunset, I've got to get on. Perhaps another time—'

'No, it will just take two minutes, I swear. And then you'll see.'

'Sunset? You mustn't waste any more of Debs's time,' says Rose-May.

'No, please, just watch for two minutes, that's all I ask,' I beg. 'I'll go and fetch it. *Please* wait.'

I run up to my room, grab the DVD, and come rushing down. My hands are shaking so much I can barely get the DVD out of the case and into the machine.

'Whatever are you playing at, Sunset?' says Mum.

'Look, Mum! Look, everyone!' I say.

360

Bilefield's Got Talent flashes onto our television screen, with shots of the whole school cheering.

'Sunset, for heaven's sake, Debs doesn't want to watch a school concert!' says Rose-May.

I fast-forward right to the end and then, oh then, Destiny walks onstage and starts talking about her mum.

Debs is squinting at the screen. 'Who's this girl? She's dressed like you, Sunset.'

Then Destiny opens her mouth and starts singing. Debs sits up straight and stares at the screen.

'It's my song,' says Dad.

'It's that girl!' says Mum. 'Sunset, how dare you—'

'Shut up, Suzy. Listen to that *voice*,' says Rose-May.

'She's incredible!' says Debs when Destiny takes her bow. 'Who *is* she?'

'She's Dad's other daughter, Destiny,' I say.

'She's *not*. She's just some mad groupie's child. She's just fantasizing,' says Mum. 'Of course that girl isn't Danny's daughter.'

'She *could* be,' says Rose-May, freeze-framing the DVD and staring hard at Destiny. 'Look, she's got the right hair, the same cheekbones, even the same stance.' Rose-May looks at me. 'You know this girl, Sunset?'

'Yes. And she *is* Dad's daughter, I'm sure of it.'

'*Is* she, Danny?' says Debs.

'How do I know?' says Dad.

'She *can't* be,' says Mum. 'Her mother's a liar. I bet she won't let that girl have a DNA test.'

'Calm down, Suzy. Let's think about what we've got here. This could be *huge*,' says Rose-May. 'Here's Danny, and here's Danny's long-lost daughter, who just happens to have the most amazingly powerful rich voice I've ever heard coming out of a kid's mouth—'

'We can break the story on my *Little Darlings* programme,' says Debs. 'Think of the coverage – and the tabloids will be fighting to do a tie-in feature.'

'I know *Hi!* would be interested,' says Rose-May.

'No!' says Mum.

But Dad is listening carefully. 'How would it make me look?' he asks Rose-May. 'Wouldn't it make me look bad, an illegitimate daughter that I've ignored all these years?'

'No, no, we could put a little spin on it, say how you're delighted to discover this long-lost daughter. We'll stress that you're such a loving family man that you want to welcome this new kid into your life. It could run and run. Do you know something, Danny, I can see your own reality series – this story's got everything.'

'*And* she can sing superbly,' Debs says. She turns to me and gives me a hug. 'Sunset, you've saved the day.'

Mum is still shaking her head. 'No, I won't stand for it. I'm not having this stranger's kid muscling her way into our lives – or her awful mother. What *else* is going to happen in this big story of yours, Rose-May? Are we going to have Danny Kilman reunited with his long-ago love?'

She bursts into tears. Dad reaches out and takes her hand.

'Suzy, *you're* my long-ago love – and my true love now. I know I've been a total fool and I'm so, so sorry. That thing with Lizzi – it was just a silly fling. I regretted it almost immediately. We're not together any more. I want to come back to you and the kids – please, darling,' he says, his voice breaking.

He takes Mum in his arms. For a moment she tries to push him away – and then she starts sobbing on his shoulder. Dad looks at Rose-May and winks.

'So, we have a show after all,' says Debs. 'Sunset, how do we get hold of Destiny?'

13

DESTINY

'Bye, darling,' says Mum, giving me a kiss.

I mumble bye, and snuggle back under my teddy-bear duvet. School's over for the summer. I don't have to get up for ages. I can just lie here and luxuriate. I'm so happy. Mum's OK, she's not going to die. She's got her medication now. She's still thin as a rake and a bit manic, but they promised at the hospital that she'll soon be back to her old self. I *wish* she didn't have to get up so early to go clean-ing, but she swears she doesn't mind. She'll go straight on from the university to her first old lady, but she might try to nip back later this morning, though I've told her I'll be fine.

Jack's coming round sometime. He says he'll teach me how to do a backflip. I can actually do a backflip already but I'm not going to tell him that. I quite *like* Jack, in a totally just-good-friends kind of way. I think I'll also write a letter to Sunset. It's her turn to write to me, but I expect she's too busy coping with Danny walking out on them. I badly want to hear what she thinks of my singing.

I lie on my back and sing *Destiny* softly to myself. I hear the applause ringing in my head, louder and louder.

'You want an encore? *OK!*' I say, and I start singing it all over again, at the top of my voice this time.

'Destiny?'

Oh Lordy, it's Mum back! I close my mouth with a gulp, feeling a fool.

'What's up, Mum? Did you forget something?'

I sit up. Mum is looking very strange, hanging

on tight to the end of the bed as if she'd fall down otherwise.

'Don't you feel well? Sit down quick. Oh, Mum, shall I call the doctor?' I gabble, jumping out of bed.

'No, I'm fine, I'm *more* than fine. Oh my God, Destiny, I can't believe it!' says Mum, sinking down on the bed beside me. 'I was halfway down the road when this Mercedes passed me, a huge great silver jobby, and I was staring at it, gobsmacked, wondering why on earth anyone would be driving a car like that round our estate, when it draws up right outside our maisie. So I beetle back and there's this chauffeur in a posh uniform getting out. And I think, *Blooming heck, what's going on?* And he looks at me and says, "Are you Mrs Williams?"'

'What? Mum, you're not making this up, are you?'

'No, no, I swear to God. Look out of the window and see for yourself! And he gave me this letter – here, read it – only be quick because you must get washed and dressed and we've got to be off, though he says there's no rush at all—'

'Mum? I don't understand a word you're saying.'

Mum thrusts an envelope at me. It's got my name on it: *Destiny*. I rip it open. There are two letters inside. One's from Sunset.

Dear Destiny,
This is your BIG CHANCE. There's going to be
this television programme called 'Little
Darlings' about the children of celebrities, and
this woman Debs hoped my sister Sweetie could
sing a little like Dad, but poor Sweetie's tooth
fell out and she went to pieces. Then they
wanted me to have a go but I can't sing for
toffee – so I showed them your DVD and they
were TOTALLY AMAZED. Now they want to do
a whole television programme with you and
Dad and I do hope you say yes. I can't wait to
see you if you come.
Love from your ever-so-excited sister Sunset xxx

I blink for a moment or two, and then look at the
second letter.

Dear Destiny and Ms Williams,
I am Debs Wilmott of Playtime Productions
UK. I am about to produce a series of
programmes called 'Little Darlings'. I have seen
your superb performance on the DVD, Destiny,
and feel there's the potential for a fantastic
programme with you and your estranged father,
Danny Kilman. We don't have a listed phone
number or email address for you, so I'm taking

the liberty of sending a car for you in the hope that you can come to Danny's home in Robin Hill, where we'll film you meeting each other – and then, if all goes well, we'll take you to the studios to record a couple of songs. Please phone the following number to let me know whether to expect you both.

All good wishes,
Debs Wilmott

Mum reads it through slowly, her finger pointing under each word, her lips moving. 'I can't believe it!' she keeps murmuring.

'Neither can I!' I say. 'Oh, Mum, oh, Mum, oh, Mum!'

'It's your chance to meet your dad!'

'It's my chance to *sing*!' I say, and I start jumping up and down on my bed. 'Oh, Sunset, I love you. You're the best sister in the world!'

'Come on then, my duck. The poor chauffeur doesn't want to be hanging around here for ever. The estate kids will be whipping the wheels off his car with him in it. You get yourself washed double-quick – and I suppose I'll have to phone this Debs. Oh help, I bet she's dead posh.'

'I'll phone her, Mum. Here, give us your mobile.'

I stab out the number before I lose courage. I

hear it ringing, and then a voice saying, 'Hi, Debs here.'

Oh goodness, she's ultra-posh with nobs on.

'Hello,' I mumble.

'Hi there, who is this?'

'It's – it's Destiny.'

'Oh, *wonderful*! I just didn't know how to get hold of you, and I need to see you, like, *immediately*. You are the kid on Sunset's DVD – the skinny one in black with the huge voice?'

'That's me.'

'Sing me one line down the phone.'

'Right now?'

'Can you?'

'OK. *You are my Destiny.*'

'Yay! It really *is* you. And you can come right now, with your mum?'

'I suppose. Though she'll have to tell them at work.'

'We'll probably need you for a few days, so pack your night things, darling. I'll fix a hotel room for you both – unless of course you'll be staying at Danny's.'

I think about Suzy. I don't think *that* will happen in a month of Sundays.

'Will I see Sunset?' I ask hopefully.

'Of course, darling. We want to film you with the whole family.'

'And, Debs, I know you'll want me to sing *Destiny*—'

'Yes, as a duet with Danny. I thought the two of you at either end of the stage at first, and then walking towards each other, and singing the last chorus looking into each other's eyes. It will be dynamic.'

'Do you want me to sing a solo too?'

'You bet we do.'

'Then can it be one of Sunset's songs? There's this one, *In My Black Clothes*. I know the words already but Sunset will have to teach me the tune. That's OK, I can learn it really really quickly.'

'I'll bet you can, honey. It's a deal. In fact it'll be an added bonus – *two* talented Little Darlings, one a singer, one a songwriter, taking after Dad. This just gets better and better.'

'Well, I'd better go and get ready.'

'That's right, Destiny – I'll see you in maybe four hours? Five hours maximum. See you soon!'

Mum gives me a hug as I end the call. 'Oh, babe, you sounded so *cool*, like this kind of thing happens every day of the week! I'm so proud of you, darling. Oh boy!'

'Look, Mum, you phone Louella, see if she can

cover for you, looking after all your old folks. You will come with me, won't you?'

'If you think I'm missing this you're mental! Oh, Destiny, darling, this is the happiest day of my life,' Mum squeals, and then starts phoning.

I dive in and out of the bath and pull on my coolest clothes – the new black outfit with the lacy black gloves and my beautiful leather jacket. Mum shoves more stuff in a laundry bag as she spills the news to Louella.

We go out of the front door, terrified that the Mercedes will have disappeared altogether, a total hallucination – but there it is in front of us. The driver nods and smiles and jumps out of his car to help us into the back like we're *Lady* Kate and her daughter Destiny.

'So, off to London?' he says.

'Well, in a minute,' I say. 'Could we possibly drive into the estate? I need to tell someone I'm not going to be around for a few days.'

He doesn't look terribly happy about going any nearer to the bleak multistoreys, but he says politely, 'Just tell me where to stop, madam.'

Madam! Mum gives a squeak of nervous laughter but I manage to keep a straight face. I direct him until we get to Jack's block.

'Right here, please. I'll just be a minute.'

I jump out of the car and run up the stairs and along the balcony to Jack's flat. I knock on his door, peering down at the Mercedes. It's already drawing quite a crowd.

One of Jack's big brothers comes to the door in his vest and trackie bottoms. He eyes me up and down and I get a bit worried. Then he shouts over his shoulder, 'Oi, Jack, it's your girlfriend.'

I blush – and when Jack comes to the door he's bright red too, though he does his best to look casual. He's in T-shirt and jeans but his feet are bare and his hair is all sticking up. It's clear he's just got out of bed.

'Hi, Destiny! You're early! I thought I was calling on you today.'

'Yeah, I know, but I nipped up to tell you. I have to go to London right now.'

'You didn't say before.'

'I didn't know!'

'So what are you doing in London then? Have you got friends there?'

'Sort of . . . family. And – and guess what, Jack, I'm going to be on the telly!'

'You what? You're joking me, right?'

'It's true. Look over the balcony. Just look!'

Jack looks – and his mouth falls open. 'That's a Mercedes! What's it doing here?'

'It's *my* Mercedes,' I say. 'See, it's got my mum in it.'

I wave wildly – and Mum and the chauffeur wave back at me.

'Who's that, then? Your mum's new boyfriend?'

'No, it's the chauffeur. The telly lady's sent him for me. I'm going to sing on this programme, *Little Darlings*. Isn't it great?'

'Yeah,' says Jack, looking dazed.

'So wish me luck, eh?'

'OK. But – but you are coming back, aren't you? You're not staying down in London.'

'Only for a bit. I'll come and tell you all about it when I get back, right?'

'Right. Though maybe you won't still want to be mates if you turn into a television star.'

'Don't be daft. I'll always be mates with you, Jack,' I say.

Then I blush again and he does too.

I go charging back along the balcony and down the stairs. As I'm getting into the car, Jack leans over the balcony railing and shouts, 'Good luck, Destiny!' and I give him a wave. Then, to my total joy, another door in his block opens and *Angel* peers out. She stares down at me, her mouth in a comical O. I wave at her too, jump in the car, and we're off.

'Pinch me, Destiny. I feel like I'm dreaming,' Mum whispers.

'*I* feel like I'm dreaming,' I say, giving her the tiniest pinch.

The car doesn't vanish. It's really happening. I think about the last time we went down south. This is all so different. The chauffeur is called Jim and he chats to us like he's a friend.

'What's this Debs lady like then, Jim? Do you know her? Do you think she'll *really* make this television programme about my Destiny?' Mum asks.

'She must think a lot of her to organize this car – I don't come cheap!' says Jim, laughing. 'What are you going to do on television, Destiny?'

'I'm going to sing.'

'Oh, great. Well, how about giving us a little song in the car, then? That would be a real treat,' says Jim.

So I sing *Destiny* – and Jim cheers when I've finished.

'You've got such a lovely voice you've made the back of my neck prickle,' he says. 'Sing us another one, go on!'

So I sing my way through a whole medley of Danny Kilman songs, and Mum and Jim join in too, Mum singing the chorus, Jim making twanging guitar noises.

'I've always been a big Danny Kilman fan,' he says.

'Destiny's . . . related to him,' Mum says proudly. 'He's going to be on this show.'

'My goodness! You're clearly going to be famous too, Destiny. I shall be boasting that I gave you a lift in my car to all my other clients,' says Jim.

I'd be happy to sing for the whole journey but Mum makes me rest my voice.

'You need to preserve it, darling. You don't want to sound all croaky when you meet Debs Wilmott.'

I'm starting to get a bit nervous now. When we stop at the motorway café I can barely eat. What if it all goes wrong? What if this Debs doesn't like me? What if I make a mess of the song? What if Danny takes one look at me and says, 'No, you're definitely not my daughter.' How are we going to meet up anyway? I thought he'd gone off with this Lizzi girl.

'Do you think they'll let us in the gate this time?' I whisper to Mum.

'Well, I'm not having you climbing that wall again – you'll tear your leather jacket!' says Mum. 'Don't worry, darling. I know it's going to be fine this time.'

When we turn off the main road to Robin Hill at long last, Jim stops the car and starts talking on his mobile.

'We're at the end of the road,' he says. 'How do you want to do this? Do you want me to drive right up to the gates?' He listens and then nods. 'OK, OK, I'll tell them,' he says, and rings off.

'They think it'll be more effective if you approach the house on foot. They want to film you meeting Danny. We'll wait here, and the sound recordist will come and get you both miked up.'

'Oh help!' says Mum. 'Not me too?'

She starts scrabbling in her bag for her make-up and then gives my nose a dab of powder too. We see the television people coming. Mum squeezes my hand.

'Isn't this *exciting*, darling? Look, your very own camera crew! You're famous already!'

'It won't spoil anything, will it, Mum? We'll still be us, you and me?'

'Of course we'll still be us, silly girl. Oh, I'm so proud of you. Come on, we'd better get out of the car.'

There's a camera man and a sound recordist and a girl in ripped jeans who turns out to be Debs herself. She gives Mum and me a kiss on both cheeks, as if she's known us all our lives.

'This is fabulous!' she says. 'We want to film you as you meet Danny for the first time, OK? So you two just walk up to his gate, and Destiny, you say something on the intercom – just say your name, that'll do – and then the gate will swing open and you'll both walk up the drive to the front door, right? Don't look at the camera, either of you. Just act totally naturally, OK?'

It doesn't feel at all natural having a mike attached to my T-shirt and a camera man walking backwards in front of me – but Mum grips my hand and we walk along the road and stop at the gate. We look at each other.

'Go on,' says Mum.

I take a deep breath and press the intercom. 'I'm Destiny,' I say, my voice all shaky with nerves.

The gate clangs slowly open, and we go inside and walk up the drive. We round the corner and the door is open, and there's Danny standing there, smiling at us. Mum gives a little squeal and pushes me forward. I walk towards him, my legs wobbling, and he opens his arms wide and gives me a hug.

'Hello, little darling. I'm Danny. I'm your dad.'

I hear Mum give a sob behind me. I know how much this means to her. My eyes are dry but I blink hard as if I'm holding back the tears.

I cling to this stranger until Debs yells, 'Cut!' looking ecstatic.

'You little one-take wonder! That was incredible,' she says.

I edge past Danny. There's Suzy scowling in the hall, holding Sweetie's hand, Ace on her hip. And there's my sister Sunset, a twin in her black clothes. We stare at each other, giggling shyly, and then we hold hands, squeezing tight, as if we'll never let go.